THE NIGHT IS YOUNG

SELECTED WRITINGS

BY

BARBARA LOCKHART

The Night Is Young

For information about this title, contact the publisher:

Secant Publishing, LLC
P.O. Box 79
Salisbury MD 21803
www.secantpublishing.com

ISBN: 978-1-944962-27-2 (paperback)

Library of Congress Control Number: 2016951839

Printed in the United States of America

Cover art by Lynne Lockhart, used with permission.

Several of the stories in this collection first appeared elsewhere, as noted:

First Green Shoots, in *Generation to Generation,*
Papier Mache Press;
Desk Work, in *Oceana Magazine,* Ocean City, MD;
The Strawberry Field, in *The Greensboro Review,*
University of North Carolina;
The Crab Feast, in *Requiem for a Summer Cottage,* SMU Press;
The Second Death, in *Indiana Review,* Indiana University.

For Lynne Naomi

ACKNOWLEDGMENTS

Since much of the work in this volume has been written over a period of time and in between novels-in-progress, there were a number of people to thank along the way. In the beginning, the workshops at Johns Hopkins with Gary Wilson, at Bennington with Richard Ellman, the MFA program at Vermont College with Walter Wetherell and Chris Noel, and the revision work with Southern Methodist University Press with editor Kathryn Lang, helped me embark on the murky waters of writing. To each of them, my heartfelt thanks. Your words of wisdom have stayed with me over the years.

And to my daughter, Lynne, who so generously shares the footprints of her artistic journey for the covers of my books, the walls of my house and in places far and wide, I hold deepest gratitude and an enormous amount of pride. To Paul, Lynne and Scott, thank you for your abiding love and support, always.

CONTENTS

Beginning with Puckum

The town sleeps.

Though it is spring, Christmas angels still cling to the lampposts on Main Street. The wind coming in from the fields rustles tinseled gowns and wings. With trumpets posed, the angels wait with patience exemplary and particular to all things out of season. Soon, soon they quiver, there will be something to herald. In the road ahead. Coming. Just you wait and see.

They wait, mounted to the poles like hollowed egg cases from last summer's grasshoppers, while their spirits long to burst free of their angelic selves. Can you blame them? They remember spring, the scent of lilacs as husbands in rolled-up shirtsleeves pushed lawn mowers and children ran in and out kitchen doors, back when their own hair was dark and their breasts were firm. They once lived with purpose and verve—or so it seems to them now.

Their children grew hairy and bald in turn, their husbands mellow and toothless. Then everyone they knew disappeared altogether like flakes of paint in colors that used to be. Now spring breezes stir the angels—is it possible?—and they answer the April air, the wafts of ammonia on the fields, honeysuckle along the roads, marsh mud at low tide, the churned earth ready for spring planting. Their curse is that they cannot forget anything.

Despite themselves, they have wisdom now. And so, on occasion, they take to wafting through the night, appearing in the dreams of the troubled to comfort and guide them. It is no less a service than any of those they've already performed and surely more useful than waiting for next Christmas.

They know as they pass the paled wood exterior of the drug store that bears the sign *The Drug Store* that on its counter lie cures and placebos in little white bags standing on end, inscribed with names and dates like insistent epitaphs. Indeed, they know. Hadn't their own demise begun the same way? With the pharmacist's young, bespectacled, sympathetic face high above the dispensing counter? Mournful, really. Orrin was his name—"Just one in the morning, Miss Mary. Can you get the top off by yourself?"

Now they float past the old train station restored to partial glory and vinyl siding, follow the tracks to the sewing factory where they once may have made polyester bell bottoms with matching vests, and, drawn by the light of the Pepsi machine outside the E and W Quik Stop Market, pause under the sign that says *Breasts and Wings—Moist and Crispy.*

Then, willy-nilly, they are in and out of curtained windows on clapboard broad-front houses, around upholstered easy chairs relegated to front porches, through pet doors and attic vents to curled heads and bald ones resting on foam pillows—two for $9.99 during Saturday's tent sale at Fox's Outlet Store. They slide across tables lined up along Main Street for tomorrow's yard sales and land on the lawn of St. Mark's First Baptist Church right in front of a *For Sale* sign planted there by Nily Realty, then float on to the bulletin board in front of the Second Methodists of Zion Church that bears the simple inscription *Hallelujah.*

They swirl around the tire planters filled with brown vestiges of last September's geraniums sitting in front of a house with no steps—the front door painted shut and windows shaded with aluminum foil. Around back, they slip past the clothespin bag hanging next to a row of permanently stained jeans with flies unzipped and pockets out, on a backyard wash line and then billow past a bathroom sink, painted blue and awaiting summer bird bathing, then on to the blinking traffic light, amber-not, amber-not, answered by red-not, red-not at the intersection of Main and 393. Swinging left, just over the wires, they head toward the pickle factory, which patiently awaits its season, the cucumber harvest. It is visited this night by lovers who are loathe to go back home to Prospect Heights Housing Project down along Gold Rush Lane and Lincoln Drive, where children lie tangled, four to a bed, breathing kerosene vapors, for the air has the chill of December. Here the spirits dart in and out at a maddening rate as if to fan away danger for they have never ceased worrying over the very young.

The town sleeps on.

They sweep past the Soul Carry-out which heads them north beyond the brown shingled elementary school and its *For Sale* sign swinging with a whining creak—the sign of the defunct—abandoned for the sake of integration at last. Not so the cemetery, with its World War I doughboy in knickers and hat, who faces west and leans on his rifle as he leads his following of upturned fossil footprints, each lovingly inscribed, familial. His pedestal is inscribed with names of local boys who died in the war, with a line drawn between the white and the colored, separate even in death, while the town of Puckum sleeps.

The collective breaths of bodies lumped in slumber murmur farewells as the spirits rise up and over the skyscraper of flattened cars and mountain of tires at Johnson's Demolition, the cyclone fenced gate padlocked against seekers of parts for renegade Mustangs and corroded Falcons here at the sudden end of town.

Now the spirits gather speed as they fly without interruption over the vast fields of new rye, through the huge steel backbone of the irrigation system, which will, in its own good time, begin pulsing life to shafts of new corn.

They pause at the sight of a child's shoe on the step of the open front door of Bounds' cottage, which sags at the edge of the field, its roof weighed down with dried trumpet vines and Virginia creeper, decay and time. They cross the threshold only to sail out again through an upstairs window and hover for a hummingbird second near an open mailbox, move on again as though they fear they could be seen with the coming of dawn, up over a wall of trees and scattered brush, out past newly plowed fields painted with lime, around Taylor's city of silos and granary storage awaiting the combine's gathering, through the splendiferous odors of the chicken rendering plant, higher, higher now so as not to wither away from the killing stench (for spirits are delicate in the presence of certain odors) and fly now, like the first birds at the crack of dawn, past long, flat rectangles of turned earth edged by macadam, then dirt road, then shale along a long lane and a single cedar tree, then to a house, a particular brown-shingled house with a high peak spiked with lightning rods and two leaning chimneys, a porch toward the east, a barn to the north, and a high, open window yawning at the south. And enter there—to come upon an old woman staring into the dark with sleepless eyes. They will bring her remembrances of her days and tender words whispered long ago. It is the least they can do. Soon the old woman closes her eyes. They leave her then with her dreams, knowing that for those who have lived a long luxury of days, sleep will bring back that hour when the night is still and forever young.

First Green Shoots

Mary opened the junk drawer in her kitchen and poked through plastic lids, bits of string, and sticky toothpicks even though at first glance she could tell her paint brushes weren't there, those long-handled, skimpy-haired wonders as familiar to her as her own hand. She hadn't seen them for a while, though for how long she really couldn't say, and her paints, the yellow ochre and burnt sienna, those tubes sculpted to messy, crinkled forms over the years—they must have a little bit left in them, she told herself as she groped the dark corners of the drawer. In her bedroom she yanked open the nightstand drawer with her collection of hairnets and eyeglass cases from Dr. Paul Ryland, now deceased, and then pulled open her top dresser drawer with its brown rolls of stockings, scraps of wrapping paper and crushed bows. Lifting her head to the wall, she stared through it, thinking.

The dining room hutch.

In the left drawer, she gently pushed aside the graduation photograph of Edna, her daughter, also deceased, and the candle snuffer, stubs of red Christmas candles and crocheted hot plates, a toy train from Luke, her grandson, now grown with a son of his own, and her favorite rhinestone button.

"Cora took them, and the paints, too, I betcha," she said out loud, Cora being Luke's live-in girlfriend, like a wife, you know, but not a wife. Not a wife at all. Mary noted the pale green rectangle on the wall surrounded by a sea of smoky green and saw again the painting that once hung there, the white clapboard two-story farmhouse, and the chickens that strutted along the fence by the hollyhocks, and the door to the porch kitchen through which she used to find her mother brushing back wisps of grey hair and warming cinnamon toast on the great yellow-enameled cook stove.

"I might climb up to the attic today and get them back, put them right where I had them. All my paintings, every one. Gone for—it was spring when they'd moved in and now the corn's almost ready—five, six months ago? Shoulda put my foot down right then, at the start," she mumbled. "It's still my house. It's like I've been asleep or something, waiting for them to leave." It seemed important to say this out loud, hands on hips, practicing.

And where was the hand pump painting? The one with the cornflowers growing around the table where they kept the tin drinking cup? And the chicken painting, with Frank the rooster, feathers dappled white and black to match his stippled walk as he chased her brothers out of the yard with a fury she hadn't seen since.

"I feel just like that today," she announced to no one.

"What's that, Grandma?" said Luke, coming toward her and scraping his heels on the wood floor. Couldn't he at least pick up his feet when he walked? Him with his bare chest and hair down to his shoulders. Who would have thought men would become more cave-like in the present, wanting to travel back in time?

And another thing. Besides the paintings, there was the Raggedy Ann doll in the wagon. The one she'd made for Edna when she was four. She hadn't missed it right away, but one night while watching *Jeopardy!* on TV, she'd looked down beside her chair where the wagon had always been and felt as though she were sitting on an island.

Why had she allowed it, this stripping down of her life?

Was it because none of them, including her, ever thought she'd outlive this so-called *visit* of Luke's and Cora's? Well, they have another think coming. This old gal's feeling pretty good today. Coming back. She can even see better.

Oh, she doesn't mean to seem ungrateful. The rooms she and her Joe shared in this cottage had grown dark without her knowing it. Darker still when he died eighteen years ago. Until Cora and Luke moved in, she'd lived alone with her rag rugs scattered comfortably over the worn spots on the carpeting and overgrown bushes blocking the walk. None of it mattered. She spent her time filling the walls with her paintings, surrounding herself with the best moments of her life.

She shrugged and looked at the new arrangement of chairs, the bowl of plastic flowers on the TV, the front door flung open, and the new curtains that billowed out across her armchair. She had forgotten (along with a lot of things) to let the outside air in. And there were new sounds in the house as Kevin, her great-grandson, trampled across the floor and Luke called to him in a singsong voice, "Kevin, Ke-vin. I'm gonna get you, Kevin."

"No—no, you're not, Daddy!" His squeals reminded her of Edna. She trembled. Kevin leaned on the seat of her armchair, which was just high enough for his elbows to rest on, and peered up at her with the same dark eyes she'd seen in her sleep—like Edna's. "You're old, Great-Grandma," he said. Her face must seem like wrinkly old elephant skin to him. She skimmed her fingers over his vernal cheek ever so lightly. A tinge of peach. Maybe yellow ochre and cadmium red light together.

"Yes," she said, then turned her head away. "Luke? Where are my paints? Do you hear me, Luke?"

"Grandma, what you startin' in for all of a sudden? I tol' you I don't know. Maybe they're with the boxes of things we put in the attic." He had shaved. His chin was wide and strong.

It was a good sign.

"Well, I need them. I think I'll be needing them today. Do you hear me? My eyes are better, and the light is good for painting this morning. And while you're up there, you can get my pictures, too, and that Raggedy Ann doll in the wagon. There's even a stretched canvas, I think."

It was useless to ask. He somehow grew up, got opinions about things, and saw himself as boss. An opportunist. "Let's go live with Great-Grandma," he probably said to Cora. "We'll stay, you know, take care of things—and someday we'll get the house." She didn't begrudge him. He was her only heir. Half Edna. You could see it in his eyes. His best feature. Luminous, they were, and mournful at times. She couldn't deny them anything.

Things might have been different if Edna had not died when Luke was four weeks old. How different everything would have been. Why, *why* was her only child taken? She shouldn't ask, but ask she did, for years—until she just plain got tired of asking. Edna's eyes closed forever as she lay on the stretcher. Mary wasn't supposed to see. The doctor pulled her back and stepped in front of her to shield her from the sight. Blood stiffened Edna's dark, flowing hair. Blood stiffened in Mary's veins as well. Dead still. And Bill, Edna's husband, the driver who had escaped with not even a scratch, held his head in his hands, stiff with fear. It was the drinking, she knew, though he never let on.

The reshuffling after that. The scramble to change everything. Bill married again and Mary and Joe fled Baltimore to return to Puckum, the gentle, country town of their childhood, like children running home for Band-Aids with hurts too big to heal, while Luke had a new mother, grandmother, aunts and uncles and cousins—Mary only saw him summers on brief visits. He was lost to her, too. Until now.

"Kevin, want to walk to the gas station with Daddy?" Luke

asked, pulling his Grateful Dead T-shirt down over his stomach. "Daddy wants to fix the bicycle tire this morning."

Mary tried again. "What are you going to do, Luke? I need my paints, I tell you."

"Thought I'd ride my bike some and strengthen my legs, Grandma. Maybe lose a little of this weight. Besides, the gas tank's low and the check doesn't come for another two weeks."

What would Joe have said? *Get your ass out of here and get a job. It don't look to me like your back is all that bad.* She would have silently agreed, but she would have defended Luke. Things hadn't been easy for him. The hands that held him as a baby were different every week, aunts and friends pitching in to care for the infant, who began to scream in terror at the strange faces. She had had her turn but he only grew worse when she held him because of her trembling. All she could see was Edna with her arms reaching out for the baby she couldn't hold. Mary couldn't believe in a heaven after that. Edna would surely go to heaven if there was one, but what kind of heaven would it be if you couldn't hold your own baby?

Through it all, Luke had been spoiled. How else could she explain what was happening now? A man who didn't work. Who lived in his grandmother's house. As a matter of fact, who lived in sin in his grandmother's house. Under the guise of taking care of her.

All those years without Edna and Joe, all she could think about was a family around her. She wanted a kitchen like Mama's, with nine children scrapping and teasing and bread on the rise on any given day. Steam at the windows. When she was ten she would wipe away the steam and peer out at very nearly the same scene as the one outside her living room window today. The road to Cambridge banked with snow looked the same then as now, even in the cold light of a setting sun. Where did Luke put that painting? The children were sledding along the icy road—last licks before Mama's call for supper. She missed them.

She'd lived too long. This house would have been Luke's by now. Eighty-four. How did that happen? On her last birthday she called Meredith, the town mortician, about the family plot and he said he didn't think there was room for her but that he would check.

"Might have to put you in vertically, Miss Mary," he said, in his dry, gravelly voice. Mary smiled to herself and wheezed.

"What's so funny, Grandma?" Luke asked.

"Nothing."

"Want anything from the store?"

"King Syrup and two paintbrushes, a wide one and a thin one."

"Grandma," he drew the word out like he was being *very* patient with her. "They don't have paintbrushes at the IGA."

"No, but Shockley's has 'em. He always keeps a few around for me."

"Now, Grandma. What you want them for? You ain't gonna paint today, and proly not tomorrow neither."

"Either. Yes, I will. I just have to find the paints."

The cookie jar. Could she have put them in the cookie jar? The day Cora and Luke moved in and began cleaning up the place, she had been painting in the kitchen, her easel propped up against the window sill. She painted the crepe myrtle in the yard, not that she had a crepe myrtle in the yard but the one at Mama's, where the bush had stood outside the kitchen window, humming with bees in the August heat. Cora had just been saying the paintings in the kitchen had to go. "Everything looks lopsided in the paintings," she said as she stood with her feet planted on Mary's kitchen linoleum.

"Maybe after you take some painting classes. They got them at the Arts Center where you learn how to draw first?

10

Luke could take you down," she said, with a twitch at the corner of her lips that might have been a smile if she'd let it, her hoop earrings swinging.

Luke let the screen door bang. The loosened screen curled away from the door frame and bounced crazily.

"Luke," Mary called. "Pick up a yard of screening and some nails for that door, will you?" She heard his boots scrape on the porch, and Kevin say, "Go now!"

"Got some money?" said Luke. "I'd get it but my check won't come for another two weeks." She knew. Lord, she knew. She reached for her black leather bag on the bureau.

Later, in the kitchen, Cora appeared at the threshold with an armful of wet sheets. "How come you don't have a dryer?" she said. Mary ignored the question—not all questions were worth answering. What was it she wanted to tell Cora? Oh, yes.

"Did I tell you I had art lessons once?" she said. "There was a Mr. Moss who was teaching classes in Cambridge. He was a very exacting man—painted graphically, like a Disney cartoon, you know? Well, he was trying to get me to tighten up on my style. 'More defining lines,' he said. 'Then fill in the colors. Start with a completed drawing and fill in.' But I just couldn't do it that way."

"You mean like paint the numbers?" Cora could be beautiful. Not every minute, but now, in this minute, with her fleshy arms around the sheets and her eyes that soft green, looking hopeful about everything, looking as though nothing mattered but those sheets if she were to be able to stay in this house. She was trying to have a home and a family like everybody else on this God's green earth. What binds women together is the nesting urge so deep in our beings.

"What I do is," she said to Cora, because she had never

11

said out loud what it was she did and she thought Cora might understand, "I paint the whole picture together. I mean I keep adding layers while the painting grows. Everything changes as I paint. Big clouds of color like a camera that isn't focused. And then the images come in. Well, sometimes they come in—as if I have to call them from far away."

Cora looked down. She was determined to get the laundry done. She'd chip away at the house and the chores and make a home, and Mary, because she, too, had a mission this morning, turned and reached for the cookie jar on the shelf above the stove, the silly brown elephant sitting on its haunches and waving its chipped trunk toward her in greeting. She raised the sailor hat lid. Ah, of course. There were the paints, the arthritic tubes waiting for her like a secret. She left them there and replaced the lid. Now she needed some paper, or a board. Canvas would be better, of course, but paper would do. When Edna was little, she'd painted on paper. Those paintings were gone now, but they were the foundation for what came later. Maybe she had some watercolor left. Then she was going to need some gesso so the oil wouldn't bleed through the paper.

The only painting in the house she hadn't done herself was the portrait of Edna that used to hang over the fireplace. She had a picture of her on her prom night that she took to Ella Murphy over in Cambridge. Ella didn't want to paint Edna at first, but Mary told her whatever she did would be fine, that it was impossible for her to do it herself. She tried, but Edna kept changing on the canvas. She'd turn her head or look down; her nose never looked right or the space between her lips and nose was too big. She remembered Edna too many ways or was it that she painted Edna moving through a huge space, from childhood to twenty-one, and gone, all in one painting? There was simply too much to tell. Perhaps Edna would have painted. She'd won that prize in high school.

She probably would have done things, and Luke would have had good examples to live by instead of an alcoholic father and a disinterested stepmother. Why did Luke put Edna's portrait in the attic, too?

Through the kitchen window, she watched Cora throw the sheets over the line in big bunches, and stick a clothespin in the middle of each mound. Somehow Cora had missed a basic or two and didn't know the pleasure of a line of clean, billowing wash on a clear day such as this. Maybe Cora wouldn't mind if she showed her how to hang them properly. Maybe the question really was could Mary stand to see laundry bunched up like that all day? Maybe it was a matter of compromise and wisdom and getting along and deciding what really mattered. Mary didn't know. She'd let them have their run of the place. It had been a cold, hard spring. Their coming was like the first green shoots of the daffodils. But it was not like family. It was company that stayed way too long.

"We're worried about you, Grandma, staying alone," Luke said, like her sisters who decided five years ago it was time Mary sold the house and went to a nursing home. They talked her into the Meredith House. One week of hanging her stockings over the footboard of her bed in a chairless room and she walked out. Told them she wasn't ready for playing cards and nurses checking up on bowel movements. She took her house off the market and showed up in Mr. Moss's art class, where she began using a dry brush for watercolor. The apple trees along the fence. Sold that one at the art show in Cambridge. Should never have parted with it. The best one she ever did. She knew people in the class shook their heads—that Mary, dabbing with a dry brush—you can't tell her anything. Yet hers was the only one sold.

Holding onto the back door frame for that first step, she planted her foot solidly on the cement. Would Joe have an old piece of wood paneling in the shed? He made that doghouse out of paneling not too long ago. Ha! She caught herself. Twenty years ago, at least. Yet, it was as if he were still in the shed somewhere, along with the wood scraps he was always using up and saving remnants from, his fingerprints still on the wood, the oil from his hands catching the dust of twenty years. The wood should be ready by now. Ready for her.

"Grandma? You all right?" Cora called. "You want help down them steps?"

"The wash isn't going to dry like that, Cora. You want help hanging it up?"

"Well, if it don't dry, I'll walk it up to the laundromat."

"I'm all right," Mary said and stepped gingerly down to the walk toward the shed. She felt Cora's eyes on her back.

How many times did she watch Joe's back disappear into the shed? The changes between Baltimore and Puckum bent him. He never stopped grieving as he went about building birdhouses and doghouses to sell. Although he wasn't an old man—fifty-eight was not as old as she had once thought—he had come home to die. She had always been grateful to him for rescuing her from her job at the telephone company and the switchboard at Puckum when everyone thought she was past marrying age. He whisked her off to Baltimore and she never once missed the clapboard farmhouse and the noisy clan of brothers and sisters, always believing that she and Joe would produce a crop of kids on their own.

She knew he wouldn't fail her. There was a piece of paneling wide enough and high enough leaning against an old door. She brushed the dust off with her sleeve. He always did understand about her painting, when she had to pull into herself like a turtle. Her hand trembled now thinking about him, his red-brown hair, the way he looked at her in the early days. She never forgot.

As she headed for the house, she stopped and leaned the

piece of wood against the wash pole. She couldn't help it. Cora was out of sight and she was free to remove the clothespin from one of the sheets on the line and tug at its edges, smoothing it out and lining up the corners so the sheet hung free as a banner to the summer breeze. Before she knew it, all the laundry was assembled like a line of ghosts against the blue sky—Kevin's shorts and Luke's shirts, Cora's nightgown and Mary's housedress—they made a family, didn't they? Shoulder to shoulder, waist to waist?

The walk back to the house was difficult with the piece of wood and besides, she was tired. Cora met her at the steps.

"What chew want that for, Grandma? We don't need that board in here. Where you gonna put it? Here, lemme take it."

"Now don't you go putting that back, Cora. I've got plans for it. Put it right in my room."

From her bed she could see Luke and Kevin coming up the sidewalk. The fields that lined the road to Cambridge were amber with dried corn. The town, walled in all summer, waited for harvest. She'd block out the Agrico grain tower and concentrate on the right blue for the sky, maybe paint Luke and Kevin walking in bright T-shirts and jeans in the lower left corner. Kevin broke loose from his father's hand and ran toward the house. The screen door banged.

"We got Grandma brushes! But Daddy got no money left for the syrup."

She heard Luke say, "Where is she?"

"In her room with a big board and the cookie jar." Mary envisioned Cora rolling her eyes as she ran her hand through her hair, tossing back her head, her hoop earrings swinging, and Mary grinned to herself, wheezing puffs of air from the back of her throat as she perceived this insistent old thing she had become, sitting on the edge of her bed, still with pictures in her head and none on her walls, waiting for her brushes.

Luke lumbered into her room, the heel of his boot catching on the threshold, the roll of screening tied with a string under one arm and a paper bag in the other. Something, something was so familiar about him, yet she couldn't name what it was, only that he drew Edna near.

"You okay, Grandma?"

"My room is bare, Luke."

"No, it isn't! Look at all the junk in here. What's in all those plastic bags, anyhow?"

"Rags for those rugs I make. Just you leave them be. Luke, I need my paintings."

"We were just trying to clean the place up for you." Innocence and vulnerability, that's what it was. That look about him that struck a chord, moving her beyond his dark hair in sweaty rivers along his neck, the black T-shirt, black boots, and soiled jeans—the uniform of his age—the softness of his paunch at twenty-six, older than Edna now.

She sighed. "Luke, dear, you need to find something of your own to do. Remember the glass etchings you made that summer when you were sixteen? You would sit in Grandpa's shop and sketch roses so beautiful they were ready to be plucked. And then you etched them on the glass windows from the old greenhouse."

"I know. I was thinking about it. You can't make any money doing that, though."

"Hmm." Mary stared past him. Was he going to miss the boat, this child of Edna's? She wished she could say, *Get a job or leave. Marry Cora. For heaven's sake, live right.* That's why old people die off, she told herself. Their ways are as old as they.

"It's too hot today to get the paintings out of the attic, okay? But I'll fix the screen in the door," he said as if he'd just decided he really should do what she asked but there was always the chance she would forget and then he wouldn't have to. But maybe he would sometime find work, marry Cora, move on—he didn't know—but not today. *Proly not till the Grateful Dead T-shirt wears out,* Mary thought and began wheezing again at her joke, but stopped suddenly, remembering.

"Luke, I can't imagine why you put away the painting of your mother. At least get that one out for me, please?"

"It's not exactly put away."

"Oh, my God, you didn't throw it out, did you?"

"No, nothin' like that. I put it in me and Cora's room."

"Why didn't you tell me, or ask?"

"I was gonna put it in the attic with the others, but it seemed like I ought to look close, study it, you know? Now I can look at her every morning when I wake up. She looks so perfect, like she should have had everything go right, know what I mean?"

"Let me see." It was as if she'd never seen the painting he was talking about.

He put the screening down on the floor with the bag and followed her to his room.

"I hung it careful and all. It's on the wall that don't get sun. You didn't say nothin'—I thought it'd be okay."

It was too easy. Edna all fluffed up in that dress. Like he said, perfect. Not alive. That was how the doctor put it. He didn't say she was dead. He said, "She's not alive."

"Look," said Luke, "if you want it back in the living room, I'll put it back. Cora don't think much of it being in here anyhow. You okay, Grandma?"

She wondered why they kept asking her. She must look bad. Maybe her bobby pins were falling out. She patted her hair as she walked back to her room. Luke was right behind her.

"Look out," he said. "Don't trip on the screening."

"I see it, I see it. My eyes are good today. You got the brushes in that bag?"

There was a cotton rag in the plastic bag beside her bed

with which to clean the piece of paneling. Maybe she should dampen it first.

"Would you wet this rag for me, Luke, please, and close the door on your way out?"

The silence in her room was an old friend she had been waiting to see for a long time. She wanted to nest in her memories but also to swoop back and forth through the years with twigs of this and that and make something new. The paint tubes were stiff but the colors still brilliant. There was enough for a few more paintings. Here was not just blue, but cerulean blue, French ultramarine, and cobalt blue for the sky. She would bring in the corn with cadmium yellow, yellow ochre, and a touch of raw umber, and Luke's and Kevin's T-shirts with ivory black, vermilion, and her favorite, burnt sienna.

No, wait. The burnt sienna was for the doll's hair. She'd put the doll back in her wagon. No, Edna could put the doll back in her wagon. Her hand would be on the doll, dimpled like Kevin's hand. Kevin could help her. Edna would be wearing her white dress with the blue ribbons. She might turn her head and look like Kevin does, right at her, the same eyes, dark, dark brown, almost black—so black Mary could see herself reflected there. "Look," Mary would say, "Do you see a little girl in my eyes, Edna?" Look quick because little girls grow up. They disappear in a blink. You have to bring them in. You begin dabbing burnt sienna, and who knows, one long-buried moment might come back through the mist.

And on that stretch of canvas she'd been saving—it must be in the attic, too—she knew then to begin with Edna's eyes. Once she got her eyes, she could even put Luke in her arms and Edna would, at last, be smiling.

18

Desk Work

I stood in the kitchen pulling leftover meatloaf out of the refrigerator. It was late; the sales meeting at Wesley Insurance where I worked had taken longer than it should and Brian was on his way in, probably hungry. I was down to one kid these days. The other three left a while ago, but Brian hung on. His father left years before the kids. Lucky for me Brian was in no hurry. Seeing what he could do around the farm to help, he seemed satisfied with welding jobs from neighboring farmers. We got along okay except for those times I came home from meetings ready to chew the steering wheel, but that had nothing to do with him.

"What's that?" I said as he came in the kitchen.

"What's what?"

I pointed to the box he held in his arms. There was something alive in it, I just knew.

"A chicken."

"Aw, c'mon, Brian." I knew it came out Bri-yen, and the tone was one I used when he was twelve. "Not again!" He was always rescuing things, and the last time he saved a chicken that fell off a truck on the way to the processing plant, it grew up to be a rooster and claimed my yard as his own, attacking me every time I stepped out the door. Brian had to bring him down to Big Mary and hated every minute of it. Neither of us could stand to wring the rooster's neck, and that's what Big Mary could be counted on to do, which is exactly what it was raised for, to be somebody's Sunday dinner. Brian took it hard, though, and wouldn't eat meat for three whole weeks.

Now he grinned that sly grin of his and said, "Yeah, I know. But it was lying on the side of the road. Don't worry. It's not going to make it anyway. Just thought I'd make it more comfortable—be lousy to die in the cold." He had me there.

Without being sentimental about it, I will say they raise them in standing-room-only accommodations, ten thousand at a time in those expansive chicken houses that sprawl behind most of the farmhouses around here and some dark night the chickens are loaded up in those wooden crates and the next thing they don't know is they're traveling on a hook along some conveyor belt. That doesn't seem fair although I do like chicken very much, especially stuffed.

The land is flat here. The wind brushes over it without interruption. Only the sky offers variation, a vast, eventful, multicolored, overturned bowl. When the corn is down, the fields lay brown-gray against the horizon so even an odd-shaped bush can hold interest as you go down the road and try to imagine what it could be. Virginia creeper, looking for vertical opportunity, will settle on a telephone pole and wind its way along the wires. I know one place where it looks like a dinosaur leaning across the road. So a lone chicken would certainly attract anybody's attention. There's plenty of time for your conscience to bother you if you don't stop. For Brian, I knew it was not possible to drive past that chicken.

But I also knew that Brian loved beating the odds. It was the idea of a marvelous escape from the black hand of death that intrigued him, an escape from a destiny so sealed and calculated that there were no options. Although he never came out and said it, he believed we were all recipients of extraordinary good luck and fortune, and when we weren't, there was an intervening hand that would save us. There were times I wanted him to tell me that, although I wasn't inclined to believe it.

He put the box inside the shop right next to the wood-stove and stoked the fire a few times during the night. The bird was still alive in the morning and Brian looked triumphant as he came through the back door for breakfast. He loved chickens and missed not having them around. We got rid of the last flock when feed got too expensive.

"Are you going into town?" I said.

"I could. Maybe get a bag of feed." He pulled his wool cap high on his head and looked dunce-like, his eyes wide and innocent, like the thought had just occurred to him. I knew it hadn't.

"I thought that chicken was supposed to die, Brian."

"Yeah, well. You ought to talk to him and pet him every once in a while so he'll know the yard is yours, too."

"You sure it's a he? Maybe we've got a hen." I'm usually better at thinking positively in the morning.

"Not sure yet. You need a ride or something?"

"I've got to take the car to Troy's for a lube and oil. I could use a ride back. I've got too much to do to wait." There was always desk work. No one, not even me, knows exactly what I do when I do desk work, but I spend hours at it. Everyone, especially me, needs a preoccupation of some kind—space in which to figure things out. Sometimes it feels more like an obligation to something larger than what is at hand, or a distraction from the realities where I play at getting organized or dream. Don't know how I could stand it otherwise.

So off we went, one car behind the other, edging along the vast rectangles of corn stubble rows, exhausts belching white in the cold November air, while the chicken warmed itself by the stove. Big Mary's place was closed up tight as we passed, her rusted maroon and cream Thunderbird gone. Her cat curled on top of a few logs by the door of her weather-beaten shack. You always knew Mary was ready for cold weather by her woodpile, or ready for spring by her freshly tilled garden. Today, the woodpile looked neglected.

On summer days, when poppies and coreopsis scattered around her front door, the old yellow upholstered car seat in her yard looked inviting enough for a chat, and we sometimes did just that. I wondered if she still had her chickens, and whether she'd like one more. Or maybe a chicken for Sunday dinner. Her tall, black body, thick as a man's, seemed bent the last time I'd seen her, her hair almost white. Maybe she'd gone off to Florida to visit her son, which she sometimes did, taking the Greyhound from Cambridge. We drove on.

With the leaves down, Puckum looked particularly bleak, showing plainly the peeling paint and windward lean of old houses on Main Street. Tables were set up for Saturday's yard sales, the town's main industry, where the expression "What goes around comes around" originated. Still, the town was its gayest on Saturdays, with rainbows of jackets, dresses, bedspreads, and curtains strung out between the trees and blowing in the constant wind like so many welcoming flags. I headed toward the stark white storefront behind which was Troy's Auto Service.

He was under a '79 Nova in his cave of a garage. The cinder-block walls soaked up the grey November light where cracks encouraged ivy to come in from the cold. Years of oil stains patterned the cement floor while a bare light bulb hung over the workbench. Another light moved toward me out of the dark; Troy worked by portable lighting like a miner. You could tell he was a good mechanic by the way his shirt was always tucked neatly inside his belt and his still-dark hair was slicked back. The man had *pride* and nurtured well the oldest cars in town. I imagined him as a teenager—the same black hair in a pompadour, low-slung jeans, and loafers—loving cars. He probably grew up in this town although I didn't know for sure. He just had that look about him. He probably was born when this garage was built in the late thirties, and grew up hanging around the two gas pumps out front, which he sawed off the last time prices went up.

Now he put his hands in his pockets, hiked up his work pants and said, "Time for another lube and oil already?"

"One hundred forty-four thousand miles is nothing to neglect. Can you take my car this morning?"

Funny how you lay people aside and only connect them with a certain performance. I see Troy regularly, every 3000 miles and then forget him until the numbers roll around, our clocks ticking away till next time when we exchange pleasantries and then go on about our business. That's why when he called me once and said he'd saved an old windshield wiper motor out of one of the wrecks because he noticed last time I was in that mine was wearing out, I was amazed that he'd thought about my car in the interim.

"Well, I've had some good news today," he began. "My wife got up and walked around—with a little help."

I realized I was supposed to know about something. It's been happening on a regular basis. I used to complain to Charlie, my ex, "You never told me," and usually he hadn't, but I was beginning to think I just didn't remember.

"Has she been sick, Troy?"

And just as if I'd slapped him, he turned his head to one side and said, "You didn't know? I thought I told you. She's got cancer. Of the pancreas. Doctor told me we'll be lucky to have her till Christmas. Thought I told you last time you were in."

Maybe he did, but the news echoed through that shop and around my ears as though someone had hit the nearest fender with a sledge hammer. I had seen his wife only once, a tall, slender blonde with a cigarette between her fingers, who followed him around the shop and answered his telephone with a serious look as the cigarette hung off the edge of the desk. I was sure this was the first time I'd heard about her illness.

A while ago, when the kids all graduated from high school, Troy figured he could finally take it easier, so he began to close the shop on Saturdays. Most people in town were annoyed, but Troy told me he figured it was time to have weekends with his wife, especially since he'd just bought a Boston Whaler and they could do some fishing. I pictured them hauling the boat to the town ramp and loading it up with the cooler and fishing rods and pushing off, free at last—free of kids, free of Saturdays at the garage and its mortgage. Since this was around the time of my divorce, I envied them. The images of a couple still wanting to be together on weekends nibbled around my brain and emphasized my own situation. I remember how comforting it was when I mentioned to Troy at one of my 3000-mile intervals that my husband had left, and he looked at me straight and said, "What? Is the man crazy?" That was pure nice.

"My God, Troy—I'm really sorry. My brother had the same thing. I know what you're going through." Dumb thing to say. No one knows what anyone else goes through. Troy stood there with his hands in his pockets and hiked up his pants again. Then he nodded his head, adjusted his shoulders and looked as though he wanted to say, "I've never done this before. I don't know what to do. I don't believe it to begin with," like he had to tell people and maybe if he said it often enough, he would believe it.

A few minutes later when Brian picked me up, I told him about Troy's wife.

"You told me about that the last time you had the car in," he said patiently, like he was getting used to me forgetting things. I tried to pass it off with the excuse of too much desk work, but Troy *had* told me—and I was upset about not remembering.

What I do remember is having young Troy Jr. work on

my car. He married, and although he was younger than Brian, had an infant son. He loved to tell me what the baby was doing at every one of my 3000 miles. One day, he called me and asked if he could borrow twenty-five dollars which just didn't make any sense at all. I didn't know him that well.

"Are you in some kind of trouble?" I asked. It was his wife's birthday, he explained; he already owed his dad and didn't want to ask him.

"Sure," I said, because the suddenness of it spun me around a little. But when he came into my kitchen ten minutes later, I knew what it was that made him race pell-mell toward that twenty-five dollars. He couldn't look me in the eye, and was flushed, sweaty, and antsy.

I remember saying to him, "You're lucky, Troy Jr. I don't usually keep that much money around here."

"I'll pay you back tomorrow, soon as I get paid," he said, dancing on a spot on the floor. Of course, he didn't. I waited a few days and then called Troy.

"I think that boy's got major problems," I said, "and I just thought maybe you ought to know if you don't already."

"Yeah, I'm sorry he got you." Troy sounded weary. "He's hit nearly every one of my customers to support his habit. Don't give him any more, okay? I'm trying to get him into rehab. Trouble is, he was in before, but soon's he got out, that dealer was waiting for him on the corner."

Troy lost a lot of customers around that time, but I hung on, knowing there's a time we can't help what our kids do. Troy charged me a lot less for the lube and oil jobs. I always asked about Troy Jr. and for a while things stayed the same. Then one day Troy announced that Troy Jr. was back home with his wife and had a new job. You could just see the trouble lift right off Troy and he did a lot less shoulder adjusting.

Brian bought a ten-pound bag of feed, enough for one

chicken for a few months. Guess he figured he was in for the duration. I tried to ignore the whole thing, but when I got up in the morning that chicken was leaning against the shop door. It was beginning to grow wing feathers, and a comb and a wattle, portentous signs of things to come. Spurs would be next.

Brian said, "See how he doesn't stand up by himself? That's because there's no room in those chicken houses for them to stand on their own, they're jammed in there so tight. His leg muscles are still weak."

They didn't look weak to me. That rooster was doing a good job of scratching up the garden, which didn't matter in December but would come spring. And those wing feathers— soon he'd flare up at me anytime he wanted. He was already practicing at the back door, half flying, half jumping up the steps, leaving slippery presents.

One morning I awoke to the strangest whine and after blaming it on the refrigerator, I realized it was the rooster practicing his crow. It was a rather lonely sound, raucous at the edges. When something gives voice, it's a hard heart that doesn't listen, so that's why when Brian came into the kitchen for his breakfast and announced that he'd decided to bring the rooster down to our neighbor, Big Mary, I had mixed feelings.

"Well, he's beginning to crap all over the step," he said, "and I'm just about out of feed again. I guess I shouldn't have saved him in the first place."

"He's had a taste of a real life for a while, and that's something," I reassured him.

"Yeah, and now somebody'll have a taste of him! You can't mess with destiny too much, I guess," he said, and dug his hands in his pockets. I'd noticed that stance in him before. It bothered me. I wanted his innocence and optimism back.

Just after Christmas, the odometer spun around to

147,000, but I waited till 148,000 appeared. Then one morning when I was on my way to the post office, 148,503 rolled in and I decided to see if Troy had any time for a lube and oil.

Troy doesn't have a hydraulic lift. He climbs down into a pit, carrying that light of his. When I walked into the garage, my eyes squinting to adjust to the darkness, he was just pulling himself out of the pit with the light draped over one shoulder, the black cord trailing behind.

"Hey, is it time for a lube and oil already?" he said, and wiped his permanently stained hands on a rag. "Guess you saw it in the paper—my wife died last week."

I stared at him. So much could happen in 3000 miles. "No, Troy. I didn't know. I'm so sorry."

"It was terrible at the end." His hands were in his pockets and he hiked up his pants and adjusted his shoulders. "She was home. We talked about it and she thought it might be too hard on me, the memories, you know, if she died at home. But I told her I don't want it any other way. Imagine all the trouble she had and she still thinkin' about somebody else." His eyes turned watery then, and red.

"We had thirty-five years together," he went on, "and only about eight months when the boys weren't around. They kept coming back you know, between girlfriends and marriages, and she put up with all of it. Long as I live I never will understand—she was such a good person—you know—why—why she had to suffer so bad. I got one boy up at the house now and by God, I'm glad he's there. I couldn't stand the loneliness."

"Yeah, that's the hard part," I heard myself say. "Somehow you never picture yourself being alone." And then I hit a fly ball, the one that I'd kept inside for so long, I had no idea it was still there. "At least she didn't leave because she wanted to." My voice cracked. So long, so very long ago, it was Charlie who had left; there was no earthly reason for me to care about it any longer.

"Yeah," he said softly, looking me in the eye. "Yeah." And then quickly, maybe because he wanted to distract me which is all we can ever do for one another, he said, "We had plans. We had plans for five years from now. We were always plannin'."

He didn't know, of course, what was ahead of him. You get educated, *pay your tuition,* as Charlie used to say. I knew about the hurt of peering into empty closets, of knowing that at last something you had only heard about but didn't believe would ever apply to you, had dropped in your lap, and that nothing you touched would ever be the same again—that midstream, the current and wind had gone against you, accompanied by the nagging thought that you could have prevented it somehow, and forevermore you'd listen to the wind and the refrigerator in whining conclusions and dream again and again the most vivid dreams about someone coming back to you and laughing again, and on waking you'd mourn the past perfect and wait for some vague thing to come and rescue you.

The car would be good till 151,503. I jotted the number down on a slip of paper and put it in the glove compartment. Heading toward the farm, I met Brian coming the other way. We stopped and rolled down our windows. The wind stirred up the papers I had on the rear seat, confusing my notes—all that desk work and some of my conclusions.

"Just brought the rooster to Mary," Brian said. "She was glad to get him. Said she just got out of the hospital after having cataracts removed. She had on those thick glasses they give you." He was shivering in his jean jacket, his hands stiff and tense on the steering wheel. "I didn't want to stare or anything, but you know what? She's got socks tacked up around the door frame to keep the draft out. I couldn't feel any heat coming from her house so I helped her get the stove lit, although she insisted she could do it herself. Can you imagine? To live so long and be sick and alone and not be warm? How can that be? I'm going to split some wood for her. She's low."

Funny how things work out. If he hadn't saved that bird off the side of the road, he'd never have gotten that particular piece of education about Mary. Maybe there *was* real purpose in our scurries across this earth. We sat there a moment wrapped in our separate vehicles, staring into each other's eyes and I knew to my toes what a good son I had. That's something in this old world. He'd better leave home soon or he'd be taking care of us old buzzards forever. And me—I'd come this way so long without Charlie—I knew I could handle the rest.

I saw my life widen all the way to the distant horizon of trees. I was a part of everything and separate from it, too, a lover of wide spaces and only a dot in them as well. I had no right to ask for more than I'd had—I'd never been without food or warmth—and Troy, although he didn't believe it just now, had been incredibly lucky with thirty-five years alongside someone he was truly grieving for.

I'd look in on Mary myself although she was probably going to brush off any offers of help. And then I got to thinking—what if you were a man who'd just lost your wife and the refrigerator was bleak with a single pork chop and a stale slice of last year's fruitcake, and someone, say, an old customer of yours who understood something about you, was to bring you an apple pie? Would you think she was after you too soon or would you just think that she'd missed your wife's funeral and wanted to comfort you in some way? Would you think she was a good woman and that because you'd just had a good woman, you might want another one to keep away the cold? Or would you think that nothing really good could come in a one-horse town that squatted down in these frozen fields? Or was it only a question of *when* would you look across the wide abyss and dare to dream there might be something more?

The Strawberry Field

It was a June dusk that lingered over the field reluctant to let in the night as the dark green strawberry plants, lush with fruit, lay in muddied rows. At the edge of the field and on the dirt road leading to the plain, asbestos-shingled farmhouse, a flat farm wagon stood piled high with baskets and other things, among them a large scale and an aluminum lawn chair on which sat a young man in his mid-thirties. In the lengthening shadows, his tanned face showed lines as intricate and delicate as the smallest branches in winter, and on his head, his thick, black hair churned as if it didn't know which way to go. He watched the girl standing on the ground before him with interest as she daydreamed, staring at his knobby work boots. In her hands she held a white, two-handled enameled pot full of strawberries.

J.D. had been watching her pick them for about a half an hour now, and she picked quickly, stooping and rising, stepping over the rows and searching, stooping again and waving her white arms through the leaves as she looked for the best of them till the whole of her movement seemed like a dance. Now she'd have the berries weighed by his wife. He grinned down at her and waited for her to look up. When their eyes met, he quickly looked out across his field.

His field. Over which the irrigation spray shot out with engine-driven force that rattled leaves and dug the ground, spraying wide over the tangled vines of the sugar peas and the wide, deep green rows of strawberries. The system was new this year, a measure of security against drought and disaster. It made him confident, as did the pickers who'd pulled up from the surrounding towns, places like Eldorado and Shiloh, and broke the peace with car door slams and shouting. They dragged an assortment of pots and baskets out of car trunks and carried them to his wife, Louise, who weighed them, wrote the weight on the bottom with a thick, black marker, and sent the pickers off to the more abundant areas of the field. She worked hard, that Louise, he'd give her that, harder than he, some days. And she got the bills paid, although he wasn't always sure how.

The girl at his feet was the last of them for the day. The sun, just disappearing behind the blue-violet clouds on the horizon, sent shadows that had softened to a charcoal everywhere, except on the dirty blonde hair of his wife who took the pot from the girl. He wished he'd sent Louise up to the house earlier so he'd be the one doing the taking.

She read out loud the figure she'd marked earlier on the bottom, "One and a half pounds," swung the pot onto the scale and called out, "Four and three quarters, a little over." She figured quickly on a small white pad, all too aware that her arms were fleshy and her figure lumpy, as if she'd had many children, although the child playing under the wagon was her only one and not even her husband's. Only adopted by him. A fact that she never forgot, like a business deal she still owed on. She tried not to envy the slim figure or good looks of the girl before her as she took the money, dropped it in the cash box, and gathered up the change. She was sure J.D. was having a good look, though.

"Right pretty, ain't they? You makin' jam or pie?" she said, and counted into the girl's hand, slowly fingering the quarter, nickel, and dimes. Whether or not he realized it, she was paying him back with her determination to make a go of things, calculating late into the night how they were to have enough to keep the tractor going, the pumps pulsing, and the chickens in the long smelly houses behind her fed. Meanwhile, her own small garden lay bare inside the small straggly hedge that surrounded it, bone dry—but that was all right for now. Everything in good time.

"Thank you," she said and smiled. "Come back, hear? They'll be right for another week or so."

The girl nodded. Louise saw J.D. grin wide, take the girl all in, up and down and across, and heard him say, "Feels like April, don't it? Been chilly enough and no rain," and then the words that seemed of such little or great significance that she was almost satisfied, "You live around here?" and the answer, "Eldorado, off Yellow Dog Road."

He knew the house which had been brought over from just across the Delaware line, delivered in two halves, each on platform trailers and set at the edge of a field of winter rye last spring. Modular homes always looked temporary to him, and he wondered if anyone had ever picked up stakes, split the house in halves again, and gone off with his half on the back of a trailer.

Regarding the girl, she looked as though she'd just graduated high school and was too young to have a house of her own, although she stood there holding that pot of strawberries and looking at him like she didn't take stuff off anybody. It made him look from her to his land again, needing to feel the importance of his possessions, all that responsibility, proud at the way the water shot out of the irrigation system over the peas and soon, soon over the strawberries again as it rotated. He may as well have said to her with a sweep of his hand, "This is who I am, all this..."

He felt his wife's eyes on him as he turned and winked at

the girl, but he ignored her. And now, because the girl herself glared at him, he looked away again and concentrated on the changing light as the sun broke through the clouds and drenched everything with the last orange-gold rays. He lost himself in it, in the color of his hands and arms and the darkening fields, in the blaze of clouds and even his own house, which was transformed into something beautiful and substantial, and when he finally glanced back, the girl had turned to go, the pot of strawberries on her shoulder, those slender hips hardly swaying.

At midnight they came like thieves to get the chickens. Chicken dreams didn't include being swept away, and generally they were quiet when the men packed them into wooden crates for the processing plant, but not tonight. They were stirred up and squawking as though best-laid plans and pent-up desires had been thwarted. The men worked quickly, and within an hour, five thousand chickens were on the truck and quiet again. J.D. looked around for escapees and finding none, waved to the men as the truck rumbled off, feathers flying. The empty chicken house seemed eerie now, larger, smellier, hollow as a gourd. There was a mile of manure to clean up before the new batch of chicks arrived in a couple of weeks. He looked forward to their delivery, although there was a lot of work to be done before and after they came.

He sat in the kitchen with a Bud Lite, enjoying the sight of moonlight glancing off the barn roof and slashing across the old silo, listening to the moths hitting the screens, a far-off owl, a whippoorwill in the tree closest to the house. But these sounds did nothing to erase the pleading sound of chickens that lingered in his ears. He imagined it, of course, but wondered what it would feel like to be packed in a crate and hauled off in the middle of the night. Did they sense what was going to happen to them? The sound persisted.

Annoyed, he gulped the last of the beer and climbed the stairs, where the sound grew louder even through the drone of the irrigation system, and he understood, finally, that it was Billy, Louise's son. He liked the kid well enough, although it had taken a while to get used to him, and he liked him even better as he got older. He was five now, and not much trouble.

Entering the bedroom he and Louise shared, J.D. said, "Hey. Hey, Louise." But the damp mountain of flowered cotton nightgown that was his wife breathed deep and long—he'd have to check on Billy himself.

He didn't need a light, the moon being so bright across Billy's bed where the boy cried and gasped as though he'd been crying for a long time. Odd that Louise didn't hear him. "Billy," he said. "It's okay, buddy. What's wrong?" He felt the kid's forehead precisely the way his mother had done when he was little. "Ah now, Billy—you feelin' bad?"

Back in the bedroom, he laid his hand on his wife's shoulder and shook her. "Hey. Hey, Louise, get up. Billy's crying. He's sick again."

"Hmm?" She opened eyes that were grey and bloodshot. "Oh. Oh," she said and got up, her hair askew and the gown sticking to her jiggling hips as she scuffed her way barefooted to Billy's bedroom.

He undid his boots, slid off his jeans, and lay on the bed, his hands tucked under his head as he stared up at the ceiling, thinking of the girl. There were plenty of ways to keep things a secret. All anybody had to do was ride down any number of seldom-traveled roads and park by the woods, she being willing. Something told him she wouldn't be, something in the way she cocked her head when she looked up at him, something in the way her long, bony fingers curled around the handles of the pot, something that told him now as he thought about it that she was very capable and sure of herself. He liked her even more.

Louise came back holding Billy in her arms as if he were still a baby, his eyes half-shut, cheeks flushed.

"I think we should carry him to the hospital. He has a fever—104."

"Naw," he heard himself say, although it was more like a test, not a real refusal. "He'll be all right. Can'tcha give him some aspirin?"

The hospital was an hour away and it was already two in the morning. Tomorrow there was that mile of chicken manure to clean up and she had to weigh strawberries. The kid did look bad though. Not breathing right. Goddamn.

"All right," he said. "If you think so," and started to pull on his jeans. Louise laid Billy on the bed, covered him with the sheet, and hurriedly pulled a dress over her head on top of the nightgown, her face pale and worried looking when her head emerged. She wiggled and tugged the fabric down with her hands, glancing at Billy every other second and slipping into lace-less tennis shoes all at the same time. She smoothed Billy's hair and scooped him up as easily as she'd picked up bags of chicken feed, her arms used to hauling. "Ready?" she said.

He nodded, imagining that the girl would pull a dress over her head in an entirely different way, her white arms coming through the sleeves like swans' necks, the dress slipping down over her slim frame like silk. Or that stuff in the Victoria's Secret catalogue—satin. It made him want her. Which was stupid, he knew. He knew, too, they had to pass her house on the road to the hospital and he'd watch for it and look for a light and what kind of truck her husband had, even though he knew that was stupid, too, and it would come to no good. He was still thinking about her when his own truck rattled down the long lane at the edge of the strawberry rows and passed under the irrigating spray, which drummed the windshield enough to blind him for a moment. He heard the boy, each breath a struggle, more like a gasp. For his last birthday, J.D. had given him a toy John Deere tractor that Billy dragged wherever he went. One of these days he'd be big enough to help out.

They were quiet most of the way and Louise must have thought he was worried about Billy because it seemed like she was trying to comfort him, or justify getting him out in the middle of the night.

"It's always better to know what's wrong than to be guessing and worrying. They can get him started on an antibiotic or something, I'm sure," she said to him as well as to herself as her body swayed with the play of the truck. He nodded to the windshield and pulled his cap farther down over his eyes. He was aware that she watched the child in her arms and didn't see him look at the small, white, modular house on the left. It was dark. There was no truck, no vehicle of any kind parked outside, only a bicycle leaning near the back door. Two-thirty in the morning and she wasn't home. Wasn't it a black Saturn she had climbed into the afternoon before?

He peered ahead, the road parting, the truck devouring the dotted line. His thoughts turned to the farm, what he had to do. He had nine acres in strawberries, planted four acres that first year, which were mature now. Louise planted an acre and a half by herself, down on her knees. Had to have strawberries, she said. After that they'd rented a planter like they did for the tomatoes, six head sitting across the back, dropping the plants down the chute. They planted four different varieties so they'd have berries for a longer picking season. He had U-Pick signs on the main road, plus an ad in the paper. They'd do okay. The peas should be ready for harvest by next week and then he'd plant soybeans. He owed big time on the irrigation system, but this batch of chickens would help.

He knew his fields like the back of his hand. Knew how

much fertilizer, what balance, and how much moisture in the ground at any given time. He had the dates burned in his brain, when to spray herbicide, when to drop the seed, when to turn the watermelon vines, when to harvest tomatoes, when the next batch of chickens would arrive. She did the books. He admitted he ought to do more there. Half the time he didn't know exactly what he owed, what he made. But she did. Didn't spend a dime on herself. And looked it. He felt old when he looked at her. She had looked better when Billy was a baby, like she was some kind of Madonna then, her hair in curls around her face and that baby in her arms. She looked so happy it made him want some of it.

He wondered if the girl had kids yet. He didn't think so judging by that flat stomach and those narrow hips. Women who had kids looked different. Not in the obvious ways like weight gain or bulging stomachs. He didn't know what it was exactly, maybe the way they held themselves, as if they were always wrapped around a kid. They got softer and more solid at the same time, always listening, laughing quietly as though they were satisfied and didn't need another thing. Louise was like that at first, but then she got caught up in the farm work and always seemed tired and distracted, a little bossy, telling him what he could spend. Truth was, he didn't think about her much—not that he didn't care—she was just there. But maybe that was because she'd blended in so well with his plans for the farm. In the four years of their marriage, they'd both become tied to the land and to the rhythm of the crops, and now it seemed as though neither one had a choice about anything.

He stared at the center-line in the road ahead of him and listened to the boy and the whine of the truck. It occurred to him that he was speeding through a life that had become a blur. He wanted a few landmarks, something to say, "Hey, here it is, something significant and unforgettable. You're really living now."

It could be meningitis. To come down with a fever that quick when he was all right in the afternoon and through dusk reminded Louise of the time when her kid sister suddenly got sick. The doctor came every day for a week and hung anxiously over the baby's crib. Finally the fever broke and her sister began to stir back to life. They had better medicines now. He'll be fine, she told herself.

She felt his cheeks burn under her touch. Might be one of those darned ear infections again, she thought, as she studied his shock of dark, silky hair. He could easily pass for J.D.'s son although he had his father's round face, which was full of remembrance for her, but hope too, that she would give Billy a better childhood than his father had had. It was because of him that she made herself get up out of the mire of her first marriage, get on her two strong legs, and use her two strong arms for something good. The weight of Billy's head on her arm had become almost unbearable, and she shifted so that his head rested on her breast. It was chilly and she hadn't thought to bring a blanket or anything, so anxious was she to get in the truck and speed into the night. For Billy was her light, at the heart of everything, all of the work down on her knees, the strawberries planted at her insistence like insurance. She thought of the strawberries as hers, hers as sure as her own arm. J.D., truth be known, made her feel uneasy at times, precarious as a red-winged blackbird on a reed of grass. He *was* a reed of grass, blowing every which way. Changing his mind fifty times about those four acres till she finally said, "Strawberries, that's it. I'll do 'em myself." But it was other things, too. He had a wandering eye. Even now, she felt tenuous riding in the truck with him, as if he might pull over and ask her to jump out. She wasn't stupid. It was only a matter of time before he found someone younger and slimmer, like the girl who came by at dusk. Easy come, easy go. She'd heard him say it a million times. Though if he wanted to split, he had another think coming.

It was only on the farm with her feet on the ground that she felt safe, like she had an important part to play. Even before the installation of the new irrigation system, as she looked out the back door and saw the field blossom despite the dry spring, she felt a strength and a sense of belonging she couldn't explain, a feeling that everything was as it should be even though the farm wasn't hers. She'd been taken in like an orphan in a way. An orphan with child. God knows why he wanted her so bad but he did. And she was delighted. Those good looks and thick, black hair, all that attention that summer and fall after the vacuum she'd lived in, he opened her heart like a June morning. As time went on, she became more and more intent on paying him back for his kindness. He needed her steadiness; he wasn't good at handling money, and neither was his first wife, who all during their first harvest hung out at the local bar.

But that was history. Now it was strawberry season, a reason to sing in the kitchen. The daisies that sprung up among the runners and the timing of their blossoming and the ripening fruit always seemed like a holy arrangement, evidence of a divine plan. She had put in the tender plants herself with Billy playing in the sandy earth close by, row after row after row. Two things gave her purpose, centered her, made her breathe deep with satisfaction: her child and the harvest. She'd married a father for Billy, found a place for them both, and planted for their future.

Which was why strawberry time was as grand as a festival to her. All spring, she waited for the sweet smell that would soon hang over the fields. The cars that pulled up along the road always seemed like her party guests. She loved hearing the kids call and chase each other and steal mouthfuls, loved the old women who gracefully stooped and rose stiffly, patient in their slow way to find the most prolific spot, where they stooped again, careful and respectful of the berries, chatting with her the whole time like family come to visit as she filled her own baskets. She loved the company of the young women as they straddled the rows and shared the gossip from town, scooted kids along, and enticed them to help by saying, "Look at the size of these, will ya!" And she loved the surprise of the biggest berries hidden under thick, dense leaves, the heat on her back as she gathered, her hands stained red, and later, the weight of the cash box as she trudged up to the house at the end of the day. And then the smell of strawberries in her own kitchen, berries so big and thick they prickled her skin as she washed and stirred through them, feeling abundance, so much abundance, and with it safety from the hunger she'd known before Billy was born, when Billy's father had a habit that sponged up everything not nailed down. She was used to doing without, including food, and when she finally got herself out of it, she swore she'd never depend on a man again.

And she wasn't dependent now, although it might look like it to him. She stopped watching Billy's face for a moment to look up and see an entire field of fireflies darting low over a stretch of soybeans as if they were stars let loose to run wild. Watching them set her mind at ease, but only for a moment. She was sorry to be pulled away from the farm just now. The berries wouldn't wait; only her child could pull her away.

J.D. was relieved to hear the doctor who examined Billy say, "Chicken pox. He's got some on his back. Take him home, give him aspirin, and be sure he gets plenty of liquid." He was satisfied about the aspirin, but Louise responded with a stony look—the fever hovered at almost 105—and her expression didn't change when the doctor patted her on the shoulder.

He was dog-tired and could only think about whether he was going to get to clean the chicken house or tend the cash box in the strawberry field—as if he had a choice and as if the chicken house couldn't wait. Mainly, he thought the girl might come back and he could talk to her without his wife there if he tended the strawberries.

"Let's go," he said to Louise, more gruffly than he'd intended. "Like I said, aspirin woulda done it," avoiding her grey, bloodshot eyes and the puffy rings beneath them. When he looked down at the small, blotched face on the examining table, it reminded him of berry stains and he felt anxious, as if hunters lurked in the woods through which he was walking. It was a vague feeling and probably there were no grounds for it. The kid would be okay in a couple of hours.

When they got back to the farm, Louise took Billy into their bed and J.D. slept in Billy's room. He didn't mind being in the kid's room—he could see the barn roof from the window and the old roofless silo where dozens of vultures perched on the top edge, a macabre sight but usually comforting in the way that familiar things offered solidity. However, tonight he thought of stirring them up with a blast of his shotgun. It was time for them to move on, he thought. The birds had been there since he bought the place, back in 1991 when his folks made him an offer he couldn't refuse. "Done with farming," his mother had said, looking down at gnarly hands. "We're heading for the mountains. Always did seem too flat on the shore for my tastes anyway." One hundred and fifty acres and all the equipment.

When he met Louise, she had Billy on her hip, over to the Sharptown Carnival. He watched her for a while carrying that baby, passing by all the stands and rides, just looking. He figured she didn't have much, not even a wedding band on her finger, and would be appreciative. He'd figured right. She was a worker and took nothing for granted.

He dozed off and slept lightly till sunup, which didn't seem like any time at all.

Louise stayed up to the house with Billy all day. He still wanted nothing to eat or drink and lay listlessly in front of the TV. J.D. went back down to the field after lunch and with the sun and mosquitoes beating down on him mercilessly, he squinted and yawned from the lack of sleep while he weighed baskets and pots and wash-basins full of berries. Just as he had hoped, the girl showed up sometime in the afternoon, and when he turned to receive her same white double-handled enameled pot heaped with berries, he jumped a little at the recognition, like a thought that took form before his very eyes.

"You're back! Makin' more jam?" he said as if he cared what she did with them. Actually he did care; he began to think about watching her eat one, suck on its redness with those juicy lips reaching out like a kiss. Yeah, kiss a berry. He would like to watch her tongue search through the red meat of it, remembering everything there was to know about redness and sweetness, the berry's optimum moment, like love appearing at the right time or whatever it was that made him so helpless in this moment as she stood before him, smallish breasts poking out that pure white T-shirt.

No," she said through even, white teeth and a sweet upsweep at the corners of her mouth. "I'm not much of a cook. I either eat them fresh or give them away to my friends. They'll never be better than they are with the sun still in them."

"You got that right," he said. And then he weighed the berries and told her how much but after that he couldn't think of one single thing to say, his mind being as empty as the chicken house floor, except for his kid being in the hospital the night before. So he said that. "We took our boy to the hospital last night." He was afraid it sounded like an excuse for something he thought she might be expecting.

"Sorry to hear that," she said and waited. He felt her eyes on him. "Is he okay?"

"Yeah. Came home and he's up to the house now. Chicken pox. Up all night, out in this sun, I'm standin' here half asleep. You by yourself?"

"You mean today or all the time?"

"Well, both, if you want to say."

"Ah-uh to both. Just bought a house—money my mother left me."

"Oh. That's right smart. Can't go wrong with that." He noticed she shifted her weight, the pot being heavy and all, and just at that moment he saw an older woman come toward him with baskets so full the berries kept rolling off the top. He turned from the girl for a second to help and heard the girl say, "Well, bye."

He snapped back around. "What's your name, anyhow? You like line dancing? They got it up to the American Legion on Tuesday nights. It's a good way to meet people."

"It's Celie, and maybe I will. Thanks." She walked off to the black Saturn parked on the side of the road.

He was weighing things; he could get away every Tuesday and learn to line dance after strawberry season. Louise would never leave the kid for a half a second.

When he went up to the house around supper time, Billy was still lying on the couch watching TV. Whether or not he was really watching it, awake enough to understand the language of the Teletubbies, was debatable. It was chicken pox all right: a few more bumps had shown up, and his fever had dropped to 103. Louise called softly from the kitchen, "Supper's ready," in a voice that was calm and matter-of-fact enough, just so polite and sweet it made him feel like she knew what and who was on his mind.

In the evening, Billy still wouldn't take anything, just lay there with his eyes on the screen and his hot head heavy on the pillow. It was eerie the way he didn't move or say a peep. In a while Louise gave up trying to get him to drink and with the TV still on and turned low, she went to the kitchen and began pulling off the green caps of strawberries, slicing each in half and piling them in her largest pot. She was just measuring out the sugar when she heard J.D. come in from the chicken house and climb the stairs to bed. "G'night," she called out to him. He grunted, as though too tired for a word more.

She laid the jars she'd been saving all year on the oven rack and lit the stove. The stirring took a long time, and as she stood over the thickening red jam and tucked strands of hair behind her ears, she thought about the cash box and wondered how much he took in while she was in the house, maybe enough to pay for the visit to the emergency room. In a while, she checked on Billy. His eyes were closed. She put the thermometer in his mouth anyway, and waited, rubbing his arm gently. 104.5. "Billy," she said. "You've got to take this for Mommy," and she gave him a baby aspirin to chew and a drink of water. He immediately fell back to sleep. "Chew it, Billy, come on, and drink this for me." She waited again and tipped the glass to his mouth. The glass clicked on his teeth. He took a gulp, then coughed a little but lay back down. She smoothed his T-shirt, feeling the heat of his body through it, and covered him with a light blanket. *Waiting is hard*, she thought. *It's like a rubber band of minutes stretched out.*

The house this quiet, her husband already gone to bed and her son sleeping and nothing but the crickets and fireflies outside the screen door to keep her company, she felt in possession of things. The fever would break soon; she willed it so.

In the kitchen, she watched the light red foam cling to the side of the pot and stirred it away. *Stirring away impurities*, she thought, as she scraped some off the top of the syrup and dropped it in the sink. She stirred some more, and then stood the hot jars upright on a towel and began to ladle the jam into the funnel that she held over the jars, never dropping any on the cloth or down the side of the jar, leaving space at the top for the paraffin wax. The berries swam in their thick, sugary juice like exotic fish; they were part of a kind of worship, a summation of the years and hours she'd spent down on her knees planting and harvesting. She had twenty-one jars ready. If she hadn't been blessed in other ways, she was in this: a son, a good harvest of strawberries, and a home. A good husband? She guessed he was a good husband. Better than the last. She wished for more to talk about. Maybe when they'd had kids between them, there'd be more to talk about. Billy still felt like just hers. Before she melted the paraffin, she checked on him again. He was sound asleep.

She moved closer to him to see if his fever had broken. He was very still, though he felt slightly cooler, and then with a heart stab she saw that he wasn't breathing, which couldn't be. She leaned closer, her nose to his ear and pushed away what couldn't be—couldn't be—no, she screamed, no—no—no—no—and shook him and breathed her breath into his mouth and screamed again and again and again, waking J.D.—she screamed, her face in her hands, and ran to the kitchen and back again to Billy's side and back again to the kitchen and took a jar and poured the jam like berry blood over her hands and down the sink and felt no pain and every pain there was, again and again, senselessly pouring another jar and another, screaming into the teeming June night.

He was too late to stop her. He ran to the couch—to the

telephone—trying to control his shaking finger on the buttons—
9-1-1— and then toward Louise whose hands—was it blood?
He couldn't understand, and it was as though he was watching
from afar as he plowed through something thick as jelly to
reach her, calm her, hold her, not understanding it was destiny
coming to crush down on them.

"For chrissake, Louise," he said, "Jesus and Mary." Over
and over and over.

People were nice. J.D.'s folks drove up from North
Carolina and even people they hardly knew gathered at the
roadside cemetery off Blink Horn Road. The minister said a
few words despite the fact that they'd never been to his
church, and the funeral director, someone Louise had
graduated high school with, said, "You ought to sue him, that
doctor who told you to take the boy home. If it were me, I
would," and he put his head down and looked at his shoes.
He wasn't the sort who usually voiced opinions, Louise knew.
"Ain't right, Louise," he said and patted her arm. Louise kept
her bandaged hands in her pockets, her eyes angry and dark,
hanging on to that anger, huge as a medicine ball in her heart,
afraid that if she let go of it she'd never stop crying. It
shouldn't have happened. It just shouldn't have, and her mind
couldn't grasp it, even now, staring at the hothouse daisies
arranged in sprays over the casket. Billy was back home,
playing, waiting for her to come in the door.

J.D. watched her through the weary, hot summer,
watched her push her plate away without hardly touching it,
watched her burst into tears when she heard music, heard her
sob once when she was walking through the strawberry field.

"I miss him," she said simply when J.D. put his arms

around her. "I can see him here between the rows. I'm scared someday I'll walk out here and I won't see him no more."

"I know, I know," he said, although he guessed he really didn't. "There's nothing we can do but get used to it," he said, as though he spoke from another county.

Slowly, her hands healed, and by the end of summer she took to working long hours with the hoe, chopping off the maverick vines that shot out from the strawberry plants across the rows. Some of the leaves curled and turned brown and she fretted that there was some kind of blight in them, but each morning, she pulled on leather work gloves and hoed some more. When she got up to the house in the afternoons, she clenched her teeth when she pulled off the gloves and spent the rest of the day with her hands held out in front of her as though they were still cooling.

"I'll do that with the tractor, Louise," J.D. said to her. Her obsession was beginning to frighten him. It was senseless, her doing by hand what he could do by machine, almost like she was staking a claim, maybe ready to take what was his, proving her attachment to the land. He was torn between thinking she owned the strawberry field in some way or was only needing to care for something.

"That's all right," she said. "Got nothing else to do."

So he left her to it, thinking the work might help her. He told himself that her tenacity was all she had, that she loved the fields as much as he. She slept in Billy's room now, unable to put away his things or wash his sheets, unable to clear away any traces of him.

Then one morning she got up and called a lawyer. Just like that. "Malpractice," she said, her eyes burning. He had a sense that he hadn't yet seen the best or worst of her and that he didn't really know what she was capable of. She took things hard, like underground water that ran deeper and deeper, cutting chasms in the earth. He could only watch her helplessly. He checked the books once. As far as he could see, she never missed a payment and still took care of things.

He saw Celie riding her bicycle every once in a while down on the state road as he drove truckloads of tomatoes to the cannery. He tooted his horn and waved, but that was all he had nerve for. She'd faded in his mind except for those moments when he saw her on the bike, her long, slim legs driving the pedals, leaning into the wind, the sight as pleasurable as an old song on the truck radio, reminding him of his first wife and wild days.

One day, toward the end of tomato season, he stopped the truck and waved her down. "How errr yooo?" She slowed and stopped the bike a few feet ahead of the truck and waited, turning toward him and smiling. He got out of the truck. "Not workin' today?"

"I teach school. One of the reasons is I get the summer off." She laughed then, eyed the truck and said, "Got any spare tomatoes?"

"Got any spare time?"

"For you, you mean?"

"Yeah, that's what I mean." His audacity amazed him.

"Aw no," she said. "You're married."

"What if I wasn't."

"I doubt it, anyway. You lost a child, for God's sake—your wife..." She stood there judging him, as if losing a child should seal him in.

"You like Eye-talian tomatoes? They call 'em plums?"

"Sure, any kind of tomato's okay."

He climbed up and got a handful, which she put in the basket of her bike. Seconds later she was off, his eyes following her down the road, the smell of tomatoes from the nearby cannery thick enough to make him sick.

He started going out in the evenings, tried line dancing although there was no one there that interested him, and wound up at Johnny's a few times, chomping down a few beers, after which he slept in the back of his pick-up all night just for the hell of it, or so he told himself. Louise questioned him when he got home but didn't raise a ruckus over it, although she had a mournful look about her he couldn't stand. He never missed a day in the fields except when it rained, which wasn't too often that fall. Even harvested all the soybeans before first frost, had them in storage down at Shiloh right and proper.

When he looked at the books again, he saw that the payments had been made on time for just about everything except the irrigation and realized there'd been no entries for the strawberry money. At first he didn't mind—she could have it if it gave her comfort—as long as money that was owed got paid. But the irrigation now, that worried him.

"I paid the lawyer with it," she said.

"Where's that gonna get you?" he shot back.

"You'll see. I'll buy this farm and pay for the irrigation besides," she said, hands extended in that odd way, arms bent at the elbows and tucked in close to her body, palms up as though she still carried something invisible in them, although all J.D. could see were her scars. She wanted him to be reminded and he hated the reminder.

"Louise, I want out of this." He didn't know what made him say it. It seemed to be the way they were headed.

"Then it'll have to be you what leaves. I ain't leavin'. The only thing I got now are them strawberry rows and I ain't leavin' 'em. So you go right ahead and do what you gotta do, fool around all you want—but I'm stayin' and Lord knows, I'll take the farm if you mess up too bad. Sure as I stand in this kitchen, I'll take this farm."

"The hell you will," he shouted, but even as he did so he

knew her words were a significant marker in the road. She was bluffing, of course, but he looked at her long and hard when she said that, weighing things. She had grown trim and her arms were empty, held out like he could save her again and she'd let him, almost daring him, her grey eyes narrowed with a determination that shocked him. He thought of the pleading sound of the chickens, and all at once he saw how everything had been decided with the planting of the first of the strawberries. And with that, he saw the brevity of things: of Billy's days—especially Billy's days—the thought of which caught in his throat and made him think how like the brief season of strawberries they were and much like his own days, his wasted search and pursuit days, and Louise's short-lived happiness, and the girl of his imaginings. And tugging at his sleeve, with no time for sorrow, was the persistence of things, the need to run the soil samples for the first fertilizer runs over the fields, his wife's arms wanting to be filled, and he saw the compromise the weak must make with the strong and how there wasn't anything to do but begin again come spring.

The Puckum Family Restaurant

In the summer morning stillness, a man and his cane plodded along the sidewalk in front of the big, old houses on Main Street, the heat of the day just now settling on his shoulders. In his early fifties and still dark-haired, he was heavyset and moved unhurriedly, as though he were comfortable with his station in life, devoid of ambition or stridency or aggravation, as though this June morning itself was enough to wake up to. He crossed the street and when he came to the lot where the Five and Dime used to be, a space now turned into a small park of sorts, he found the gossip bench—a phenomenon peculiar to Eastern Shore Maryland towns—and sat down.

Both hands rested on the cane as he gazed into the street through black sunglasses, giving the appearance at first glance of someone who might be sightless. He had a smallish, flat nose, adding to the pancake appearance of his face. The smile he gave his friend, Bern, who now appeared around the corner, did not disturb at all the roundness of his face, but disappeared into it.

"Hey, Alton," said Bern. "Goin' in?" and he nodded toward the door of the Puckum Family Restaurant with its faded orange and white striped vinyl awning.

Alton used the cane to hoist himself up. "You up all night like I was? Man, some kinda noise," he said, as he shook his head and the flesh under his chin shuddered.

Bern sprang for the door. "What, Fay again?"

"Her own fault. Shoulda left Clay in the jailhouse. Bailed him out Saturday. Don't know what in hell for."

A strap of sleigh bells tacked to the door of the restaurant jingled as the men entered. Bern, his powerhouse legs blackened by thick hair, shirt unbuttoned over his shorts, was already soaked with perspiration. He pulled out a handkerchief and wiped his neck before sitting in the booth. His jowls sat like the bottom end of a ripe pear beneath the too-small Shorebirds cap which he didn't bother to remove. When two cups of coffee immediately appeared on the table, he never looked at the person who brought them but as Norma May scuttled off to the kitchen, he glanced at her hips, which completed the daily ritual: the coffee, Norma May returning to the kitchen, and his targeted glance, a rapid succession of events he took for granted as much as his own breathing. Charlie, the proprietor, from his wheelchair by the last table in line with the TV, was absorbed in *The Sun Paper*. He called to the kitchen without looking up, "You got somebody." The TV, high on the opposite wall, showed a weatherman apologizing for the heat.

"Already got 'em," said Norma May.

"Hey," Charlie said then and nodded at the two men.

"Hey," said Alton, although he was trying to finish what he'd started. "Couldn't get away from the screamin' and yellin'. I finally went out on the sleep porch. All's I want is my room, my hall, my bathroom, and my porch. That's what I'm payin' for and that's what I'm usin'. Might be wrong but that's the way I feel 'bout it."

"Yeah. You got a right," Bern told him. "You know that bill for the cable? Suckers charged me twice for the same thing. Got channel 2 and 4 but that's it. Lost 8 and 12. Flippin', flippin', flippin' those channels and nothin's happenin'." Bern shook his head.

"If it can be fixed, I can fix it," offered Alton. "I can fix anything, any damn thing you got."

"Naw. This ain't the hookup. This the bill they screwed up on. I'm switchin' to Prime Star. Fifty channels. They got channel 5 and 13 and 16 and all. 47 and 22, 43, 96..." and he kept on naming all the channels he knew while the door opened again and the sleigh bells on the door sounded like Christmas and Rog, dressed in a multicolored Hawaiian shirt, sneezed in, hair tousled.

"Hey," said Alton.

The Hawaiian shirt sat down, sneezed again, face red, explaining, "Hay fever. Shoulda took my pill but I didn't," sneezed once more, coughed, too, and blew his nose, a strawberry of a nose hanging off his face like a welt.

"You're probably allergic to that shirt," said Alton.

"And then there's channel 52 and 55," Bern went on, "and if you get the second plan—they got different plans—you pay extra but you get more channels, 'stead of having it all one price, you get 102, 108, and they have some in 200, like 211 and 231 and then you got a choice—the movie channel and the sports channel and like that." He paused then, looked at the Hawaiian shirt and said, "That's some shirt."

"Got it over at the Nearly New Shop."

"Where?"

"Right there in town. Got a pair of pants look like they'd just been creased. She said some doctor come in with pants he only wore oncet or twicet. Got 'em for three dollars."

"Look," said Bern. "I had fifty-five dollars for Saturdy, Sundy, Mondy, and today, Tuesdy, and I only got three left. I'm watchin' my carbohydrates anyway. I took my pulse? It's all over the place."

Norma May brought Rog some coffee and whipped out her pad. "You ready?" she said without looking at any of them.

"Pancakes," said Alton.

"Just the coffee," said Bern. "56, then it was 72, on up to 77, then dropped to 49. They say they're coming out with a wristwatch you can wear that'll take your blood pressure reading, too. 'Course now I can go get a reading every morning right up there to the medical center. You know what the gal there told me? She said that they can't guarantee that stuff I take once you open it if you don't use it right away so she told me there's one thing you're doing wrong if you stick it in your lunch box and keep it there and don't use it, they won't guarantee it'll be right—you can't count on it. I told her I was glad she told me so now I use what I open, and I think my heart's gettin' regulated. 'Course I guarantee if I go up there this morning, I'll get a reading I won't like. I check myself but I get a different reading than they do. Ever time."

Alton lost himself in Rog's shirt—bananas, leaves, parrots, and flowers in profusion. It made him think of a place where he could do anything he liked, naked if he wanted to, but he thought it was probably the lack of sleep that made him think that way. He'd finally dozed off just before dawn and dreamt about a room with a door that was wallpapered over. He couldn't get in the other room, although he knew there was somebody he felt deeply about on the other side, somebody from long ago was all he could say for sure. He just didn't remember. To think of it now, it was only paper that kept him out and he wondered why he hadn't torn the door open.

"Rog," he said. "You want some pancakes?" Rog would say no anyhow, and then watch him eat, which made Alton uncomfortable. Norma May never even asked Rog what he wanted, as if he were invisible. Rog didn't seem to have a connection with anyone but the men at the restaurant, and no dreams for anything more. He didn't talk to women much, had no luck with them. He lived over the store on the corner, whereas Alton lived in the big house around the corner and next to the drugstore, at Fay's house.

His friends thought he had it good living there, and he did. Lucky for him Fay ran into a bit of bad luck when she married Clay and had to rent rooms, not that Alton wished bad luck on anybody. He knew her since elementary school when she was a little stick of a thing who jumped if you said *boo!* He called her *scrawny* to her face once, *ugly and scrawny,* actually, and he had leered in that chicken-shriek way he and Bern did when they talked to girls back then. He remembered the way her grey eyes teared up and how they narrowed to little hateful slits that set him off shrieking again. A small victory from the past that bothered him now. She probably remembered it, and he tried to remember what she'd done to deserve it, and couldn't. He thought about her mother and how she never told on him and Bern when they chased the train and hung on for a ride if they could catch up with the last car. She could see them plain as day from her porch, but she never told. He'd always liked her and the house she lived in with its wraparound porch, stained glass attic window at the peak. He thought of it as classy, or at least it had been classy a long time ago when Fay's mother had it. Alton's mother had always lived above one of the stores in town, and they'd sweltered in the August heat. He'd always wanted a house with a porch, and now he even had his own sleep porch.

"If I watch the carbohydrates," Bern was saying while Norma May plunked bottles of King's Syrup and Natural Choice Fat Free Imitation Maple Syrup on the table. "I can maybe lose some weight," and with that his huge hands hugged the two containers of syrup to his chest as he leaned on the table. "I checked myself just before I came down and it was 62. Five minutes later it was still 62 so I'm doing better. If I get one of those wristwatches, I'll know by the minute."

A fly set on Bern's knee but he never felt it, since it was

entangled in the trap of his leg hair. Alton nodded. It was all you had to do when Bern was around.

"Hey, Rog," he said to the Hawaiian shirt. "I like the touch," and he pointed to the Styrofoam cup beside a wax begonia on the window ledge. *Roger's water for the plant* was printed in large letters with a black marker. The other plants, hanging high, were plastic.

"Yeah. Come in here last night and that thing was gasping."

When the pancakes arrived, Alton took off his sunglasses and began cutting one-inch slices, first in one direction, and then in the other direction, stopping to mix in the syrup with the pile of cubed pancake, gathering pieces from the sides and pushing them up toward the middle like he did with mashed potatoes until every piece was soaked with syrup. His mother fixed pancakes like that for him when he was little. Anybody watching could tell she was probably a good mother by the way Alton fixed his pancakes. She probably did a lot of things for Alton to make him so comfortable in the world that he couldn't have things any other way.

Like that tin sign on the wall, that antique Aunt Jemima sign, straight out of his childhood. That friendly, shiny, round brown face, toothy smile, bandanna and apron and all. Now that was comfort. Along with that colored kid with patched pants licking his thick lips advertising O' Baby Chocolate Drink, saying,*"Ain't that somethin'?"* Something, it seemed to Alton, he could always count on—this place staying the same —something to hang on to. One time a colored social worker came from Cambridge and mentioned to Charlie those signs might be offensive to some people, but Charlie just told her he was a collector of memorabilia and that those signs were worth a lot of money. "All those colored customers I have, not one's ever complained," he told her. "That's history." Charlie was laughing about it the next day. "Don't think she even noticed the one that says *Pickaninny Drink 5 cents.* That one's getting kind of faded. Next thing you know the Gay and Lesbian League'll start complaining about the one that says, *You got a fairy in your house? Try White Fairy Soap*," and he wheezed and coughed his way back to the kitchen. Old Charlie was still walking then. Alton tried to remember when he'd last seen colored in here.

Charlie was lucky. No one went against him. And Alton Abbott was lucky. He'd be fifty-one next November, retired on disability and considered himself not bad off at all, except for last night's lack of sleep and having to hang out on the sleep porch so he wouldn't hear anything. Secretly, he did want to hear, but he felt ashamed listening, like he ought to do something. That Fay, though, she brought it on herself. He'd been reading the paper and watching *ET* when he first became aware of the door slams and raised voices. He was surprised at the male voice, Clay's, no doubt—deep and harsh as a bulldog's, through the oyster shell and horsehair plaster. Alton could swear the sound began a kind of crumbling that he could hear sifting down inside the walls.

Bern sliced through his reverie. "Oh, what the hell," he said, and since they were the only ones in the place, yelled to Norma May, who must be somewhere in the kitchen, "Bacon, two sunnysides and hash browns."

"Got that?" said Charlie, his eyes on the TV and the five-day forecast.

"Rog?" said Bern.

"Maybe some toast—white," Rog gasped through two-three sneezes.

"I'll give you mine," Bern said.

The train engine went by on the tracks just beyond the corner store. It whistled long and low, diminutive, too, like a mere formality. Time was when Puckum was at the hub of things in the summer, when cantaloupes and canned tomatoes were hauled daily over those tracks, back when Alton and

Bern and Rog were kids and the houses freshly painted, all of them occupied by people they knew by heart. Now, there were Mexicans and Puerto Ricans in many of the houses, migrants who stayed, and there were no freighters or passenger trains behind the engine, which just seemed to be keeping up appearances, keeping the tracks slick. It seemed a hopeful thing to do, but Alton wondered in a dull, vague way why anybody'd move an engine from here to there and never have it pull anything. Annoyed, he said, "Where's that train going?"

Rog stared out the window, not listening. Bern said, "What train?" And it was true, that by the time Alton thought to say anything, the train was long gone.

The sleigh bells rang again. Like a breath of steam, Skin came in. Undershirt inside out, chartreuse shorts unzipped, and those skinny legs adjoining the wide shorts and thick work boots, Skin spun around for no particular reason, but maybe just so they could see the back of him, that he had a back and a bone in it, although he waited for a whole minute for Rog to notice him and make room on the bench.

Alton said, "You hear anything last night?"

"Jeez, yeah. Some fight. But I drifted off about ten-thirty. I got tired of listening. Each time, they go through the whole routine, back when *he* had to marry her and *she* says if he hits her again she'll call the cops." Coffee appeared for Skin, and Bern got his eggs, the whites hanging off the edges of the plate and the bacon fast-cooked and contorted, the potatoes soaked in bacon grease. Packets of butter and jam lay in the middle of the platter with the toast piled on top. Bern picked those off and passed them to Rog.

"Did you hear him smack her?" Alton said suddenly. Skin shook his head. Maybe he'd imagined it then, that *whap* that sent tingles up his spine.

"No, but that don't mean he didn't. I guess she'll be after the rent I owe now that Clay's back. She gets feisty when he's around."

Alton looked down and chewed. Bern picked up about the train. "From here it goes to Federalsburg and then on up to Denton, I think. I seen it once cross the road at 394. It was around 9:02 so I figure it gets to Denton around 9:46 if it stays that slow. 'Course it picks up cans at Phillips' in season but right now they're just checking the lines, keep 'em from gettin' rusty. Besides, they got to keep the train going because of the sign."

"What sign?"

"The one just outside of town, as you come in on the right: *Puckum, on track since 1854.*"

Alton finished the pancake bits and sat catty-corner now, arm over the back of the bench behind Bern, feigning nonchalance about the fact that Bob Dole on TV was talking about Erectile Dysfunction.

Bern turned to the screen and said, "Man's got to say things out loud that never ought to be said."

"That's why he waited till after the election," Alton heard himself saying.

Bern said, "Man, if I never got to fuck again—I could live with that. But I say to myself—what if I couldn't fart?"

Rog snorted, put his head down and slapped the table, even though he'd heard that one before. Alton was safe here with Bern and Rog and Skin, though Skin was a come-here from Baltimore. Come ten years ago to work at the cup factory. They all three worked at Silo. "What time you go on?" he asked Skin. His friends had told Alton he ought to apply for a job there since Styrofoam cups didn't weigh near as much as chicken feed and he could probably handle it with his back, but Alton never did, liking things just as they were. Most things, anyway, but just now he was feeling tired and unsettled, the sounds of the fight between a man and woman still in his ears, and the curiosity he held about what they must have looked like, their faces contorted with the revision of their unhappy history, the erupting violence between them, the lovemaking afterwards, the harsh whispers in a sudden self-conscious attempt to keep quiet the cruelty of actions that matched the sounds he'd heard, grown wilder now in his imagination. His skin prickled and his groin rippled.

"Four," said Skin.

It was after eleven, he thought, when he'd heard the first smack, and a thud that sent the walls crumbling and sifting again, and Fay's muffled cry, then Clay's croon like he was talking to the sweetest thing that walked, although Alton knew what came next. He felt stirrings again just remembering her cries.

That's what had upset him and sent him down a road he hated to walk, or crawl, or gasp. Because he knew that with the sound of the smack, he'd get an erection, as though he was loving what he heard even though it appalled him. And what with blood pressure medicine and his weight and smoking (although he quit when Charlie coughed his way into the wheelchair) and no female companion and all, he didn't get erections for a long time so that the first one surprised and pleased him until he realized it was the violence he'd heard that caused him to have one. With Clay in jail, Alton didn't think about it once, even when one time Fay answered the door and she was in her bathrobe. No, that's a lie. He did too think about it, knowing it wouldn't do him any good. If she should turn to him, he probably couldn't do anything about it anyhow. Except now he knew what it took, and because the thought frightened him, it would all just have to stay inside his head, the sound of the smack repeating itself to him at odd moments, like a pleasure he couldn't resist that waited for him against his will until it *was* his will, and he began to conjure up the sound whenever his hands were idle.

"No," she had said from the safety of the door opened

just a crack when he'd knocked to see if she was all right, under pretense of a leaking toilet. "Sorry, I can't help you—Clay's not here," never admitting Clay was put in jail a few nights before, her light hair brushed back neatly from her face, her skin rosy like she'd just come out of the bath. He could smell cologne like the scent of contentment, a fact that left him wondering what she had to be so content about unless it was because she was alone and she could do as she pleased. Unless it was because she'd finally gotten even with Clay. None of which included Alton. He had no right to think he might have a chance, did he? Maybe he should never have rented a room there to begin with.

Out loud, he said to Skin, "Well, you'll miss the shenanigans tonight bein' as you're on the night shift."

"Why do you think she puts up with it?" said Rog suddenly.

"Because he's her man," said Bern. "Simple as that," and he tapped the table on the last word.

"What's that supposed to mean?" Alton said.

"Some people have a game goin' on, is all I meant. A little roughing up gets 'em turned on."

And there was Alton, between a rock and a hard place, knowing what the words meant, but not wanting to believe them about himself or about Fay. With Clay, it was the drink, he was sure. With Fay, maybe she figured that was all she deserved: love any way she could get it.

Norma May was writing on a piece of plain newsprint spread across the next table. The black marker squeaked, the letters uneven and hurried, her hands roughly veined, efficient, plain and hard, the kind of woman to bring coffee and nothing more. You could see Charlie needed her and she knew what she was worth, no bones about it. You could see that in the way she snapped the lid on the marker and took the paper and the staple gun to the varnished pine board hanging outside the door and held up the sign with fleshy arms and clasped the trigger, *snap* with a hollow sound from the board, *snap, snap*—each corner, *snap*: announcing chicken and dumplings, chicken soup, and steak sandwich. The words, *pies—lemon, apple*, stood out by themselves at the bottom. You could see how she asked little but a few tips on the table and a paycheck at the end of the week, how she actually invested nothing of herself although she did everything she was supposed to. Was that her protection?

As for himself, what had he invested? He'd been content with his room, his hall, his bathroom, and his porch. The words he himself had said, taunted him. He'd gotten what he paid for, no more. He'd wanted so little—until now. Maybe that had been his protection.

Bern mopped up the last of the egg, wiped his mouth, dug out the three dollars and put them half under his plate. He stood to go, pulling at his shorts on the inseam to unstick them from his damp crotch, saying he had to walk up to the P.O. and mail off his cable bill, or else. Rog followed, the colors of his shirt dizzying as they caught the sun's hot rays beaming through the window. Alton lifted his hand from the table in a half wave. Then Skin got up, too, calling out, "What about the plant, Rog?" to which Rog stopped and emptied the cup in the gray soil.

"Hey, Norma May, fill the cup, okay?"

Charlie glared and Norma May nodded. "See ya now," she said, lighting a cigarette, her brown-gray eyes dull and cold. "Where's the remote?" Charlie said to her without looking up.

Alton watched them and turned away. Far as he knew, Charlie had never had a woman. But, Alton—he should have stepped in when Fay answered the door in her bathrobe—just stepped in and closed the door quietly behind him, watching to see if her eyes would tear up and then get narrow. And he, Alton, would do it right, with tenderness, take the hate out of those grey-filled cat eyes, tell her she was even prettier than her mother had been, and hold her for a long, long time—as long as it took. It'd be like getting a plateful of pancakes and syrup ready. He knew it would, and that he could. Erasing forever the sound of that smack, her muffled cries, all his doubt and shame.

And what would he have said? He didn't know, his mind blank about the sequence of things, but maybe she'd have said, "Yes. Come in a moment, will you, while I call the plumber and you can tell him yourself what's wrong."

Then he would have said, "Fay, are you all right?"

She'd have denied everything bravely at first, but finally she'd have admitted that Clay treated her badly and she was tired, so tired of it all, and wanted someone who'd treat her nice, someone who'd rescue her. It dawned on him then, he was neither rescuer nor knight, neither exciting nor excited, and worse, not excitable, not in any normal sense of the word, a fact he still refused to believe although he thought he understood how he, too, harbored what he despised. He wouldn't listen again, he decided. He might even have to give up his room, his hallway, his bathroom, and his porch.

He believed he was a good man, although he'd done nothing to help her and that pained him. But he was what he was.

And slowly, slowly, with his stomach full and feet like sacks of feed, he rose and passed through the door of his own heart to the incongruity of sleigh bells ringing and the enveloping heat of the day, to Main Street, where the old houses stared back at him and walls quietly fell to powder.

The Trunk

Returning from the dentist, Midge pulled into the garage. Slamming the car door, she glanced to her right like she always did, for no other reason than she liked to look at the trunk there against the wall. She never forgot to look at it. *Force of habit*, her mother would have said. Now that Midge was in her sixties, her long-dead mother appeared with a clarity that had grown more so over the years, so that now her mother's voice often came back in that precise simplicity of hers that neatly summed things up.

The trunk had sat in the garage for years, humpbacked, scarred and scraped, black iron bands wrapped around its edges, the finish darker with each passing year, its brass lock dull and pitted. Dating from the 1880s or earlier, it offered an invitation to wonder who'd owned it and what had been packed in its dank interior. She'd saved it as she'd saved so many things from those first decades at the farm—not able to part with any of the bits and pieces of her life, the visible measures that marked time into segments—when the kids were little, when they'd put up the barn, when they'd had the pigs—the image of Timmy at thirteen now flashed before her, that year he raised three pigs and they'd gotten out, escaping into the deep woods, and how he had torn through the brambles in panic at the loss, coming back looking a bit wild with scratches on his face and burrs in his thick hair, but triumphant, the three pigs scampering before him.

That's how it was. Flashes of this and that—remnants floated by her. But along with that, as she looked back at her long-ago marriage around which all her adult life had been centered, there was a renewed determination to save something, put things to new use, pass on in good condition. She'd always loved redoing furniture, and there were some nice things that lingered like abandoned orphans in tucked-away places like the tool shed, chicken coop, and garage. This determination of hers was strengthened by what her older friends were telling her, that later, she might not have the inclination. She couldn't picture that happening. Not really. She'd always just gone on. But the toothache she had since last week, so minor a thing, set her off.

She was surprised when Bill Seidel said without his usual brightness, his golf tan looking a sickly yellow under the bright light that hung from a steel arm over the dentist's chair, "Not good news, Midge. It'll have to come out, but then you might consider an implant." As she pictured herself with a gaping hole in her mouth, his words had left her feeling this could be the beginning of the slide downhill. First one tooth, and then the shifting of the others, then loose teeth, then eating only soft foods—and on and on.

But it was only a tooth, she told herself, staring down at the trunk. Bill had hesitated to tell her the implant would cost $3000, and when he did, he blushed, knowing, after being her dentist for thirty-one years, that the suggestion was an embarrassment financially. She stared back at him. "No other options?" she asked. "Not really," he said. "I think the root canal has a fracture, although it's difficult to tell for sure. We'll give you penicillin to calm down the inflammation."

Come to find out, he still was Roger's dentist, a fact that he never let on all this time, but something she'd heard Timmy say. "I met Dad in the dentist's office. Looked like he was flirting with the hygienist, like what else is new." She pictured

Bill leaning over Roger with his fingers in his mouth, and then washing his hands for the next appointment—hers. She'd met Roger when she was sixteen—that was fifty years ago!—known him through thirty years of marriage and five kids. Sixteen more years followed in various stages of separation and divorce. The present connection of the dentist's fingers in her mouth and his was certainly laughable. Strange the way links kept cropping up, more frequent now since Roger had chosen to move back to the flatlands with his new wife.

And the trunk was another link. Roger paid no attention to her bringing things home from auctions during their marriage, but she'd managed to furnish most of the house with items bought for seventy-five cents or a dollar in the early years. The trunk had been seven-fifty, an extravagance she remembered, and the clothes inside were a dollar extra, clothes too small for her large bones, dresses with tiny waists and puffed sleeves, but they fit Marly at age ten when she was still in pigtails. Marly, after playing with them for years, had grown up with a love of the 1900s era. Many a time she'd mount the round lid of the trunk, and pretend it was a horse and years later, when she got her own horse, she'd lay her saddle on the trunk, which by then had been relegated to the pony shed and filled with tack.

It still was a good trunk, solid, made of pine and reinforced with oak strapping, but in the previous wet spring and summer, green mildew had grown over the scratched finish. When she lifted the lid, there were the chipped and rusted Christmas balls that had belonged to her mother-in-law lined up in the old sectioned boxes. There'd been a time when the children's faces were reflected in those balls, at those wonderful Christmases with Beatrice. Now they sat as stubborn vestiges of the bitter years since Beatrice had died. For it wasn't until his mother was gone that Roger took it in his head to leave. Better that she never knew. She had certainly loved her grandkids.

So. All that history. That was exactly why the trunk needed a new life, she thought, letting the lid slam shut. She
dragged the trunk onto the sun porch and looked at it for a
long time, remembering when it had stood at the foot of their
bed, how they'd first used it to store blankets, and for some
reason, old letters, neat packets done up with ribbon that
began *Dearest Midge,* and ended with *Love Always*—from
Roger's days in the service. Once, he banged his knee on the
corner of the trunk and told her to get the damn thing out of
the house. From there it wound up in the pony shed.

They had grandchildren themselves now, she and Roger.
Another one of those links. And if one of them didn't look
just like his grandfather—Damian—with his large eyes and high
forehead, the delicate chin, the thin, wiry body. It was the
child's cleverness she so much enjoyed, his quick wit at age
five, those sidelong glances with a hint of devilment behind the
smile. Putting Roger's and Damian's baby pictures side by
side, it could be the same child. She was partial to Damian.
He told her once when he was three that she was his "favorite
woman," which still made her laugh whenever she thought of
it, and because he embodied the sweet ongoing-ness of
something she couldn't lay aside, she decided the trunk would
be his. She swept off the cobwebs, wiped off the mildew,
propped the lid open to release the mildewed air inside, and
put the boxes of Christmas balls in a garbage bag.

From then on it was pure pleasure. With the first sanding,
the characteristic pale yellow of white pine emerged and the
trunk began to look as though it had been built yesterday. She
thought of the wood as forgiving and constant, even patient,
lying underneath the layers of varnish all those years. With the
trunk set up on a table, she returned to it in the first of many
sunny fall afternoons, sanding while the blackbirds darted back

and forth by the thousands, lit in the trees and at the slightest sound whirred to the sky. Just outside the porch, yellow chrysanthemums shone like a thousand suns, and she thought she couldn't think of a better way to spend an afternoon.

Using a fine grade of sandpaper until the wood was completely bare, she sanded for about an hour, until the wood was silky to the touch and the heads of embedded nails shone. The ridges where the handles once were placed had been smoothed out. She lay down the sandpaper and thought she'd go for a walk around the perimeter of the farm as she was in the habit of doing each day. The sky stretched horizon to horizon without interruption of cloud or building, and she thought about how the space around her was filled with a world that went on without bother. She felt slightly out of breath suddenly, and so when she reached an open area, she stretched out on grass that had already dried after first frost. She'd done this many times before on sunny days. It was peaceful as death must be, a friend, really. With the sun warm on her face, she closed her eyes. A bug crawled on her arm. She could tell it was a daddy longlegs by its lightness and the spread of its legs. Still with her eyes closed, she brushed it away. Then she heard the flap of wings overhead. Something big. Eyes open now, half-blinded by the sun, she jumped up at the sight of a vulture not five feet above her, ready to land close by. She flapped her arms wildly, and looked up to see seven more buzzards circling overhead. She shrieked, still flapping her arms. The birds in the sky kept circling, and the vulture nearest her swooped upward to join them. "Not yet, damn it!" she shouted, wondering if they sensed death as horses or dogs sensed fear in a person. She headed back to the house now, glad she had something to do.

Once back on her porch, she ran her hand along the sides and top of the trunk and began sanding again. Just a bit, and a little bit more, as if she hated to be done with this first step. It was a revelation, this connection to its beginning. She thought about how easily the years could be stripped away, not like her own body with its rumpled, patchy places, or the lines on her face, impositions on skin you'd think would be worn smooth from facing the wind.

Inside the trunk was another story. When she tore out the old lining of blue taffeta she'd put in years ago, she saw again how roughly hewn the inside was. Running her fingers over the deep marks left by the saw blade, she could imagine the blade cutting into the wood and the muscled arm that swung back and forth, back and forth. She'd line the inside. Maybe even lay a page from today's newspaper under the lining for the next person who fiddled with the trunk.

Closing the lid again, she thought it seemed much too light against the dark cedar shingles of the house, like something as yet unclaimed. The carpenter who made it—did he stand back and admire it at this point? Or, having made hundreds of them, did he carelessly, thoughtlessly, lay aside his tools and reach for his supper of corn cake and bacon? Because she was sure it was made by someone without means, someone not bothered by perfection, someone in a hurry. The metal was of the cheapest grade and the oak reinforcement along the humpbacked top was unevenly bowed. The covers for the ends of the long-gone leather handles had been made of tin and tore when she removed them. They were unsalvageable. Was the trunk built with plans for a quick departure, done quickly using scraps that were lying around, making do—all of it as familiar to her life as the washwoman history of her own great-grandmother? Down the line, they were all good at making do. It was what made their ancestors strong and adaptable. She wondered if the present generation was as easily adaptable, as well prepared for mishap or being without, lost in an environment where nearly everything was disposable, easily replaced, a world that presented endlessly new, albeit confusing choices, a place where she could no longer choose even something so simple as a telephone without exhaustive research. It made one hesitant to the point of catatonic. It was good to be able to return to something from an old, old past. Like the house she'd lived in since the children were small. Like the farm itself, with its circle of trees and wide-open fields lying yellow this October with the leaves of soybean, just like they always did.

She worried about applying the varnish because she liked the plain, homespun look of the trunk and she had no idea what it would become. With the first brushstrokes, the wood darkened a bit, taking on a deep amber. Astonishingly, the sanded wood seemed dead compared to this new color, which seemed to hold depths of gold with hints of orange and red and brown in the change of sunlight. Not like anything she'd refinished before. Not like the color that the trunk had been before she began to restore it either. It was as if the years were reflected, made finer, put back in each layer of varnish until a color emerged that was unlike any other. It had been brought to life. The glide of the brush and the even coat, the smell of varnish and the deepening color absorbed her. The trunk glowed. It harmonized with the sun going down and the soft orange in the low clouds. Satisfied, she wondered if it would hurt the finish if she left the trunk in the night air.

She stood back, planning tomorrow: the grade of steel wool, the alternation of it with yet another coat of varnish—at least three times more—and then the blue denim lining she would make with pockets sewn in for secrets or special treasures, the brass plaque with his name, *Damian Scott,* nailed to the lid, the red velvet ribbon with a huge bow for Christmas. For Damian. She knew happiness when she felt it. She knew a good thing when she saw it. A bit of a stretch for a five-year-old, but it was a treasure chest, she'd tell him, for things he wished to keep away from everyone. He'd grow to appreciate it through the years. "My grandmother restored that trunk for me," he'd say. She'd tell him it was from the days when people traveled by horse and carriage. She'd encourage him to wonder about what it once held and where it had been.

The restoration of the trunk took longer than she expected. Or was it that she lingered after each step, actually hating to see it finished? She sewed the pockets in the lining just as she'd planned, glued it in and glued on the trim, shined the old lock until it looked like new. Marly had painted a cowboy roping a steer on a piece of the denim and Midge put that inside the lid. Tim had reinforced the back of the trunk where the wood had split. Christmas Eve she was still working on the trunk, installing an inside hinge for the lid. At the last minute, she realized a locking hinge was needed so that the lid would not slam down on Damian's slender young arms. In her haste she'd measured wrong and the holes wound up in the wrong place. She drilled new holes and covered the mistakes with Elmer's glue so the fabric wouldn't fray. Finally, there wasn't any more to do, and with the handsome, shining trunk standing in the hall with a huge red bow on top, she admired it again and again as she passed through, but she mourned the finishing of it, too.

With penicillin, her tooth had stopped hurting long ago, but now there was a dull ache, a pressure around her heart that had been occurring mid-afternoons in the days before the holidays. She felt it now, as she considered all the things she still must do before taking off for Christmas Day at her youngest son, John's. All the family would be there—the boys and their wives, Marly and her boyfriend, the grandkids running rampant through the house. Roger and his recent wife, Anastasia, would be there, too, but she told herself she would not let that ruin her day with the children. It had been

72

so long since they'd lived together, she and Roger, long enough for her to be over that by now. For the sake of the children, she would get through it smoothly, graciously. Christmas was a habit not to be broken. For the sake of the family. Besides, other divorced people did it all the time, shared the holidays with the grandchildren, smiling at each other across the dinner table, didn't they? She'd manage it.

Although the trunk was bulky and difficult to grasp, she was able to lift it onto the back seat of the car on Christmas morning. After packing a mountain of presents on the front seat, she went back into the house and spent the next hour trying on five different outfits, not deciding until the last minute to wear the black velvet with the jacket of red-and-gold-roses design. A bit fancy for a family celebration, but still. She fussed with the dry old wisps of grey around her face, cursing them, and finally gave up. It was important to look good—self-possessed and happy. She was. Despite all. The pain in her chest had lifted.

Somewhere along Route 62 she stopped at a diner for a newspaper but, needing change for the machine, had to go inside. The trunk sat like a jewel in the morning light, and the red bow atop the high, round lid could easily be seen through the car window as well as the seat full of presents. She was careful to lock the car.

The woman behind the counter waited on the customers before Midge, her thin frame spidery behind the extravagance of slices of lemon meringue and cream pies in the showcase. Her hair was dyed dead-black, probably a while ago for there was a ribbon of white at the roots as she bent her head to work the register. With hair that white, she might have been Midge's age even though clumps of dark, tight uncombed curls hung around her shoulders. One could guess what the woman wanted to look like, what she might have thought she looked like, what she had looked like years ago. Somewhat. The same hairstyle, kept up with more effort now. Maybe she thought no one would notice. Maybe she no longer cared. Her skin was lined like the rough wood of the trunk, and her lips slipped loosely around her words without a wall of teeth behind them. Midge noted the print on her thin T-shirt, *Bud's Gas Station,* and how the shirt hung without the interruption of breasts, how the woman looked like a skinny kid, her arms no bigger around than Damian's. Working on Christmas Day. No wedding band. Minimum wage, no paid holidays, no pension, no luck. Maybe kids still hanging around, not making it, or maybe they were far off somewhere, while she existed on coffee and cigarettes. A lifetime of force of habit and making do. Getting by—by the skin of her teeth or less, much less. Probably renting a room somewhere, with a little artificial Christmas tree from Goodwill. Probably leftovers from the restaurant for supper, a lighted cigarette afterwards.

Quickly, efficiently, the woman took the bills of the customers in turn and gave change. Midge knew she was staring yet she couldn't help composing the woman's life, and when the woman turned to her, Midge pushed a dollar on the counter and asked, "Would you mind giving me change for the newspaper machine, please?"

"Sure, hon." The woman smiled, her papery lips closed, and stooped to reach under the counter. Suddenly she coughed a hacking deep cough, an emphysema-like, liquidy cough. Her hand flew to her mouth and the other to her back and then swooped down for the quarters from the wrapped change that must be stored there.

"Here you are," she said, handing Midge the quarters. But it was her smile that caught in Midge's throat. Her lips spread wide around nothing, a smile she had no embarrassment about, a broad smile that lit her face. "Merry Christmas!"

she whistled.

"Merry Christmas to you!" Midge said, warmed by the woman's genuineness. She was shocked in a way that poverty always shocked her, because that was a destiny she had fought against all her life, especially after the divorce. But the thing in the dark that awaited her, and about which she could do little, was ill health. It was the one indignity left.

Returning to her car with the newspaper under her arm, she began to cry. She didn't know why, except she had this image of herself sitting in her car dressed to the nines with the beautiful trunk in the back seat and family to go to on Christmas Day, while tears she couldn't stop slid down her cheeks. Would she have rather been in the diner attending customers? Distracted from Christmas rather than having to face it? No. She was guilty, that's what. Guilty for feeling so wretched when she had everything.

Now the trunk stood next to the Christmas tree, dominating the room when the gift giving began, that long parade of gaily wrapped packages and bags with tissue paper fluffed carelessly over the tops. For Alora, the baby. For Damian. For Aunt Marly. To Grandma with love. For Uncle Tim and Aunt Sue. To Uncle John and Aunt Cindy. Exclamations. And there was Damian, hands on hips, his five-year-old face screwed up, reading the brass plaque on the trunk.

"It says it's for me!" He opened the lid and said, "Where's the present? There's no present!"

Midge laughed. "The present is the treasure chest, so you can hide things in it that no one else can get a hold of. It's for your favorite things."

"But where's my present?" Damian insisted. His mother distracted him by shoving a wrapped present in his hands, this one from Aunt Jessie, which turned out to be a Spider Man figure that he immediately put in the trunk, took out, held for a minute, and put back. He closed the lid. "Nobody can get that, can they? Are there any more presents?" he asked, looking at Midge.

That's okay, she thought. He'll have the trunk for the rest of his life. She didn't expect him to view it with excitement, although she wished she'd put a large wrapped present inside. She didn't know what, exactly, as the usefulness of modern plastic toys eluded her.

Gifts for Grandpa were set aside, as he and the new Grandma hadn't arrived yet. With the turkey ready, Midge began making the gravy, John was carving, and Marly was slicing the bread she'd made in the shape of a huge braided wreath. The living room was in disarray; empty gift boxes and bows and wrapping paper lay scattered. Outside, the light was already beginning to fade to grey as she stirred the gravy, adding more and more flour until it was a thick paste, lumpy. Not her best. She jumped at the sound of Anastasia's voice ringing out a gay *Merry Christmas!* Roger scooted in bearing yet another load of presents, his tired old face hanging in a kind of permanent look of confusion and doubt he'd acquired in the last few years. He was more stooped than Midge remembered from the last time she'd seen him.

"What happened? How come you're an hour and half late?" asked Allison, the daughter-in-law who needed to know exactly what was what.

"We were waiting for our turkey to be done, the one we're taking up to New York tomorrow," said Anastasia, "when we'll visit my family."

Midge kept stirring the pan. Oh, she was gay with the children tugging at her skirt. "Grandma, come play."

"In a minute, baby," she said and picked up the youngest so the child could watch the making of gravy. "Hot," Alora said, pointing.

"Yes, love. Oh yes. Very hot." Alora began to blow, and when she got bored with that, she turned to Midge and with her lips still puckered, kissed her. Midge set her down. There was that tightness again in her chest, which now ran all the way up to her throat. She tried to clear it away, again and again. Talking was impossible. She busied herself with filling the gravy boat and finding a fork for the platter of turkey. At least she knew where everything was. At least she could say this home was a second home to her, after all the time she'd spent baby-sitting the kids. At least she could say she was close to her kids and to her grandkids. It was his family, too, but basically it was *her* family. And he was only here because she had allowed it, and after being asked, had convinced herself it was the right thing to do after all this time, that he had a right to be here. After all, he was the grandfather. At least she knew she looked good; Anastasia was dressed casually in a cotton shirt and a pair of jeans. She was unforgivably half the size Midge was. A runner. Athletic. Pert, still, in her late fifties. The woman had absolutely no ass, no breasts.

Midge was pleased to see that jokes had to be explained to her. Midge didn't chime in when Anastasia's conversation centered on bargains at the mall. What did the woman have that Midge didn't have? And what, for God's sake, did she see in Roger? That was the big question. He always looked so sour.

"Did you hear from Aunt Lucy?" Midge asked at the dinner table, looking directly at Roger.

"No," he said, helping himself to his mother's recipe of cranberry sauce that Midge brought.

"I understand she's in a nursing home. How old is she now?" Roger had spent nearly every weekend of his childhood at Aunt Lucy's. She'd taught him to fish. She was not truly an aunt, but a step-grandmother, having married Roger's grandfather late in life. She was his secretary, and one day, after his wife had died, he presented her with a ring. Being Catholic and Italian, Roger's staunch New England mother resented Lucy, but Lucy had a kind and devoted heart. To this day, she kept a lighted candle in her husband's memory on her kitchen counter even though Roger's grandfather died nearly fifty years ago.

None of which Anastasia would know, of course. That, and all the Christmases at Beatrice's with the kids clamoring and turkey sandwiches after dark and games of Monopoly and Scrabble as the kids got older, nor would she know about their own Christmases, hers and Roger's with the four boys and Marly. Anastasia wouldn't know about the time Roger used a stencil to make large footprints on the hearth of their fireplace and sprayed them with fake snow mainly for Tim, who was then five and verbalizing first doubts about Santa. Midge could still hear the shouts of the kids on Christmas morning when they discovered the footprints.

"Ninety-nine," said Roger.

"We might stop to see her while we're in New York," said Anastasia, looking to see her husband's reaction.

"No, we won't," he said flatly. "The last few times I called to see her, she was too busy."

Midge knew how Aunt Lucy disapproved of his leaving the family. It was one of Lucy's greatest disappointments although she would never tell him that. She'd always favored Roger. And she was always good to Midge, giving her an antique chair that belonged to the family since the mid-1800s. This was after Roger had left her, as if the family heritage was to be kept by Midge for safe deliverance to the next generation.

Midge quickly changed the subject.

"Guess who I met last week at a book signing in Annapolis?" she said. "Marlin Fitzhugh!" she announced. She was breathless. She had to keep the conversation going as if she were running with it right to the finish line. Anastasia stared blankly at her. Roger raised his eyebrows. "Really!"

"Yes, we had a nice chat. We talked about his new book, which is a novel, quite a stretch for him beyond his memoirs and other nonfiction. Have you read the new book by Billy Collins? He's the new poet laureate, as he well deserves to be." She was on a roll now. She was stepping out of the gloom, the constriction of her heart. She was who she was, after all. She spent a good bit of time reading. Besides her grandchildren, it was her deepest pleasure. None of the rest of the family did, except maybe Marly. Long ago, Roger had made comments about her blue-collar family, but deep down, she was aware that she'd read much more than he had, that she'd become self-educated, more confident, more the kind of person she'd always wanted to be. Besides, she no longer needed him as she once did. There wasn't anything on the farm she couldn't handle now, except maybe the mowing of the field paths, which the neighboring farmer consented to do. "I planted 250 trees last spring and have another 500 ordered for April," she said. "It's getting to be veritable forest. And the soil is a lot better than it was, especially with all the rain. The insecticides and herbicides dumped on the land when it was farmed are leaching out. We have a family tree-planting day. Even the kids turn up with shovels and help."

She was dominating the conversation now. And she couldn't stop. Soon she had them laughing, opened opportunities for them to cajole each other like they used to do. Even Roger joined in, his face uplifted, his chin forward and his eyes alive with the banter. Anastasia would ask questions to keep her going, as though she was really interested, and when politics came up, Midge and Roger agreed that Bush was a concern as was the new turn the U.S. had taken in foreign policy. Her boys disagreed, loudly. "Bush men," she called them. "Are you really sons of mine?" she teased. Roger couldn't believe it either for he and Midge shared the same political views. They were in it now, arguing, teasing, laughing, growing louder and louder just like the old days. Anastasia grew quiet, finally staring at her plate. For a split second, Midge felt sorry for her. She was really a nice person.

"Have you seen the trunk?" Midge asked Roger.

"What trunk?"

She didn't want to say the one that had stood in their bedroom, so she said, "You'll remember it when you see it," and rose from the table with Roger following her. The others began to clear the table. As she turned the corner of the living room, she caught sight of Anastasia carrying the gravy boat to the sink.

They stood now before the trunk as if it were some kind of altar. Roger stooped to feel the finish she was so proud of.

"Hardly a gift for a five-year-old," he was quick to say.

"Well, I thought it would be a permanent one, you know, one that he'd have the rest of his life. I didn't expect him to appreciate it all at once. Something like this takes time to appreciate, and maturity. I just restored it now because I don't know if next year or the year after that I will *feel* like refinishing anything."

She opened the lid.

"Did you paint that?" he said, staring down at the opened lid where the cowboy lassoed his steer.

"No. Marly did. Isn't it beautiful? And Tim repaired the metalwork and added a piece to reinforce the back. So I had plenty of help," she said, feeling mean and exclusive. Why was she doing this to him?

He studied the trunk, his turtleneck pushing on loose neck skin as he stood with his hands in his pockets. She folded her arms in front of her, thinking she'd said too much. Was she still trying to prove herself to him? Was it a battle over territory, over *her* territory? Why was she still doing that? His face was expressionless.

"Lotta history in that old trunk, eh?" he finally said, and when he looked up at her she thought there were tears in his eyes, although she couldn't be sure in the fading light.

"Yeah. So much history. Way before our time."

"I meant during our time."

"We have to pass that on, too," she said, realizing it might have sounded accusatory.

He nodded and then shrugged, the droop of his mouth like the droop of skin under his eyes. He'd dyed his hair red. Maybe at Anastasia's suggestion. He was ten years older than she. He was sad. There was no satisfaction in that, although she wanted to feel some and realized that's what she'd been trying to do. Maybe had even worked up the whole afternoon's performance on that account. Oh, there was no smoothing over their mistakes. And as she turned and spotted the baby in Anastasia's arms, the tears she'd choked down all day suddenly resumed. Enough, she thought. She reached for her coat and sang out good-bye in the semi-dark, calling "Merry Christmas" as gaily as the lady in the diner when she turned from Roger and the bewilderment of his life. He still stood before the trunk, his thin, stooped body silhouetted against the Christmas tree. If he could be happy it might have all been worth it.

She couldn't remember any other time when she'd gotten him, but there was no triumph in it, only an old, persistent grief. Damian came running in. He had a turkey drumstick in his hand. He'd wrapped it in plastic wrap and now placed it carefully in the bottom of the trunk. "For later," he announced to them both, shutting the lid. "Shh. Don't tell anybody, okay?" He looked at them both. "Why," he said with his large eyes turned to Roger, "why did you get a new grandma?"

Internally, she gasped. She waited to hear Roger's answer, but there was only the usual silence, the same one that was the reason for them not being together, she supposed. She could only distract the child, hug him, demand a kiss, and because the trunk needed a future, too, promised to bring something special next time for him to put in it. She was sorry about the trunk, sorry about the legacy they were leaving him, sorry that their history was disconnected. It was not what she had expected in life, this story that hung like a question between the generations. What she hadn't known was how fragile everything was.

She knew she'd not see Roger again. That she didn't have to had just occurred to her. She buttoned her coat and stepped into the still, cold air, well aware of the lighted house behind her, the cold dark of the car as she put her key in the ignition. The woman in the diner. She'd felt sorry for her. But maybe the woman was to be envied. Maybe she no longer expected anything. Maybe she knew that nothing could be done about any of it, that everything of importance and weight was past, which was why she could light up the morning so generously with just the brief moment of her life.

Miz Satchel

I'm doin' all right. You?

Look here, me with two turkey breasts in the cart, ninety-nine cents a pound. That's a good deal, ain't it? I come in and get the specials, you know what I mean, but I'm going to all the stores this morning—IGA, Acme, Food Lion, Meat Land, all of them—and looking through my change, figurin' that penny might turn up. Oh, you ain't heard about it? It's been on the news where it's worth seventy-thousand dollars, a 1943—and them people spent it in the grocery store! Said they had a collection of them 1943s and they accidentally spent one. Said it was one of them brown ones, only forty of them ever made, where most of 'em were silver-colored that year, you know? Said if you put it to a magnet, it'd stick. I had a '43 but it wouldn't stick to no magnet. Could be anywhere. Could turn up around here or anywhere. Thing could've traveled clear to California by now. But can you imagine? What that must have felt like to find out you spent it on something, give it in for one cent? Seventy thousand. One coin?

Wish I'd had it. Might turn up, you never know. Wouldn't that be somethin'? Get your change and find it in your hand?

How you enjoying retirement? I like it myself, but I don't like the money. People tell me, you got it made now, living by yourself, with Clyde gone. You shouldn't have no expense, nothing to worry about. But the bills still come, electric's the

83

same, oil and gas and telephone—all them's the same. Clyde, he didn't use much. I don't see no difference in the bills and they keep comin'. You know it? You know what my pension is? One hundred sixty-two a month. 'Course now I get Social Security and that's around six hundred and five a month, but that's it. That's what I got to make it on.

'Course I did myself in with that insurance policy. Pay twenty-five a month for that. It'll be enough to bury me, I guess. I'd rather get my teeth fixed, to tell you the truth.

Didja hear about the Smith boy what drowned? Seventeen year old. Been drinkin' and into God knows what else. Went out on the river in a canoe late at night and never came back. They found him next morning. I know the mother 'cause I had him in school in first grade. She took it hard. Lives out in the country, over there to Grove Road. Got them two girls, too. Sad, ain't it? Awful thing. Happened just here this winter. You didn't hear 'bout it? Was on the news and in the paper. Maybe you didn't make the connection. I feel sorry for the mother, don't you? You hear so many things about kids these days. I watch the newspapers all the time for news about the kids I had. But you know if it's news, most of the time it ain't good. Don't seem fair so many kids in trouble before they really even get started.

I hate things unfair. I'm telling you one thing—it was unfair the way they got rid of me at school. All them years workin' with kids, buying 'em little treats and all when they did good. What they said about me wasn't true. What a way to end up, saying I wasn't doing my job. Who could, working for five teachers, each one wanting ten different things every morning? I run off more stuff for them—so much paper it'd kill a whole forest of trees. Once in a while they'd get mixed up you know, 'specially if I was runnin' two machines at once, hurryin' to get everything done before the Pledge, 'cause right after that I'd get my first group of kids.

84

But these young ones, you know, they come in with ideas out of a book and forget they workin' with people. That one with the red hair—Miss Koontz was her name—sayin' I misspelled a word when I was copying something for her and she got the word *pome* right up there on the bulletin board for *poem*. Think they're something, they do. Run here, run there, me with that bone spur in my foot. All's I know is I did my best. But thirty years in the system and no one gives you any thanks. Making ten thousand a year. But I never complained about that, far as that goes. I was glad to have a job with benefits close to home and I liked what I did, you know what I mean.

The teachers were nice when Clyde got sick, and they sent me a—whatchamacallit—arrangement when he died. The hospitality committee did. I always got along with most everybody. Even that crazy teacher, the one what wore those jelly bean shoes and was engaged to her boyfriend for thirty-seven years? What was her name? She always said, "I got it good now. Why should I *marry* him? This way I don't have to do his laundry." Tickled me, hear her talk. She was always humming to herself like she had a secret too good to tell. I remember that one time the kids were supposed to have a party for Christmas and they weren't behavin' so she kept the cupcakes from them and put 'em up on top of the cupboard. Come June they were still there. She spent half the time in the bathroom with me watchin' her class. Comin' back, if there was a hair out of place, she'd let me have it. "Miz Satchel," she'd say. "Can't you control these children?" A few of 'em would snicker, you know. She gave me a birthday party once. I *was* embarrassed. Made the whole staff drop what they was doing and head for the lounge like there was some important meetin'. I saw those cupcakes on the table and it crossed my mind that they mighta been the ones on the cupboard. I shouldn'ta been thinkin' that, like I was ungrateful. They got rid of her finally, but it practically took an act of God,

somebody to write down how long she been in the bathroom
every day. Not me. I didn't want no parts of that. She worked
for the system for twenty-six years, and I'm sure she thought
that was terrible unfair—having to work that long, I mean. She
walked out of there still wearing those jelly bean shoes and that
engagement ring, hummin' away, holding onto a shopping bag
full of rolled up charts. I couldn't help it. I threw in one of
them cupcakes. Just one, though.

Me, I'll always be glad I married Clyde. He was a good
man. I been lucky. Always had my family around me right
here in Puckum. My mother, my daughter, and granddaughter
right here. Lived here all my life. I know what to expect from
my people. I can see Clyde in Lee Ann the older she gets, you
know it? He was good to her. If she needed something for
herself or the baby, he'd give it to her. "Here, Lee Ann,"
he'd say. "Take this and be sure the baby gets her
medicine." He couldn't stand it if anybody needed anything.
He had a good heart, you know it?

We took in another child, you know, and adopted her.
But she don't come around 'less she wants something, you
know it? She had a baby and no husband. Only this boyfriend.
Says he'll marry her when he's got enough money for a big
church wedding. I think it's silly and I said so, too. I told him,
I said, "You just don't want to marry her or you'd do it." He
didn't like that.

Lee Ann says, "Mom, he don't like to be around you
much because of that." But I don't care. I just come out and
say what's plain to me. He just don't want to. Never gives her
anything for that child of his, either. Never gives that little boy
the time of day. I tell him to face up to his responsibilities.
"Don't come around here talking about no big church
wedding," I tell him. "That don't hold no water with me."

I go to the flea market still. I used to go a lot more, when
I had a little more money to spend. Used to get them pencils

and erasers for the kids at school. Some of 'em would work all morning for a new pencil. Never had a bit o' trouble and some of 'em could really be a handful. But I do believe I did my job and the young teachers comin' in have got a lot to learn 'bout people. They scared they don't look good come time for their evaluations, I know, so they take it out on somebody else. I had those kids working, though. Some of the worst kids, too. They always give me the worst ones, you know, but I never minded. Lot of 'em just needed somebody to make 'em do and they loved those pencils! Sometimes I'd get little rings and bracelets and things for 'em and I'd see 'em wear 'em day after day. Once I got a whole bag of them little stuffed animals like little dogs and cats and bears and stuff. Boy, they were crazy over 'em. I'd see 'em trading 'em off at recess. No, I never had no trouble with them kids. I wonder how they makin' out now. I understand they don't hire no more aides. Didn't replace me. Used the money for something else.

But they made me go. Said I wasn't doing my job. I hate things to be unfair, you know it? When there's nothing you can do or say to make people change their mind? They think they got things all figured out and they don't. It's all a lie. Wonder how them kids is makin' out. Had one, lost his mother in a car accident—six boys in that family who didn't even know who their father was—went to live with the grandmother who was in a wheelchair. Imagine that? He'd come to school shoelaces untied, a shirt way too big for him all unbuttoned, sleeves dragging to his knees. First thing I'd do in the morning when he come to me is button him up, help him tie his shoes, and be sure his sleeves was rolled up so he could work. Half the time he didn't even have a pencil so I'd loan him one and if he did his work, he got to keep it, and he nearly always did. I'd give him a hug and he was okay after a while, I mean—he really tried—though everything was hard for him. Black or white, I don't care. After a while, you don't see the color; you see what they need, is all.

We was always poor. I mean, we had enough, but nothing fancy. Clyde's mother was the one. 'Member her livin' up by the railroad track in that shack with the goat tied out front to keep the weeds down? Now *that* was poor. And she lived there with Clyde's brother, Tommy—he was retarded, you know—till she just couldn't do no more. We went in there and the place was filthy. No running water, no heat but a kerosene heater, she all the time needin' wood for that cook stove. I don't know how she lived that way, but Clyde would check on her every few days or so until she just wasn't gettin' out of bed no more and Tommy got to wanderin' off. Found him down to Shiloh in his underwear so then we knew it was time to do something with the both of them, though she didn't last long when we brought her into town. I know poor. I know what it's like. But some of these kids—they got it bad, you know it?

There was that mulatto kid. I know I'm not supposed to be telling tales out of school—and I never did, but now when it comes back to me I want to tell somebody—want to tell the whole world that some things just shouldn't be. Don't remember his name, big beautiful, gray eyes, and curly light brown hair—stank of urine when he came to school. Come to find out, he slept in his clothes with four in the bed and his little brother would pee in the bed and it'd be all over him. I washed his clothes many a time. Kept extra clothes at school I got at a yard sale for him. Sometimes when kids come to school in clothes all wrinkled—I found this out talking to a seven-year-old—she didn't know what a dresser was. I was trying to explain it and she said, "We just put our clothes in a pile on the floor and when morning comes, we put on whatever we can get." She was white, too. Had a white mother and father, though he was in jail for a time.

That's the mother that couldn't pay the electric and gas and it got shut off. She made the kids sleep outdoors with a campfire. Told 'em they was going to have fun camping. Got to hand it to her. She tried to turn something bad into good. But then come to find out, she got arrested for fooling around with a minor. Found her in the woods with some fifteen-year-old boy. Said he was just a friend of her boys.

Some people make a mess, don't they? And it don't need to be that a way.

Had one kid, third grade, would worry me to death about his sister in kindergarten not having her snack. She got free breakfast and so did he, but he'd come to school and have to walk his little sister down to her class and he'd say to me, every single day, same thing, "Miz Satchel, Miz Satchel"—he'd find me no matter where I was—"I know Sarah's supposed to bring a snack and we didn't have nothing. Do you think they'll give her free milk? Free crackers?" No matter how much I told him they'd feed her, he never rested his mind about it, like it was all up to him. He was all pale and stringy himself, like he knew what it was like to be hungry. I never seen a kid so worried, like the sky was going to fall any minute. I used to think now what could have happened to him to make him so worried all the time? Come to find out, four kids, father in jail, mother on the couch with baby number five in the oven, he the oldest, feeling like it was up to him. What those kids ate at school was all they ate and he knew his sister was in half-day kindergarten. I didn't think he'd live till ten with all that worry, you know it?

I bought little treats for her sometimes, if I had anything, and I told the kindergarten teacher about it, too. I just know I did what I could. When a kid was sent to me, I'd try to help them any way I could, whether it was school work or something else.

These young things fresh out of college, they just don't know. And the people in charge use big fancy words—*challenged* is one of 'em. Fightin' words, they are. The kids are challenged all right and they got nothing to fight back with at first. Then they grow up and that's all they know—how to fight.

I seen things. Nobody can tell me different than what I seen with my own eyes. Lot of kids can't do in class, and they get left behind, even while they're little. Then they just push 'em through like they're invisible. That one teacher said I ran off the wrong papers for her, said I got 'em mixed in with third grade—said I couldn't keep nothin' straight. These papers she was so crazy about, half the kids couldn't do 'em anyhow. Lotta times, that's what I was supposed to do with 'em—help 'em fill out those durn papers. Kids didn't know what they were doing to begin with, couldn't read.

Sometimes I get to thinking. I didn't cry when a kid was sitting in front of me and thinking how hard everything is. And I couldn't do much about it. Now, all I do is watch TV and go to the grocery store to pick up what's on sale, waiting for some bit of luck like finding a '43 penny, but then I think about those kids and tear up. They never get lucky. Least I had what I needed comin' up, a mother and father, food on the table regular, clean clothes. What have they got? Where do they fit in? And how are they ever going to make it? I see names in the paper all the time, kids I worked with—three are in jail right now, one stabbed his brother, one is in for rape, one shot somebody—and I don't know—as little kids you could never do enough for 'em, and now it's too late. I hope someone's looking, someone's got those little kids in their heart, know what I mean?

Something new showed up on my income tax return. Have you seen it? It says *poverty level* on mine. Made me laugh. Didn't make me feel no better really. Boy, I got something now, *poverty level*—like some kind of disease. They don't know, do they? They just don't know what *poverty level* really is. Worse yet, how to make it go away.

Well, I'm on my way to Sav-a-Lot. Good to see ya. You take care now, hear?

Crab Feast

Just he and Dad were in the boat this morning. He loved it without Davey or Anne around, when Dad talked to him about things he was planning—and he was always planning something big.

Greenfly felt like his boat. His father never actually said it was, but ever since last summer he was allowed to take it downriver alone to the red buoy where he'd watch the gulls circling, telling him where the fish were. For his eleventh birthday just last week, he got a Mitchell Garcia reel, Model 301, the model for left-handers, from his dad and a Shakespeare rod from his mom (she said she liked the name), both of which he kept in his room next to his bed.

From the first time his father rigged up a roller for the trotline—he was nine then—it had been his job to tie bait on Friday mornings. He'd reach into the bucket of salted bull lips (which stung if he had a cut on his hands but were good to dangle in his sister's face and gross her out) and knot them on the line every foot and a half. He never tangled the line and was careful to drop it round and round in the bucket ready for his father to use on Saturday.

You could lay half a mile of line without having to get a license, Pete told him, and he ought to know, being a waterman. During the week, Michael went out with Pete in his workboat, the *Miss Linda*. *Time I need a new boat, it'll be time to git a new wife,* said Pete, winking at him, although

Michael's ears got stuck on the sound of the word *time,* which seemed to come out of Pete's nose as *toim.* Not that he got to dip for crabs, but he did cull them while Pete dipped, and the best part was Pete was a storyteller. When he was young, he had sailed skipjacks on the bay, *seen squalls come up so fast they could put a boat down in two minutes.* But it wasn't the stories so much as the way Pete told them, his voice a singsong of strangely pronounced words and his eyes slits in his sunburned face as he squinted out over the water. Michael thought Pete was like a mooring pole, thick and grey, and always the same no matter what the weather was. Michael didn't have to *be* anything when he was with Pete; he just tied up to the mooring pole and did what he was told. Got paid for it, too. Secretly he hoped one day he'd have biceps as big as Pete's, which were thick around as Michael's waist was now.

On Saturdays, he crabbed with his dad. Just before sunup, he listened through his sleep for his father to stir and whisper, *Michael!* They'd pull on their clothes in the dark and sneak out the door into the dead quiet. Except for the *Miss Linda,* they had the river to themselves.

When he was a little kid their house seemed gigantic. But now, from the water, it looked small, the roof lower than those of the other cottages as though it had sneaked in like a cat on the prowl. He thought of the sleeping shapes of his mother, brother, and sister, and of the privilege to be out with his father alone, the two of them taking turns as they aimed the boat along the line and scooped up crabs in the wire net, the air so still and quiet that the putt-putt of the motor and the swish of the net as he plunged it into the bright water seemed loud enough to wake Davey back in the cottage, something Michael didn't want happening. The sun was just rising; its rays bounced off the tin roof of the barn across river, blinding him for a second, just long enough to make him miss a big one. His heart sank. *Awww.* The crab was saved by the glance of sun on the water and he by his father's quiet *that's okay.*

Sometimes he was not so lucky. Sometimes he couldn't do anything right. "Bring the boat farther up on the beach, Michael, for chrissake! Can't you see the tide's coming in?" or, "Put the crab tongs on the hook in the hallway—How many times do I hafta tell you!" or "How about the boat cushions you left out?"

"Well, nobody's perfect," his mother said and told him a story. "When you three were little, Michael—you might remember this—we had a sailboat called *Flying Tern.* Your father forgot to tie it up one day—this was back when we rented a place down here before the cottage was built—and we were eating lunch when Dad said, 'Looks like someone else has a yellow *Flying Tern* just like ours.' The boat was way out in the middle of the river and Dad turned to me with a dumb look on his face, and said, 'Where's ours?' Mr. Phillips had to take Dad out in his boat and tow the boat in. Your dad's just trying to give you the benefit of his experience, see?"

He laughed, but he shouldn't have. His dad could figure out anything. Theirs was the first new cottage on the point in fifty years, and he'd built it on a lot everybody thought was too small and swampy to build on.

They finished the line and his father leaned over the edge of the boat, the peak of his hat shielding his face. Steadying himself with one leg against the boat's side, he lifted the line from the roller with the net handle and gently dropped it back into the water. The river took it with a soft sucking sound. His father never missed, although Michael missed a lot, and they'd get hung up in the line and have to stop the boat. He was glad his father was dipping this time although dipping was his favorite job. You had to concentrate hard especially if they came steady on the line. Then you didn't even have time to turn around to empty the net into the bushel basket because you had to hold it tight against the flow of water or you'd lose what you already had.

"Hungry?" his dad asked as Michael culled the crabs that were too small and flung them into the river. He nodded. He was always hungry. "We'd best go in then. Let 'em get on the line good for the next run."

"When do we start building the bulkhead, Dad?"

"Soon. We have to get a tractor, too, some fill dirt, couple hoses."

He had gone with his father to order the gigantic sheets of corrugated cement at Robbins and Robbins. The sheets lay stacked on the ground, grey and stiff, rippled like the water when the wind starts up. They were longer than his father was tall and just wide enough for him to pick one up with his arms outstretched. They were so heavy his father had to bend down, lift one end to shoulder height, and then walk his hands down the sheet in order to stand it on end.

"Cement and asbestos. Something new," he panted as he lay the sheet back down. "Pretty soon everybody'll be wanting corrugated cement for seawalls. And this is what we'll do. We'll get a long hose, see, and I'll shoot water down where we want the sheet to go and the water pressure'll dig a trench for us down on the river bottom. When we get the sheet in place, you sit on top and rock it side to side while I keep shooting water down there to loosen up the bottom. Okay? Think you can do it? It'll be like riding bareback till you toughen up a little." Green eyes looked at him, man to man. "Then when the sheet is down two, three feet and holding steady, we'll go on to the next one and when they're all in place and we've got a wall, we'll use the tractor to push the fill dirt up to it and pack that in on the land side. Guess we'll have to prop it up on the river side till everything settles. I've still got to figure something out for the top edge, though, to steady it. Especially where it curves around." His father narrowed his eyes and squinted. Creases ran from his eyes down toward the sides of his long nose. "Unless we just take those two-by-eights and bolt them on and gradually tighten the bolts to conform to the shape of the wall. Yeah, that might do it. Are you with me?"

You bet. He loved it when Dad was excited like this. Every meal he sat with one knee sticking out from under the table, a knee that had a life of its own like a wind-up toy. Up and down it bounced, up and down like a spring gone wild. The floor vibrated and the dishes rattled until his mother said, "Justin, can you stop that? It's driving me crazy." He'd stop and get that blank look like she'd gone off somewhere else even though she'd keep nodding at him while he went on planning.

Now, quick, before his father revved up the motor for the ride back, Michael put into words what he was worrying about. "What about the beach part, Dad? It won't be as much fun as it is now if we build a wall across it."

"No, uh-huh! You're right! We're going to leave the beach alone and end the bulkhead right where the beach begins. We'll build a stone wall from the bulkhead to where the beach starts to slope down to the water. You're right—we want the beach! Glad you're thinking about it. Here. Take us in." He moved from the stern and allowed Michael to take his place. Michael thought things just couldn't be better.

The motor was out as far as it would go and he made a smooth arc toward the cottage. He saw Davey run from the house and splash into the water. His father pointed and turned around to warn Michael and Michael at the same time began to slow the motor. He knew what to do: cut the motor and pull on its back end to tip it forward before the prop hit the sand. In the sudden silence, he heard Davey call out, "How many?" Next it'll be Davey's turn, and then Anne's, but Michael wished they could have stayed out all morning, just him and Dad.

Company came in the heat of day. Car doors burst open, floats and coolers were pulled out of the backs of station wagons, kids leaped from car to back step to beach having changed their minds about entering the house. The Wurtzes, Hannah and Giles, were their neighbors from the city, but Rosemary didn't know the Lesters, Truman Lester being a co-worker at the new computer firm Justin had just joined. Truman's wife, Nancy, was perfect in her green miniskirt and yellow sandals. Her blonde hair swung smooth, a gold fluid mass that changed shape with every step. Each family had three children around the ages of Michael, Anne, and Davey.

Soon the big room held food offerings on every flat surface—Tupperware containers filled with potato salad, brown bags of tomatoes and corn, plastic bags of potato chips, six-packs of Coke and beer. Tennis shoes, towels, T-shirts, life jackets, shorts and duffel bags littered the floor. Hannah, Rosemary's friend, marched in with two huge loaves of bread she had baked in the shape of fish. Her wide cheeks pushed up her glasses when she smiled and she was constantly adjusting them. Built like a football player, thick in the back and chest, rolled waist and narrow hips, her weight was the one thing she seemed powerless to conquer although if her boys were built like her, she'd have pigskin stars. Rosemary guessed Hannah already disliked Nancy's perfection and Nancy, too, and became uneasy at the disparity of her guests.

Everything was a bustle of running feet, splashing water, and shouts from the women to the children, from child to child. Hannah's husband, Giles, round as Hannah, offered cigars to Justin and Truman and the men clustered around the crab float to survey the cottage.

"Comes in a kit, every piece precut, just the shell, of course," Justin was saying. They scanned the boats, puffed away on the cigars, pulled a foot up onto a step or a cooler to lean on a knee with one elbow. They talked about investments and vacation homes. Justin's done it, they agreed. He was way ahead of them, although they were "looking around."

Truman and Giles decided to take out the catamaran and pushed it out gingerly, way past the harbor before even attempting to get on board. When they did, they lingered around the mooring pole and the catamaran bumped into the side of the cruiser moored there. The sail luffed. A puff of wind came up and the catamaran moved backward toward shore. Justin swam out to them and called out instructions. Finally they were off with the wind slipping off the sail. "Let it out a little," Justin yelled, cupping his hands around his mouth. The catamaran bobbed on an incoming wake, then eased on out.

The boys gathered on the neighboring pier and took turns jumping into one of the tractor tire tubes while the three girls, Anne, Amy, and Nancy's daughter, Lisa, hung onto the other tube. Two of them climbed up, straddled it, and giggled as Lisa pulled herself up, but then all three slipped off into the water. They tried again and again, shrieking at each dunking while Hannah settled on one of the lawn chairs and took out her knitting, one eye on the children. Rosemary joined her while Nancy disappeared into the house to change into her bathing suit. Evelyn, Justin's mother, arrived. She sat down briefly and called to the kids. A minute later, she waded into the water with her bathing cap stretched over her newly coiffured hair. She preferred to be with the kids. Widowed twice, she mostly listened to the chatter of young mothers and didn't say much. The kids, at least, made her laugh and she had a genuine appreciation for them. "Grandma's here!" they yelled.

Justin started up the motor to the rowboat and invited Steve, Hannah's boy, to dip for crabs. Motioning and laughing, he promised to come back for each of the kids in turn. Misinterpreting, Chris, Hannah's youngest, just Davey's age, jumped in the boat. "Michael, pass me another life jacket, will ya?" Justin called.

Rosemary watched, counted kids, listened to Hannah, wondered lazily what was keeping Nancy so long. She watched Evelyn and admired her graceful swimming stroke as she felt the sun burn her legs and wondered dully where the Coppertone was. "Michael," she called, "put on some of this!" Suddenly self-conscious at the thought of Nancy in a bathing suit, she pulled in her stomach and wondered if she would ever again wear a bikini. Lying back on the chaise, she caught sight of Evelyn stretched across one of the tire tubes, paddling and kicking her legs.

Hannah was knitting like Rosemary's aunts. Her motions were smooth, and the wool gently flowed through each loop on the needle to a new loop in easy progression. Rosemary studied her fingers for a moment and thought about getting her own knitting, then decided against it.

"I think I'm going to take some courses, Hannah, in the fall, I mean—at night."

Hannah glanced sideways at her but her hands went on. "What kind of courses?"

"English—literature, poetry—kind of pick up where I left off." She surprised herself but saying it out loud established something. "I had some college before we got married."

Without enthusiasm, Hannah said, "Sounds neat. You don't have enough to do? With three kids?"

Rosemary shrugged. Hannah seemed much more content than she. She felt the afternoon breeze begin like an afterthought, rolling those fluffy cumulus clouds along with it. A picture postcard day. She closed her eyes and listened to the children splash and squeal, listened to Hannah's talk, the flags flap, the pages of Nancy's *Redbook* flutter. This is nice, she told herself. Everyone's having a good time. All because of Justin. When she opened her eyes, colors swirled around her. Nancy came out of the house in a scant bright yellow bikini, her face made up with fresh lipstick and mascara, her blonde hair shining. The children sparkled, never still, a perpetual round of wet, brown bodies in red and orange and green suits, diving, jumping, shouting, laughing, wet, bare feet slapping against the old, grey wood of the pier that splintered the nearly cobalt blue of the water and sky. Flags rippled American red, white, and blue, Maryland gold, red, and black; towels sprawled with Disney characters in purple and pink lay over striped lawn chairs; the catamaran's huge orange and black sail slid across the horizon; sleek, white cruisers bobbed alongside mooring all along the point catching blinding flashes of sun in windshields and Nancy's brilliant red toenails bloomed at the end of the green and yellow webbed lawn chair—the whole great rush of life, of summer, of every blade of grass, of their very own beach and the boats, her children, like all of her hope, strong, promising, churning about her. The other cottages lay sleepily along the narrow shore, but theirs was teeming with life. She drifted in and out of listening to Hannah tell about the Pillsbury Bakeoff she'd entered, watched her hands shape her words as she told about the men in tuxedos who lifted the finished breads high above their heads as they carried them to the judging table, watched her laugh through the exaggerated movements of her huge arms, the graceful sweep of her knowledgeable hands, the bright red half-finished sweater in her lap, her reddish-brown hair in wisps around her face and thought, *Hannah is beautiful in a way I hadn't noticed before.* She laughed with her—not just because of the story—but because of everything she saw, everything that filled her. At all this happiness. And Justin now coming toward her, but too hurriedly, the tendons in his neck strained as he said, "Where's Mom?"

She looked out over the water for the black inner tubes, and could only account for the one the boys were using. Justin ran into the house, calling, and Rosemary called to the children, "Where's Grandma?"

"Maybe she went for a walk," they answered. "She was in the tire tube, Mommy," Anne said, and they both looked out to the river. There was something mid-river. Could it be the tube? Pushed upriver by the tide and wind? Panicked, Rosemary screamed for Justin.

"Look! Way out!" Seeing only a small black dot now, they couldn't tell whether there was anybody on it. Suddenly Anne dove off the pier and began swimming out to deeper water.

"No, Annie, come back! It's too far! Anne!" Rosemary shouted, but Anne's slim golden arms paddled crazily while her head stayed underwater. Justin ran toward the rowboat. In seconds, he pushed the boat to deeper water, tipped the motor forward and down, and yanked on the cord. He caught up with Anne now in water over her head, put the boat in neutral and reached for her arm. After he pulled her in, he revved up the motor and headed out.

Rosemary stared hard at the black dot. "Please, please," she said to the air. The kids had gathered on the beach. "Everything will be all right," she said and reached out for Davey. Hannah began throwing towels around her shivering children. Nancy stayed on the lawn chair, her legs still crossed, her ankles slender and smooth, toenails sticking up like little red flags. Rosemary ran for the binoculars. The screen door slammed behind her as if to shut her off from hearing or knowing anything she didn't want to know. She could not believe harm would come to Evelyn or any of them. Evelyn was an excellent swimmer. The afternoon was hot and sunny and the flags flapped gently as if to reassure her, but in her mind she saw dark clouds, whitecaps rolling in any minute, complicating everything. That's how it was—in the midst of a good time—when you least expected it...

She searched the horizon with the binoculars, but in her fright she couldn't even find the boat. She took the glasses from her eyes and put them back again, trying to aim better. The boat was slowly coming toward her and she couldn't see whether or not Justin was towing the tube. He probably was, and Evelyn would surely be on it, annoyed that Justin had spoiled her ride.

There she was—drooped across the inner tube, her head lying on its side in a helpless aspect that brought tears to Rosemary's eyes. There was no one she felt closer to than Evelyn. The dignity Evelyn carried Rosemary emulated. She'd known acceptance and love from Evelyn unlike any other in her life. Evelyn wasn't moving—she must be resting, and horribly frightened. Oh, the terror of underwater space. Unseen depths. Unimaginable quietness. On the surface so beautiful—glancing rays, mirroring skies, expanding sunsets—below, so deadly, so dark.

The boat danced in place for a while, Evelyn probably refusing to get aboard. She never could manage that first unsteadiness of putting a foot in the rowboat. The boat headed toward shore now, slowly, carefully towing the tube. The children were back diving off the pier. Nancy remained on the lawn chair browsing through her *Redbook,* and Hannah took up her knitting again. Truman and Giles were still out on the catamaran. Rosemary paced on the shore. When Justin pulled the boat onto the beach, she reached out for Evelyn, whose legs wouldn't support her. Her face was as white as her hair and Rosemary felt her tremble as they staggered together toward the sand, Evelyn's weight against her.

"Well," Evelyn said, trying to make little of it with a faint smile. "I didn't want to let go of the tube, you know—swim back without it—the children enjoy it so. But once I began drifting, the current was swifter than I thought. I just couldn't paddle hard enough to steer the darn thing," she said. "I'm okay. Just let me sit awhile. My arms are a little achy." She was shaking. Justin brought her a bit of vodka and orange juice and she asked for her beach jacket as she sat in the nearest lawn chair. Rosemary covered Evelyn's legs with a towel and looked up to see Justin pass by Nancy's lawn chair, trailing his hand across Nancy's neck and back, sweeping her hair to one side, an action so fleeting Rosemary wasn't sure she was seeing it at all. She must be mistaken.

He disappeared around the side of the house and came back carrying the enameled steamer pot, a signal the kids did not miss. In a second he was surrounded by dripping children. Davey said, "Let me, let me," but Michael already had the tongs down in the crab float. "Aw, you get to do everything, Michael," he said as Michael pulled the crabs out one by one and Anne slammed the lid on the pot after each crab. One hung on to another and let go just before Michael got it in the pot. The crab scrambled sideways toward the water. Kids jumped out of its way, screeching.

"Give Davey a turn, Michael. Just let him try it once," said Rosemary, but it was Anne, dutifully helping Michael, never asking for attention, who Rosemary saw clearly in this moment. The sight of her diving off the pier and swimming toward her grandmother, taking things in her own hands at such a young age—she was the valiant one. Rosemary, close to tears now at the relief of seeing Evelyn in the lawn chair chatting away to Nancy, bent over to whisper in Anne's ear, "Anybody ever tell you what a good kid you are?" Anne smiled back and shrugged as if no one ever had.

With the children following, Justin hosed off the crabs at the outside spigot and water poured out of the bottom of the steamer. The crabs, subdued, bubbled quietly in the pot.

"Watch out now," Justin said to the kids. "Annie, hold that door open for me, will ya?" He disappeared into the house with the pot.

Rosemary followed. She just wanted him to look at her, reassure her in some way, help her ward off the doubt she felt. Would he, did he, do more than look at other women? He did spend Monday through Thursday alone in the city. She'd never had cause to suspect anything. She would not wreck the status quo with suspicions and accusations. He would enjoy it too much. It was an ego thing with men, she decided, and said instead, "Do you think your mother is okay? She looks awfully pale."

He nodded. "Oh, sure."

Then there was a rush of kids between them. "C'mon," Davey called. "This is the best part." He meant the crabs scratching the side of the pot as they cooked. Usually he covered his ears, but today, the others would be as horrified at the sound as he.

"Eew!" said Kevin, Nancy's boy, about Michael's size, his nose screwed up. "You cook 'em alive?" He looked at Justin and then at Rosemary and back again as if they were murderers. "Eating a crab that's dead before you cook it will make you sick," Rosemary explained.

"Timer's on," Justin announced, a fact she could see for herself. "Who wants to go for a swim?" But the children listened to the pot as Rosemary began laying newspaper on the table. Then Davey gave a yell. The crabs, escaping down the side of the pot, dropped off the stove and onto the floor. Eight of them scratched across the linoleum before she got the lid back on and laid a heavy bowl on top. The crabs' claws clacked midair across the rug like they were playing castanets. The other kids yelled and danced in exaggerated leg lifts, but her kids tried to catch the crabs with bare hands. They knew how to do it. Michael had taught them.

"Okay, okay," said Justin, bursting back into the room. "So we forgot to tie the lid on. Maybe they deserve to be let go, warriors that they are. Open the door! Down to the sea in victory! Step aside, you tender earthlings, before they sink a claw in you!" He leaped toward the door and swept a folded newspaper at the crabs, funneling them to freedom. The kids squealed and giggled, stood on couches and chairs, looked at Justin and looked away and then back again not knowing whether to trust him, eager to join in the game if there was one. Kevin shouted, "Here's one; here's one!" Michael pinned down the claws with a broom handle, then picked up the crab with forefinger and thumb around the back end behind the swimmer fins. He ran out the door and flung it out into the river as far as he could. He turned around to face them with a big grin. The hero.

"Look out!" cried Justin, bending to grab Amy's toes. She yelped and jumped, her round face red with heat, but looked up at Justin with a grin. She began to follow him around for the next hour or so, while he brought the next batches of crabs for steaming—in and out, trailing him to the rowboat until he took her out to dip crabs. Twice more the pot was filled.

Rosemary slid the red crabs sprinkled with seasoning onto trays and set them on the newspaper-covered table while the smell of crab overpowered all other smells. It filled the room, lay on her damp skin and permeated her hair as she marched back and forth through the crab steam with trays of crabs, mallets, steak knives, rolls of paper towels, cups of melted butter, a bottle of vinegar, platters of potato salad and sliced tomato and Hannah's bread.

Steam rose from the heaped crabs. Outside, flags drooped at the poles. The air was suffocating. Even the fans didn't help much. The kids jumped in the river before coming to the table and when they did come in, their hair plastered to their heads, sniffling, eyes bloodshot, they dripped puddles on the floor despite the wet towels wrapped around their middles. Justin passed around cans of beer to the grownups. There never was enough ice for the tea; the lemonade quickly warmed in sweating glasses.

They all reached for the crabs and began pulling off claws, putting the larger ones in piles to crack later and sucking sweet bits out of the smaller ones. The crabs lay burnished and plump on the trays and Giles acknowledged their glory like a grace. "Nothing prettier than a pile of hot, steamed crabs!" Justin showed Nancy the best way to break off the hard shell while Rosemary sat with a huge crab before her on the newspaper, the crab red-ugly and angry in its final revenge. She picked it up and pulled off the shell. With her eyes on Justin, she yanked its appendages vehemently—as if crabs had testicles. Sex seemed to get in everyone's way, Nancy's way, and Justin's way, and hers, she thought, as the juice ran down her arms, sex being the thing she least understood. Furious, she watched as Justin drenched a piece of back fin in vinegar while Nancy opened her mouth to receive it. *Just fooling around,* he'd say. He'd make light of it, maybe even laugh at her. The chunk of meat in her mouth wouldn't be swallowed. She looked down, afraid of revealing anything like need or hurt, or her plainness in the face of blonde competition, and broke open the crab's body to the bittersweet smell of the mustard-yellow butter inside. She stole a glance at Truman, deep into his crab claw, sucking out the meat, hammering the tip to get the last bit out. Maybe he was right to absorb himself. Maybe he was stupid or didn't care, or maybe small flirtations were acceptable and she was being foolish. *Why make a big thing of it?* she thought as she listened to the chatter, the hammering, the drone of the fans, and felt the heat melt her as she glanced up at the sweating, flushed faces around her.

No, she said to herself. *This day, this gathering, this feast, our children. Didn't he build the cottage for us?—so much effort for us? This is it. The forever people reach for.* Besides, Justin was looking at her now if only to see if she was watching him, conscious she might be offended, but that was all she really wanted—to have him look at her as though she mattered. All too quickly he was telling Giles what he thought of the president's war on poverty. Evelyn, engrossed in her crab, pulled the meat with fingers that looked too small and delicate for the task. She was silent, still pale, with a new seriousness in her demeanor. Her cheeks wobbled, something Rosemary had never noticed before, as she refused Rosemary's offer of more tea.

"Anything I can get you, Evelyn?" she asked, to which Evelyn raised eyes that said, *Am I like a child now? Do I have to be looked after like one of the kids? Counted, kept track of? I saw myself helpless today. Dependent on you to save me.*

"No, thank you, Rosemary deah," she said softly.

Hannah picked the crabmeat quickly and gathered it in three small dishes for her children, who were happily eating her bread and waiting, trusting mother would provide. We are all dependent on each other, Rosemary thought, in such close and distant communion, so trusting in the tight web of family, feelings, and words that create an aura of safety. For her it was Justin and the children. For Evelyn, it was having them live close by now that she was alone again. For them all, these were good times, the ones that would be good old days someday. She breathed deep, feeling satisfied and strong. They were so fortunate. *Don't worry,* she wanted to tell Evelyn, *I'll always love you, look out for you.* She thought about the word *always* then, as she concentrated on the lavish bounty on the table before her, listened to the hammering, the shells cracking open to reveal mysterious innards, and knew time was measured in the diminishing pile of crab, the voices around her but a momentary distraction.

Soon the children lost interest and found their way back to the water, trailed by parental warnings to stay in the harbor where it was shallow. Occasionally they ran in to check on the circle of families and complain of a splinter from the pier or a mosquito bite. The table was heaped with mountains of crab skeleton while hands reached out to push back the debris to make room for picking the last crab. Finally, Evelyn raised herself stiffly from the table and washed her hands at the sink, then drifted to the couch, lit a cigarette, and stared out across the water beyond the children to watch the sunset.

Rosemary turned on the table lamp; gnats gathered and flurried overhead. The youngest of the children, Lisa, came in crying and would not be comforted. Events run their course, lose momentum, become memory. Change sneaks up on us. Something, something is different. Justin spends four nights a week in the city alone or not alone. She lit a citronella candle and heard the whispered hiss of something caught too close to the flame.

Maybe she was staging dramas again. They would talk it over some afternoon when they were out on the catamaran and she was calmer. Justin would wind up laughing about it and then they'd both laugh. But not now. Now she had guests to see to. She needed to straighten the room, wash the dishes, bunk the kids, and help her husband, who was rolling up the newspaper around the crab hulls, his face still flushed, his eyes bright as he swept everything into the trash bag, gathering the top in his fist and spinning the bag as if it were a partner in a dance she could not know.

The Bird's Heart

He stared at me as though he might recognize me.

"Uncle Leon?" I said hopefully.

Suddenly, he cried out loud enough to give everyone around the kitchen table a start, including me and my cousins Pat and Betty Lou, and their husbands, John and Harry, and my aunts, Tante Elizabeth and Tante Dorothy. The sound was not directed toward me; neither was it one of recognition. It was a high screech like a toddler would make. It was as though a long ago terror sprang from some cruelty in his childhood, a period to which he had now returned after a long career of selling boilers and a retirement of playing golf. His cry was met by an ear-piercing scream from the very large birdcage in the corner of the kitchen. The raucous duet turned into a duel, a reality none of us were ready for: the intrusion of my uncle's plight and the warning from the bird, both in an unknowable language. Frightened, we let loose a flurry of words as ephemeral and hopeful as snowflakes on a school morning: *So how're ya doing? How's life treating you? You look the same! Not a day older! How was the drive?*

It had been a long time since I'd seen my aunt and uncle. I had a feeling that if I didn't visit soon, I might no longer have the chance, so when my Tante Dorothy called and said, "Come with me. We'll drive down and see them. It may be the last time," I was glad to do it even though it meant a long drive across the Chesapeake Bay to the Western Shore. But now, as Leon and Elizabeth sat side by side in their wheelchairs, I wasn't so sure. I wanted them to be like they were when I was a child and one of the fourteen cousins being yelled at by Leon and soothed by Elizabeth. It was remarkable the way Pat had cared for her parents, but there came a time when her father became too difficult and had to be put in a nursing home. Pat continued to care for her mother through a series of strokes that had stolen Tante Elizabeth's grace, but never diminished her faith. Her white hair was neatly brushed, her face peaceful. She was well cared for.

"That's her company face," Tante Dorothy said later. "She never allowed a crack in that wall of hers. She always believed that if you followed the rules, God was on your side." Elizabeth had been a fortunate woman. She was the prettiest of the five sisters, the one with the most children (there were four of them) and the one who was always dressed up, the only one who wore furs and jewelry, the only one who dyed her hair. Her family life seemed to go on without a ripple. One summer when I was thirteen, I stayed with my cousins for a week. One afternoon, my uncle called everyone into the living room for family prayer time and I could hear them saying the rosary as I sat on the bed in my cousin's bedroom and waited. I never felt so left out in all my life. My mother, Florence, had chosen to leave the Catholic Church when she married my father, and I don't think my Tante Elizabeth ever forgave her. From the way my family fought and struggled, I grew up thinking their family life had it easier than ours because they prayed all the time. They had the edge. Turns out, nobody has an edge.

I watched Harry, Betty Lou's husband, tap his fingers and listened to him hum "Yellow Submarine", a can of Bud at his elbow. He would always ask me, "Aren't you married yet? Can't you find a man?" I waited for the question now, ready to be put off. "What for?" I'd say. "I love being single," to which he'd turn down his lips and raise his eyebrows.

"Been there, done that," I'd say. A few more beers and he would drag out that question again, air it out like a piece of dirty laundry. Ready with my usual answer, I turned my attention away from them all for the moment. Dorothy would have said, "It's none of your goddamned beeswax."

I love opulence. Pat's kitchen was a masterpiece that must have come straight out of *Better Homes and Gardens*. I loved the array of silver appliances along the counters, ferns hanging at the windows and African violets blooming on an island counter separating the cooking area from the dining. One whole side of the room was glass, beyond which there was a deck that overlooked a wooded ravine. The tangle of bare, grey limbs outdoors only emphasized the lush greenery inside. In a corner of the kitchen, there was a roomy and considerable birdcage that held the aforementioned parrot-like bird, an idea that had probably been a stroke of genius by some interior decorator but not anyone with a musical bent. The greens, yellows, and brilliant blues of the bird's plumage exactly matched the valances over the windows. Outside, the moon rose like the face of a peeping Tom as dusk descended.

This was a reunion of sorts, though in no way like the ones we'd all experienced in the past. I have an old photograph of the five Elbert sisters when they were very young, standing from oldest to youngest like stair steps. They are wearing huge bows at the back of their heads and high-button shoes peek out from longish dresses. Beginning with the oldest, there was Freda, Emily, Florence, Elizabeth, and Dorothy, and it was because of them there'd been a bevy of aunts, uncles, and cousins in my childhood, something missing in my children's generation and their children's. Now there was just Elizabeth and the youngest, Dorothy, who had admitted on the drive over that she was uneasy about the visit. "Elizabeth was always so proud and private, you know. She may not want me to see her in her present state, or Leon either. Yet things can only get worse. I think I'd better visit now rather than later."

"Coffee, Tante Dorothy, or tea?" Pat sang out. "Marie?" I shut my eyes for a few seconds. The voices were reminiscent of other voices that had gathered at my grandmother's in the Bronx when I was a child. Somehow the voice genes had carried through the next two generations because remarkably, my aunts and cousins and I sound very much alike, with the same New York accent shining through on the word *cawfee*. I could see my grandmother's oak icebox and the round oak pedestal table, the yellow enameled stove with its thick pipe sticking into the bright blue walls over which my grandmother, in a fit of creativity, had splattered white paint, a dappled effect that matched her enamelware pots. Those days, the coffee was always accompanied by hard rolls and baloney from the deli a block away.

The bird screeched again, and Uncle Leon, excited by the sound, yelled out. They screamed at each other for a while, louder and louder, competing. The relatives merely raised their voices and continued talking across the table.

"Spell of warm weather for February, eh?"

"Did you come Route 4 or did you take the bypass?"

"Still driving that Toyota?"

Uncle Leon never looked up. He played with a Matchbox car, a white Corvette, which he rolled along the table top. Soon all eyes followed the car as if the sight of an old man playing with a toy on the kitchen table was the most riveting thing they'd ever encountered, and the most normal. Eight pairs of eyes followed the car.

Betty Lou said, "He came in wet pants. I wonder how long he's been wet and if the nursing home sent him out like that."

Leon looked past Betty Lou as if she were a shadow he

was looking through to a shaded spot on the wall where he was trying to decide what he saw there. He cried out again and the bird shrieked, a grating, raw-boned sound. I tried to smother my grin, a response that absurdity and off-key sounds always elicit. I wondered if there were some sort of joke going on that meant I had to listen to the old man *and* the bird at the same time, or was it that the bird was trying to tell us something urgent that Leon couldn't, or did the bird and Leon speak the same secret language, which controlled us in some way, making us listen in puzzlement, chaos taking over in some insidious way, something I always feared when things went sour. I was feeling disoriented and wished I could think of something to say.

"What a nice kitchen, Pat," I said.

"Yes. Thank you. John planned it and I must say it's very workable."

John, tall, lean, with serious eyes that darted here and there, a headful of thick grey hair, leaned carelessly against the counter, apart from the group. It wasn't easy to pull him into conversations. He strode to the bird's cage and opened the door. With a smile of straight, even white teeth he said, "She just wants a little attention." The bird hopped onto his extended finger and began preening. It was larger than a cockatoo and smaller than a parrot but it had the voice of a monster. "What kind of bird is that?" I said.

Speaking at the same time so that my words went unnoticed, Tante Dorothy spoke up. "If it was me, I'd open the kitchen door and..."

"Squaaaaawk," interrupted the bird.

"...let him find his own food," she continued. "You actually paid good money for that thing?"

Pat smiled and said, "It was an anniversary gift from my husband," and she looked up at John, who was throwing kisses at the bird with gentle pecking noises. The bird and he were beak to beak. He stroked its back.

The kitchen light hung like a street lamp over a lonely corner, the large oval table bare as a sidewalk, the lines on the faces heavy and grey as if someone had sketched them in charcoal. Betty Lou's rinse had a reddish tinge and her lips pursed themselves into a plaintive ripple that weighted her entire face. Harry sat sweating under the light, bulbous and paunchy, circles under and around his eyes, panda-like. "C'mon, Pop," he said good-naturedly. "Let's get you some dry pants," and he got up to wheel Uncle Leon back from the table.

Tante Elizabeth glanced at him with a look of relief. "Leon," she said obviously trying to keep up a semblance of decency and civility, "why didn't you tell us?" although from the way she quickly looked down at her lap, I could see she didn't really believe he'd answer. The question was more out of hope that this time he might. This time he just might burst out of his caul and tell us where he was and what was wrong.

They hadn't really talked to each other for a long time now, Pat told me on the phone. When Elizabeth had had her first stroke, Leon didn't know what to do. He just stood there, a child disbelieving Mother could be sick. He'd forgotten how to use the telephone. Now Elizabeth sat with her right arm resting on the pillow in her lap, her long, narrow face still beautiful and strong but pale and streaked with shadows in this light, her hair in a thick, soft fluff swept back from her face.

Seemingly embarrassed about Leon's condition, she seemed to brighten at his absence. She said, "Well, how are the kids?" slurring her words slightly, but she was smiling, maybe at the accomplishment of such a normal question at this difficult time in her life. She jumped when the bird screeched again and her arm fell off the pillow. Pat put it back for her gently, as if it were a baby bird she was returning to its nest.

"They're fine," I said, trying to say as little as possible about my brood. "Each into their own thing. Don't hear from them often enough, but they're fine."

"Eeee-oooo, eeeee-oooo," screamed the bird from John's shoulder. I had the distinct feeling the bird was saying, "Liar, liar." So what if things were not ideal or even promising? So what? I'd done all I could without the help of a husband. Why was I so defensive about everything? The bird went on shrieking with a hysteria that wouldn't quit. It was the kind of sound that sent splinters of glass through my veins.

"I'll have to put you back in the cage if you don't stop," crooned John. "Do you want to go back, hmm? Do you?" He walked toward the cage with the bird still on his shoulder. As it took little side steps higher and higher toward his neck, I waited for the bird to climb bare flesh and hang sideways, gouge John's neck and draw blood. *Then* maybe he'd open the door and shoo the bird off. Everyone watched, glad for a break in the conversation. But John only paraded around the kitchen with the bird on his shoulder, his head turned toward it, making kissing sounds, his silver hair falling over his forehead. He was handsomer outside of the band of light that coned over the table.

Handsomer than anyone had a right to be. What I couldn't understand, though, was his fascination with the bird and not even one look toward Pat who sat with her legs crossed and her complexion rendered into cream by the light. She's very pretty. Look at her, I thought, a complete family, husband, kids all married off on time, eleven grandchildren, mother, father, a big house with bedrooms enough for everyone when they wanted to stay. I conjured up noisy family get-togethers—kids running in and out, giggling, the grownups yelling, "Go on out and play and shut the door behind you—Cut that out!—Hey kids, keep it down to a dull roar, wouldjas?" like Uncle Leon used to do. I loved those times. For nine years, I was an only child, raised by an upraised hand, yet when my cousins and I played at my grandmother's, we were uproarious and no one ever noticed. In fact, I always felt it was *expected* of us. This was what you did at family get-togethers.

But none of this was in evidence now.

Pat put water in the kettle and began measuring coffee into the coffee maker.

Harry wheeled Uncle Leon back to the table. He had on new maroon sweatpants, the tag still on them. Betty Lou reached over to remove the tag. Still clutching the little Corvette, Leon began running it back and forth slowly in front of him.

"Did you have snow yesterday?" said Tante Dorothy. "Hey—!" shouted Uncle Leon to no one in particular. The others shook their heads. She went on. "We didn't have enough to stick, but it made everything pretty for a while. We played golf early in the day but by the eighth hole, it started to snow."

"I love it when it snows," said Elizabeth, looking up hopefully.

"I hate to go out in it," said Pat, shaking her head at the kitchen sink.

"Aah, a little bit of snow never hurt anybody," said Harry cheerfully. "How's that, Pop, all right?"

Uncle Leon was silent.

"Is that all right, Pop?" Harry repeated. "Is that all right?" he said again as he bent over and put his face right in front of Leon. Leon stared at him, opened his mouth as if to speak, and nodded.

"There you go!" said Harry and looked around at everyone, grinning wide. "Sometimes we connect!" He clapped his father-in-law on the back. "Way to go, Leon," he said and went back to his place at the table.

The bird let out a blood-curdling shriek. "For chrissakes!" said Harry, his face changing faster than a blink. "Put that thing away, will ya?" It shrieked again and again until Tante

Dorothy's hands flew up to her ears. She laughed then, and rolled her eyes. The others laughed with her.

"It does that all day," said Pat, "but I don't even hear it half the time. You get used to it after a while."

"I heard of a woman in Florida who got mad at her boyfriend and killed his pet parrot," I said. "It was in the paper where she plucked him out and roasted him for dinner that night, served him up on a silver platter. Her boyfriend was bringing charges. I love thinking about the expression on his face when she brought the platter to him with that skinny bird body on it, stuffed. *Breast or leg, dear?*"

Dorothy laughed. "You might think about that, Pat."

"Well," she said, "that's my bird, like I said. John promised he'd take care of it for me since I was taking care of Mom."

Another shriek—as raucous as the blare of a misfired trumpet. I shuddered.

"All right now, all right," crooned John. "We're going to put you night-night." He kissed the bird again and lifted the wire door on the cage. With the bird perched inside, the door of the cage snapped shut. John unfolded a cloth cover—which matched the valances and the bird's own colors—and laid it over the cage. The bird muttered for a while and grew silent as everyone listened, afraid to speak as though a child had just been put to bed.

For the most part, Elizabeth kept her face directed toward her lap. She looked up to glance around the table once in a while but ignored her sister Dorothy, who hadn't come all this way for small talk or out of curiosity either. To comfort. Yes. Certainly. Her big sister Elizabeth, fabulous, sophisticated Elizabeth. Proud Elizabeth. Something tore at my heart as my aunt's head bowed to receive the straw Pat had put in the coffee cup she held up to her.

Earlier, Dorothy showed me a picture she treasured of

her and Elizabeth in white dresses hugging each other when Dorothy was no more than a toddler. A rarity in the days of formal pictures. "At the photographer's up on Tremont Avenue. Round, adorable faces, even if I say so myself," she said. "I remember holding onto Elizabeth's hand for most of my childhood while my mother worked in the butcher shop with my father."

"It isn't too hot for you, Mom, is it?" said Pat. Elizabeth shook her head.

Meanwhile, Betty Lou stirred sugar into her father's tea, then pursing her red lips, she tasted it in case it was still too hot and set it before him.

I knew I was about to natter but couldn't stop myself, whether or not anything I said fit into the conversation. It was all that screeching and sorrow around the table.

"This morning when I woke up, I looked across the field and was amazed at the great number of migrating birds. Huge flocks of whistling swans had settled in the cornfields around the house until everywhere it was as white as snow. Coming over, I had to drive right through them—they were on both sides of the road. They waddled away, then rose up to the sky all at once like a huge, white blanket set to air in the wind. It was a beautiful sight." I stopped suddenly, embarrassed, everyone staring at me as if to say, "Where did that come from?"

Pat jumped up. "Would anyone like to see some movies of the family? I just had the oldest ones put on a DVD."

Leon tipped his cup and looked into it. "Want some tea, Pop?" said Harry. "Can I help you?" He started to raise the cup but Leon pushed his hand away, spilling some on the table. He ran the Corvette through the puddle, making two wet ribbons along the table edge. Pat reached for the sponge. "He-e-ey," Leon shouted, and woke up the bird.

"Rawk, rrrraawk," the bird wailed in its high-pitched way.

Higher than E, maybe high G, or A even, I thought and grit my teeth. The bird seemed to mark time, accenting the terrible poignancy of Leon the wheeled finding mobility in wheeling the toy car, and the way we, the collected relics of family, were trapped in circumstances and trying to accept them ever so politely. What if the bird's heart exploded during one magnificent grand finale of sound and Uncle Leon shouted, "Keep it down to a dull roar, wouldjas?" for one last wonderful time? My eyes watered.

John went over to the cage. "Sh-sh-sh, Baby," he said. "It's all right—it'll be all right. Don't you pay them any mind," he crooned to the bird.

"Ch-chk-chk-chk," said Baby. "Raaawwwk! Raaawwwk!"

Maybe John's getting even somehow, I thought, for his mother-in-law living with them. For not getting enough attention himself. Pat watched her husband steadily, as though glad to have him react to *something.* The cover on the cage moved and John removed it, clucking softly to the bird. "There she is! She wants to watch the movie, too!"

Pat put the DVD in the player and pressed Play. She waited, watching the screen, one foot forward, her hand rubbing her chin. Whorls of snow on the TV, wild swings of the camera, and there they are—forty-five, fifty years ago, up on the flat roof of Tante Freda's apartment building in the Bronx (they used to call it *tar beach*), and there's my grandmother, Omie, laughing with her head thrown back and the wind blowing her dress above her garters—the same thin lips, long angular face, her hair neatly settled into finger waves at her temples and held in place with bobby pins. Her lips are moving as she stands with Freda and Emily and Florence, and they dance for brief seconds arm in arm, kicking in different directions, uneven and out of step, then unhook their arms and wave at the camera, the wind blowing and blowing, ballooning dresses, springing hair from coiffures, sunshine making them all squint. They blow final kisses at the camera and look away over the rooftops, pointing into the distance. There are the uncles with rolled-up sleeves and suspenders, young blonde hair swept away from chiseled faces. Other roofs quickly—a sweep of chimneys, walls, tar, a wild collage—then kids, the cousins, which is which? There! Pat! Betty Lou! Me! Pulling Uncle Leon's elbow to come and dance with us, which he does, flipping his cigarette with his middle finger and thumb over the walled edge of the roof, laughing. There's my father, Willie, blowing into a harmonica, then Elizabeth, holding onto her picture hat, giving up and pulling it off as her hair flows around her face and across her eyes. She's laughing and reaching for the door to the stairs and pulling the door open, her arm around Dorothy, protecting her as wind belches up from the staircase and pushes Dorothy's skirt higher than her waist. The camera focuses on her legs, beautifully curved and slender, hands shyly pulling down her skirt, Elizabeth trying to help her with fluttering fingers and the wind playing with both of them as they giggle and look at the camera. Suddenly the wind billows both skirts and I could almost hear them scream as their mouths hang open.

Instead, the spell was broken with catcalls from Harry. "Hey, hey?" he shouted and banged on the table. "More, more!"

"More!" repeated Uncle Leon. I swear I heard him say it, but the others paid no attention and Leon began to study his hand, turning it over and over, back and forth, as if it were a disconnected piece of something with which he didn't know what to do. Tante Elizabeth stared at the screen, lips parted; Tante Dorothy studied and searched, called out names, translated every move. "There's Abe! Swaying—had too much—and Willie, too, see him? Leon with the cigarette, and me! Mama again! I can hear her laugh! Must have been her birthday—August."

The bird's shriek this time was more like a sentinel crow crying a warning. My eyes darted from the scene before me to the one on the TV screen and back again. Then and now, then and now. "Lost, all lost," wailed the bird.

"Oh! There's Christmas!" Dorothy announced as the camera moved to a lighted Christmas tree in Omie's parlor.

Elizabeth then and Elizabeth now stared at each other. A second later, the one on the screen breaks out in a wide smile, her hair dark and bouncing around her smooth face, eyes clear, sparkling into the camera. Children jump around her, reaching up to touch the fur piece she has just taken out of a box. She lets them pet it a minute before reaching up with both arms to wrap it around her shoulders. She is a queen posing with one arm clutching the fur and the other extended, palm up. Leon appears by her side and kisses her on the cheek. She turns her head toward his dark, curly one and kisses him on the lips, children jumping around them and laughing.

I began to cry. It wasn't like I'd just started; I felt as if I'd been crying for a long time except now tears appeared, much against my will. I glanced around at the other faces, all turned toward the screen, enraptured, searching for themselves, all except for John who busied himself talking to the bird, feeding it bits of bread through the bars, and Harry because it was before his time in the family, and Leon, who, thank God, didn't know who that was on the screen. I watched the two figures side by side in wheelchairs spotlighted by the kitchen light as their youth exploded before them. What was Elizabeth feeling? Pride in her former beauty? A few moments of release from the wheeled imprisonment of her body? Then I saw her begin a slow smile—and was grateful to see it. I had to leave the room while the bird shrieked and screamed again and again, sending missiles of sound into the kitchen, and the little car rolled back and forth, back and forth on the table. I coughed and excused myself.

It was a big house, and I walked down the center hallway.

"Hey, Marie, don't leave now—here's you, singing for Santa Claus!" called Tante Dorothy.

Uncle Leon echoed, "Hey, Marie!" It was him, coming at me in little flashes of comprehension. I wiped my eyes quickly, fanned my face momentarily, and slipped back into the kitchen. Yes, there I was in pigtails, mouthing "Silent Night," innocent of life's store. We all were. Misfortune, grief, loneliness attaching to us like burrs in later years, but here I was singing a "Silent Night" solo, probably off-key but with gusto. Oh, it was a lovely time; the movie camera scanned the faces I would have been seeing before me, faces so alive and kind as they smiled at me. I'm not sure I've ever felt so loved again.

Suddenly, Uncle Leon laughed. "God damn!" he said loudly. "Here comes Santa up the cellar stairs now! You better be good, cut out that racket, you hear me?" Heads reeled; mouths dropped open.

"Elizabeth, dance with me, Babe," said Leon. "Put your warm, delicious body next to mine!"

He stared into the kitchen light for a moment and then looked at John just beyond the band of light. John shifted his weight as if it were all a nuisance to him and he was just waiting as he'd waited all evening for the visit to be over. Leon picked up the Matchbox car without seeing it. Pat went over to him and laid her hand on his shoulder. Some of his hair stood up on end and some lay mowed down as if influenced by the confusion of thought within. John picked up the leftover bread. He slid open the glass door and stepped out on the deck.

"What?" said Dorothy, but Leon wouldn't answer. "What did he say?" she asked again. Elizabeth looked at Betty Lou and Pat looked out at the moon.

"Well, Pop. I suppose we ought to think about bringing you back," said Harry. "Did you see yourself in the movie? Didn't you look handsome? Give Elizabeth a kiss now. C'mon. Give her a kiss!"

"Stop it, Harry," said Elizabeth.

"He can do it. I know he can. C'mon, Pop, kiss her. Go ahead. Just lean over and plant one on her. Go 'head. C'mon now, Pop. We got to go so you kiss her goodnight. I know you can do it. You answered me before. C'mon, kiss her!"

"Check to see if he's wet again, will you?" said Pat.

"Leave him be," said Dorothy.

"What, leave him wet for the trip out in the cold?' said Harry.

"I mean don't expect him to do what he can't."

"How do you know he can't?"

"Here's his coat," Pat said, holding up a maroon sports jacket and deftly slipping her father's arm in the sleeve. Betty Lou watched, and when he was ready, kissed him on the cheek. "Goodbye, Dad," she said.

"All set?" said Harry. "No kisses?"

Uncle Leon stared straight ahead.

"Please, Harry," said Elizabeth, tears welling up.

"I just thought..." Harry shrugged and pulled Leon away from the table, the Matchbox car still on the table, forgotten.

The bird screamed and I hung on to my coffee mug, rubbing my thumb on its handle. Everyone watched as Harry struggled to get the wheelchair across the threshold with Pat holding the door open and Betty Lou fussing with her father's hat, a maroon and yellow wool cap that he kept pulling off whenever she succeeded in putting it on.

Tante Elizabeth's face crumbled. Tante Dorothy moved to her side. She bent down and took her hand. "It's okay, Liz," she said.

Not wanting to break the spell, I tiptoed to the birdcage

and replaced the cover, thankful the bird was silent. A slight movement beyond the glass door caught my eye and I saw John lean against the deck rail, arms folded across his chest, his face turned toward the moon. I wondered what he thought. Tonight he was like a stranger in his own home. But it's only because of the history, I wanted to tell him. Because of the Christmases and the picnics and the staying over for summer vacations and the rosary said in the living room in the middle of the day.

We want to save something out of it all, I wanted to tell him.

But nostalgia was wearing me down. While Dorothy still held hands with Elizabeth, I got a few ideas for my kitchen. I could paint the old dark cabinets a colonial green, paint the walls and try that new mottled look done with a sponge, maybe look for brighter curtains, get a few fresh plants, and repeat a little bit of my grandmother's kitchen, and my mother's and Pat's, that long line of Catholic and uncatholic women, awakening to their collective lessons in how to love and remembering how they died, how to make the best of it, how to open the doors and windows and let the pain fly out. Harry was right. My kitchen was probably too quiet with just me in it. Maybe I should get a canary. Something that sings.

Long Story Short

Omie

She had five daughters
who gathered 'round the kitchen table
Wednesdays
while grandchildren ran through the alleyways
unleashed and gleeful
until one of them came crying
with grass stains on new dungarees.
"Don't worry," she'd say,
"It'll all come out in the wash."
Such wisdom
still brings comfort.
One daughter died at 58.
The rest lived into their 80s and 90s
still loving her.
She was Omie,
always washing sheets
her boarders used,
hanging them on the long line

that stretched out to the wash pole at the edge of her yard,

the pulley shrieking with each advance,

her arms draped in white, wet sheets

she sent over the garden again and again, like sails,

there in the Bronx.

Freda Barbara

She had five babies.

Only one lived

till the age of nine when she died, too,

her blonde-white hair gathered on

the pillow for one last breath.

Helene, her name was.

Then Freda, with little to do,

knitted sweaters for all the cousins,

knitting while her Abe went

"down on the corner" every night

leaving her with her knitting needles

and skeins of colors in her lap.

She had one more baby, a boy.

"Down's Syndrome," Dr. Palmeteer said,

deciding to withhold treatment.

"She's had enough troubles,"

he told her sister,

who always wondered, *Was he right?*

She would have loved the boy.

She would have knitted only for him.
It was a terrible secret for a sister
to bear.
But then again, maybe it wasn't,
some things being better left unsaid.

Emily Rose

The tomboy
eloped with her Walter.
Had two boys back East.
Then Walter left them
and there was nothing but oatmeal
for a whole week till
he came back
after some shady deal.
They fled to California,
and settled in that company house
in Hercules,
a stone's throw from the powder plant.
Had two more boys—"Yeah—it was his birthday
and ya know who wound up
with the present?" spoken wryly in Bronxese.
That was our Ricky.
For years, old coats from Salvation Army
were carried home, washed, stripped, sewn
and braided into ovals, then rectangles

that covered the floors in every room—
wall to wall—
raiment patterned under foot
from born-again dyed wool.
A life rich in colors.
In the end
no one wanted them,
but me.

Florence Margaret

Look into the family portrait—
the middle one, face like a cherub
and dreamy-eyed
as though far away
into her inner life,
which did not include scars
or taunting sisters
and later, a moody husband.
There were two daughters, far apart,
for whom she was the storyteller,
embellishing, imagining,
stating fiction as fact.
She kept them listening.
Meanwhile, the stories grew,
and she began to live there.
Alone a long time

with the chrome on the kitchen faucet

wearing down to brass

with her earnestness

of fifty years,

she kept her spirit alive

and waltzed alone

on Sunday afternoons

in the tiny living room

as do I in mine, and think of her

missed and mysterious other life,

always longing to be.

Elizabeth Bertha

She was a staunch Catholic

all her life.

She had four children, two boys, two girls,

and had her heart set on a son

who would be a priest.

The oldest one went his own way.

The second one became a Baptist missionary

and looked a lot like Jesus,

which made the compromise easier.

If she was disappointed,

she never let on, as was her way,

but quietly took to crocheting

handbags her daughters still use,

till stroke after stroke

made her hands useless.

"You can still pray

for someone," said Pat.

"Everyone needs a prayer."

I wonder, often,

if it was enough.

I remember her now as one who loved children

and would take the time for a

conversation, eye to eye

with the child standing before her,

looking up to her,

like me,

feeling loved.

Dorothy Marie

The youngest.

There's a picture of her, just ten,

sitting on the fender of her father's

1930s car,

legs crossed,

grinning into the camera,

face tilted, a bit haughty,

maybe even naughty,

very proud and sure.

She kept that all her life.

Her hands kept busy
crocheting and knitting
outlandish color schemes,
the kind that either fascinate or
irritate, and make you look away,
disrupting your thoughts.
She could do that with words, too,
but I always told her,
"When I grow up
I want to be like my
Tante Dorothy,"
even when she was 90 and I was 74.
She listened to my woes
and told me, "It'll get better,"
and then would say,
"Would I lie?"
And no, she never did.

The Fox Fling

This morning it was the Lutheran Mission Society on Race Street. Miriam, keeping busy, had a bag of Gary's clothes to bring, that white cable knit sweater he'd bought in New Zealand where he'd written her postcards that began, *Dear Mother, Today we are...,* and there were also his navy gabardine slacks and the blazer with the gold buttons. He had had a flair for clothes that might have been a bit old-fashioned, but nice to see in this day and age. She had a picture of him in the blazer with his hair blown back from his forehead as he stood on the porch steps, his cheeks looking hollow even then, the blazer too loose and flapping at his waist.

Later, she'll go—well, it's on the list. She should be out most of the day.

The bag weighed on her as if most of her life were in it, slippery and unmanageable, its drawstring digging into her hand as she approached the Society's display windows filled with yesterday's fashions on yesterday's mannequins, gifts, no doubt, of the last department store to leave town. No new businesses had flourished here in twenty years. But it was the quiet of this Eastern Shore town that had attracted her and Francis when they had retired. That and the proximity to good sailing waters. She hadn't minded living here as a widow either. She liked being called by her first name at the bank and the grocery store and the post office. But in the last few years, the shops had been abandoned or sold to establishments that sold used clothing or furniture. Along Race Street, there were hardly any places that sold anything new.

Now as she pushed on the brass door handle of an oak-framed glass door that used to belong to Carlson's Dress Shop, the door shuddered as if in protest over her intrusion upon the town's collection of the discarded. To which she was adding her son's clothes. Which was an atrocity, now that she thought about it. Unbelievable. And too soon.

Inside, a rack of pamphlets, *Words of Healing and Strength, Guilt, Victory over Evil Spirits,* stood as proper introduction to the high, old tin ceiling that loomed with churchlike loftiness over the congregation of coats, suits, furs, sweaters, and flannel shirts sorted and assembled on wire hangers. A man about Gary's age maneuvered a carpet sweeper under the first rack of clothes which bore a sign *Ladies Suits - $7.00.* He nodded at her, smiled and said, "Mornin'!" but continued sweeping, his arm swinging back and forth in ambitious arcs.

She set the bag down and began looking through the rack. It was foolish to buy anything. The previous owner would turn up sooner or later, probably right there in the Super Fresh at the end of Race Street. Still, there was a lovely pink wool with a mink collar and fitted skirt—something like the one Francis had given her for their tenth wedding anniversary. Sweet, patient husband Francis who would have said, "Go ahead and get it, Miriam. You'll be thinking about it all week if you don't." Mink. For $7.00!

"Here, let me take that bag for you. It's for the Society, right?" asked the man with the carpet sweeper. Hair the same color as Gary's. From the back he would look—no, he was twice Gary's weight.

"Oh. Yes. Thank you. You might want to hang those things right away so they don't get wrinkled. They're in very good condition."

"Can you stay for our ten o'clock sing-a-long?" He pointed—those things of Gary's swinging so carelessly in his hand—
to a circle of those uncomfortable wooden folding chairs that
used to be part of Sunday morning punishment. "We'll get
started in a few minutes. You sing soprano or alto? We could
use a good soprano," he said without waiting for her answer.
He had one of those eager, magnetic smiles with even, white
teeth, and an open, innocent face. And he was robust. Why
was he so robust—pushing a carpet sweeper? He looked so
healthy she almost hated him.

She glanced at the pink wool, wearily trying to think of an
answer to his question, feeling like a butterfly pinned to
cardboard. *A tired, old moth more likely.* Her eyes swept
across the multitude of wool. *Well, then, I'm in the right
place.*

Smiling, she said, "I'm not much of a singer."

"Well, that don't matter a bit! Join us anyhow." He was
irrepressible and she was almost entirely repressed, grief
rampant under the surface of her skin. He went on, "Lots of
good buys today. Two dollars off everything in the store," and
waved his arm, accidentally hitting the first of the men's coats.
A plume of dust particles came alive in the sun's rays that
ended in the Lutheran portrait of Christ, the long but not too
long brown hair, the gentle eyes, the gentile, generic white
face. Outside the window, a woman walked by carrying
chrysanthemums, oblivious to the white rabbit fur jacket
draped over the green polyester pants suit on the mannequin
and the artfully opened Chutes and Ladders game board at
the mannequin's feet. A man walked by, and two laborers
carrying a ladder. Miriam turned away. "Thank you," she said
as she pulled the suits toward her by the shoulders as if they
were kids in a line at school.

"Miriam?" Holding onto the pink wool in one hand,
Miriam saw Virginia peering out from behind thick glasses on

the other side of women's coats.

"How are you, dear?" said Miriam, glad to see her bridge-playing buddy from the days before Francis's and Gary's succession of illnesses. She was surprised to see Virginia in this place, Virginia with the huge old mansion at the edge of town, her white hair coiffured in a careful French roll and her arms full of old coats.

"Looking for good wool again, Miriam. I've begun another braided rug for the downstairs hall. How are you? I've been meaning to call and see if you can join us for bridge. Maude had to drop out. She's in St. Stephen's, you know. She hated to go, but there was nothing else to do. I thought of you because you might be having time now."

"Yes. There are always things to do afterwards, I mean—things to go through, clothes and medical forms, bills—and the like. I don't think I'm ready for bridge, but maybe in a month or two. Gary's illness was the center of everything for so long, you know—I miss tending to him." Hearing herself sum up the last few months was an admission that they did happen. She could take the strangeness out of her pocket just as Gary used to count his change when there was a lull in the conversation, stare at it for a while, and put it back.

"Well, dear, I will be calling you. Anytime you want to play just give me a ring, will you? The funeral was beautiful, Miriam. The reading of his poetry was a wonderful touch." Virginia shifted her weight. Some of the coats slipped off her arm.

"Here, let me take a few for you," Miriam said. "What in heaven's name—?"

"I cut them in strips, two inches wide—that part I hate—then I pin three strips together, fold the raw edges in, and start braiding. The fun is planning the colors. This one's going to be mauve and green tones. They last forever you know—one hundred percent wool. I made one the year my first was born, what—forty-five years ago?—and it's still beautiful. Of course, the ones I made when the family was around have pieces of the children's clothes and mine and Chuck's in them. Every time I look at those rugs, I can still see one of the kids wrapped in a certain blue wool coat and legging set or that purple wool dress I wore to New Orleans for the Mardi Gras. A real fault, never being able to throw anything away, I guess. Now that I've run out of a supply of our old clothes, I buy other people's! Lord, Miriam, I never thought of it that way before! I really can afford to buy wall-to-wall carpeting now, can't I?" Virginia laughed. "But then, what would I *do*? That would be my idea of hell, you know, not having anything to do."

Miriam should add to the list: *wash walls,* although she wasn't sure why. When Gary came home, already blind despite the last series of laser treatments, she'd said with a determination and lightness she didn't feel, "We're in this together, kid," and washed the walls. Then she ordered the hospital bed and made arrangements for the dialysis as if moving through a dream, knowing with dread what was sure to come.

The carpet sweeper guy bent over the guitar on his knee, and a round-faced young man tuned up a banjo, a thick nest of plaits cloaking his head. They were the only ones in the circle of chairs, and they began with, *Will the circle be unbroken, by 'n' by, Lord, by 'n' by.* The carpet sweeper guy sang in a clear tenor voice, throwing his head back while his accompanist anchored the sound with a nasal huskiness. Their singing was pleasing and homey as though they should be in a country-western band somewhere, cowboy hats tilted against bright lights, girls blowing smoke-ringed kisses their way. They should be wildly celebrating their youth, thought Miriam, and looked down for the pink wool suit that had become mixed in with Virginia's coats. She couldn't bear the thought of it being cut up for a rug, the mink wasted, which was why she now grabbed it up from the counter to return it to the rack.

On the way, she caught sight of an embroidered, green silk smoking jacket. No, it couldn't be the same one, could it? The one she'd bought for Francis in Hong Kong on their way to Australia? She ran her hand down the lapel. Oh God, it was his. There was the coffee stain. She'd brought it in after Francis died, and it still hung chest to back with the other ghosts. Suddenly she was outraged at seeing it. She was angry at herself for ever having stepped in that oak door. She should have dumped Gary's things in the bin out back. Had it over and done with.

"Miriam! Look at this!" Virginia waved a red-brown fur piece at her. "Did you ever have one of these? A fox fling? Here, try it on."

She felt the weight of the skin around her shoulders and watched the fox's head and feet flop on her chest in the mirror. Virginia held her head back to look through the bottom of her bifocals and fluffed up the flattened fur with bent fingers.

"It's really in good condition. No hair falling out." Virginia fussed with the clasp, the black braid that fitted into the fox's mouth. "These days, if you walk down the street in this, some animal protection advocate will spray you with paint, but my— isn't the fur lovely?"

Miriam had had one long ago. It was the first thing she'd bought when she landed that job at the British Embassy in Washington. She always associated it with fresh flowers, the lilies that Francis began to send her every few days. Almost incongruous in that tiny, scantily furnished apartment: a fox fur piece and white lilies. Her hair was dark then, her nails flashing scarlet before her. What did her face look like? She couldn't remember. She slipped off the fur and was conscious of the chill around her shoulders.

Virginia wandered down the rack of furs and pulled a jacket with long, curly white hair off its hanger. She laughed at herself as she stepped before the mirror. "How do you like this?" she said. "I could do my hair to match!"

"All you need are fishnet stockings and knee boots," said Miriam, fingering the fox's paw. "And a miniskirt."

"Or how about this?" Virginia tugged at a grey cashmere coat with a huge silver fox collar, but Miriam still stood in the same spot before the mirror, examining herself in the drape of the small brown fox. It felt like only yesterday that she had heard the saleswoman say, "The fox fling is you! You can't go wrong with a bit of elegance, my dear!" Although she hadn't needed much convincing. She remembered feeling at that moment as though she'd *arrived*, that her life was her own at last and all the trials of growing up in a large family in West Virginia mining country were over. Delicious feeling, that. At first it was just taking dictation, but then quite suddenly she was "noticed" and for the two years before she met Francis, she worked in jobs with unending possibilities, arranging meetings, luncheons, and parties at the embassy. She was caught up in the social whirl she'd always dreamed of, and best of all she had begun to dance, something her father never allowed, diehard Missouri Synod Lutheran that he was. The dancing began, and then there was Francis. And the children, a different kind of dance to be sure.

"I'd love to step out in that, wouldn't you, Miriam?" Virginia was saying. "And look here, a black Persian lamb. My mother had one. Weighs a ton."

As a child sitting in church, Miriam had pressed her face into the arm of her mother's coat, breathing in her sweet cologne, studying the tight waves of fur at close range—she knew she was wasting time. She had things to do. She must go out the door and get on with it. Oh, the shocking vividness of long ago! When so much of what had gone on in the ensuing years had become a blur.

Virginia appeared before her wearing a black velvet

pillbox, her glasses gone, a black veil down over her face. She looked twenty years younger. "Darling," she said, "how would this look with my new lemon sweat suit? We used to dress, for God's sake, didn't we?"

Miriam slipped the fox fling around her shoulders again. Should she get it? She'd given the other one away years ago. When the children were teenagers, probably. Her daughter, Liza, hated the sight of those glass eyes staring at her. "Mom, don't wear that old thing again," she'd say. The boys pretended to take pot shots at it when she walked by. Except Gary. Being the youngest, he would wrap himself around her and bury his face in the fox's tail until he had to come up for air. "You look pretty, Mom," he'd say.

"Aw, go ahead, Miriam," said Virginia. "Get it. Do something crazy—it'll do you good. Tell you what. You get that and I'll get the cashmere and silver fox. We can wear them when the girls get together for bridge."

Miriam told herself if she got it, she'd drive across the Bay Bridge to Washington wearing it over her good blue jersey knit and find an afternoon tea waltz to go to, like they used to have at Glen Echo Park where she'd met Francis. Not that she cared about meeting someone now. She was beyond that. But she loved to waltz. Surely afternoon tea waltzes still thrived somewhere. Even if she only got to watch, that would be enough. She could see herself, the fox fling giving her the courage, taking a few steps to see if she could still manage it— she was sure she could—smiling again, feeling self-possessed, relishing a bit of saneness and civility, and yes, beauty, in this difficult life.

Maybe she'd spend a whole weekend in the city, visit a museum and visit Gary's partner at the Decorator's Gallery— find a piece of silk-screened velvet for new drapes for the dining room. Gary was always bringing her the latest fabric, sharing news of last night's concert, giving her brochures from the newest showings at the National Gallery and the Renwick. Now, without him, it would be too easy to succumb to the season of old lady-hood, playing bridge on Tuesdays and Thursdays, combing the library for mysteries, watching "Jeopardy!" while eating her dinner.

"Can you remove the tag?" she said to the cashier. "I'll wear it home."

Virginia struggled to take off the black velvet hat. "Wait a minute, Virginia, the veil is caught on your pins." Virginia's French roll began to unwind and her hair fell to her shoulders.

"Miriam?" Do you see my glasses? They must be on the hat shelf." Virginia looked helpless, her hair loose, groping along the rack, the black hat dangling from her fingers, *looking old,* Miriam thought, *why—just so old.*

The banjo rested on a chair now, as its player continued a cappella:

Could my tears forever flow
Could my zeal no respite know.
Rock of Ages
Cleft for me...

The carpet sweeper stroked the wrong chord and quickly threw in another one which was no better. The lady at the cash register didn't seem to notice as she began to ring up the coats, but Miriam struggled to contain herself and not laugh out loud. Discordant music always did seem to start a hysteria in her that she couldn't explain, like the time Gary was eleven and played trombone in a duet at school, his arms not long enough to play it properly, the notes flying crazily off-key into the nodding, composed, and patient audience of PTA mothers. She'd begun to perspire at the effort to keep in her laughter then as she did now, but then she'd been better at self-control. Now her laughter erupted anyway. Virginia, who was reassembling her glasses and her hair, said, "Okay, okay. Maybe I should just throw a bag over my head, go home and start again."

"No, Virginia, it's not you I'm—"

"Can you ladies manage with all them bags?" asked the cashier.

The singing had faded. Except for the musicians, the circle of chairs had remained empty.

"You ladies need help?" said the carpet sweeper.

"We're the ones what need help, George. Sure we can't get them ladies to sing with us?"

"Got yourself a bargain there," said George to Miriam, nodding at the fur piece.

"Thank you! You might want to check out the bag I brought in. There's a good wool blazer that's just about your size. Take your best girl out somewhere and dance the night away."

He blushed a bit and laughed with a shyness good to see in this day and age. Miriam opened the door and stubbed her toe on the bottom edge. The door came alive with rattles and groans as the chilly October air rushed in over them and the members of the would-be quartet laughed. Outside, Miriam listened to the steady beat of footsteps on the sidewalk and felt the light tapping of the fox's paw on her shoulder. As she turned her head in the direction of the tap, she saw Gary's face, so pale, so close to hers she wanted to brush her fingers along the stray hairs at his temple. Her breath stopped and her eyes smarted. Was his hand on her shoulder?

"Miriam, you okay?" asked Virginia.

"Yes, oh yes, dear." Miriam blinked. Suddenly she wanted to go home. "Virginia, will you come for tea?"

"I have one more errand. Then I'll be along, okay?"

Miriam sped home. She parked the car and entered the house from the back porch. The kitchen was stuffy. Carefully, she lifted the fur piece over her head and laid it on the back of a chair. Hands on her hips, she walked into the dining room and listened to the silence as she once listened to Gary's light breathing. The window was stubborn. She banged and pushed on the old wooden frame until it shrieked upward. Curtains stirred.

In the kitchen, she set the kettle on to boil, and then, because it forced her to, she stood still and listened to her heart. It was beating wildly, erratically, as though prompted by a whole series of stomach drops and adrenal shots. It seemed to struggle to beat again and then trilled crazily as if it would fly out of her back, beating its way between muscle and bone. She sat down in the chair and waited for it to right itself, waited for the cramp in her back to go away. She shifted in the seat and took shallow breaths as if to say, "Stop it, behave," but she was frightened. Her own death had only been a nebulous certainty. Was it now becoming less nebulous? Scared to move, she reached for the fox fling behind her and, drawing it to her lap, buried her hands in the soft fur. Her heart beat slowly now, heavily, as though it would forget to beat again and for a second she thought it would stop entirely, but then it thundered and bumbled too fast again, and her legs began to ache. She breathed deep and even, as though to will her heart to steadiness and watched the clock, waiting, hoping—for what?

What are you afraid of? she said to herself. *This might be a good time. As a matter of fact, a very good time,* and with that her body began to relax. She listened to the clock tick and looked at her things: the blue kettle on the stove with the bluebird perched on its spout, the table that had been her mother's, the wall of family snapshots where Gary still smiled, Francis at the helm of *Bluebell,* their sailboat, her distant grandchildren posed in outfits she had made them, her oldest son, Todd, looking stern in his police uniform before the fatal accident, Thomas, the middle son before the cancer, Liza in hiking gear in the Grand Tetons a continent away—the whole kit and caboodle of family—and when she thought of it again, her heart was beating normally. "Is it all right, Mother, if we stop the dialysis?" It was Gary's last question. "Is it all right?" The thing was she would have to—continue, that is. She saw that now. Now that her heart had quieted.

And then, because it *was* time, and because she was to have a guest for tea, she draped the fox fling safely on the back of the chair, pulled a pair of scissors out of the kitchen drawer and stooped to pick up one of the plastic bags stored in a cardboard box under the table. With tears spilling down her face, she walked methodically to the bathroom, snipping off the upper corner of the bag, and emptying its contents into the toilet. Back and forth she traveled, bag after bag, feeling as though she were killing him again, even as much as when he'd asked her that awful question and she'd nodded.

On the sixth trip, hands shaking, she was startled by Virginia's knock on the door. The bag she held slipped out of her hands and emptied on the floor.

Virginia didn't wait for her to answer the door. She just popped in. "Miriam? What's happened? What's that on the floor?"

"Urine, Virginia."

"Oh."

"Not mine. His. This is the last of him."

"There's a lot of it."

"I've been saving it. Isn't that sick? I was actually saving it."

"Come on, Miriam. I'll help you clean it up."

"Oh, God. No. Let me. From diapers to dialysis. Alpha and Omega. I will. Pass me that roll of paper towels, will you?"

"I'm not going to just stand here and watch you."

"There's no one, Virginia. Now there's no one. Every

light in my life turned out."

"I know. But somebody has to be last. I guess it's us, Miriam."

"What do you do when there's no one?"

"I guess you find someone or something else to love. Otherwise, what's the point?"

"At our age?"

"It might have to be raising roses this time, or braiding rugs, or bridge."

"Down on our knees—wiping up—so what else is new?"

"It's gotten into your rug, I'm afraid."

"Damn it. Damn everything!"

"Drat!" said Virginia.

An impotent word, too small a protest, a helpless whimper in the context of things— the sound made Miriam laugh. Kneeling on the floor, in her hands wads of urine-soaked paper towels while the sour smell permeated the room, her own laughter startled her. She glanced at the fox fling.

"Virginia," she said, "have you ever gone to an afternoon tea waltz? Would you like to?"

Virginia looked down without smiling. "I'm afraid it's too late, Miriam. I'll get dizzy. I never was a dancer anyway."

The following Sunday afternoon, Miriam, in her blue knit with the fox fling over her shoulders, drove to Glen Echo Park and the Spanish Ballroom where there was a waltz; she saw it listed in the Sunday *Post*. It wasn't difficult to find the way despite the years since she'd been there, although she missed seeing the white trellises of the roller coaster ride at the bend in the road signaling the entrance and wondered if she'd somehow missed it. But there was the parking lot, paved now, and new lighting along the pathways. When she crossed the wooden bridge over the creek, and followed the winding path, there suddenly before her was the carousel, newly painted and restored, and the bumper car pavilion, and slightly uphill, overlooking the parkway below, was the old ballroom, its mustard yellow walls darker, the red-tiled roof still in place, still beckoning with the sound of violins, guitars, and a piano emanating through its high arches, stirring even the trees to dance.

She only felt a little foolish. People dressed so differently now. Some men were in shorts, white ones with white socks and sneakers, and, good Lord, headbands—although it did make sense, she guessed. Some were dressed formally, and some in casual shirts and trousers, some all in black like tango dancers. The women—and this was curious—she was sure they had bought their dresses in vintage clothing shops, places like the Lutheran Mission Society, as if good dancing dresses were not to be found in today's department stores, ones with twirly skirts or sleek spaghetti straps, wraps sequined, feathered, and flowered. Still, it was a colorful enough blend, as if all the collected members had consented to go back in time at this appointed hour, and she was safe to enter without causing a stir, despite the white hair and her years. She lay her bag down on a chair and lifted the fox fling from her shoulders, turning to see a young man approaching. He held out his hand. "Care to dance?" he said as if programmed, as if he himself were a vestige stepping out of the past, and the words would have been a silly cliché except she'd wanted to hear them so badly. Ah! She lay the fox fling down on the chair but picked it up again and lay it back on her shoulders.

"Yes. Yes," she said again, laughing.

He was Gary's age, his last age, or Francis's when she'd first met him. Oh, it was no good wishing for it all again, she thought as she looked into his eyes, which focused now on what was behind her, steering her to a clear path. She took his hand, felt his arm on her back, guiding her. After that, there was only his face, blank and handsome, his eyes empty and unknown to her, but drawing her into perfect balance, leaning this way, then that. There was only the circle they made in their stepping and swaying. She imagined the line of their dancing in its curlicues around the floor like some long forgotten, yet consistent path penciled in while everything else disappeared around them. Yet it was her heart she must listen to as it fluttered wildly again like the wings of a butterfly. The speed with which they traveled was dangerous, she thought, as if watching from afar. At her age, and her heart's foolish unsteadiness! But there it was, what she'd come for, the heart's desire still left out of all the rubble, between the mad thunderous, capricious, and disorderly palpitations or maybe because of them. But there was no one to tell it to, no one but herself, the pair of eyes in front of her so close she knew everything about him and nothing of him. They turned and she spun round and round (though she knew she shouldn't) until he stopped her and held her once again face to face. She stepped backwards, relying solely on him to guide her through the crowd. She recognized the feeling of excitement—as if she were standing before a precipice that would be filled with her life, hers and Francis's—before anything had happened and everything was before them. Her heart would calm soon, and her breaths would slow. She would will it.

They walked back to her chair. "Are you all right?" he said, still holding her hand. He was looking at her with concern. Her face must be flushed. Her hands trembled.

"I'm fine," she said, though her heart would not slow and her head was so light it would float out through the arches as colors spun below her somewhere. "Yes, I'm fine," she repeated. "So fine," and drew the fox fling close around her, her hands deep in the luxurious fur, loving her life again, astonished at its brevity as she smiled up at him. She saw that just for this moment, she was saved from the sea of yesterdays that held so much sorrow. Now there were only the dancers sweeping her along in the culture of the waltz as they circled. Skirts flared. Faces flushed. Dusk had settled in at the windows and the soft lights made everyone young and beautiful. Soon the music would end. The dancers would smile at their partners and look around to find the next one. If only for a three-minute waltz, none would be solitary. Not even those seated along the perimeter, looking on. Not even her.

The pain in her back grew sharp. Better this than the terrible insistent succession of dementia, a broken hip, a treacherous cancer, the steady decay, the slow demise. She was not that brave, she decided. But she was brave enough to choose, maybe had chosen the minute she saw the red-brown fur, had recognized love's last flicker like a gift, as she rose from the chair with the now fierce pain in her back, saying haltingly, breathlessly, "Would you mind, sir, one more time?" Only now did she think of him, her partner, as she held out her hand and hoped he wouldn't be too shocked or scared. All that was required of him was that he hold her hand, and maybe not forget the moment. He was not in any way attached to her and for him it would only be a startling event, a lesson, perhaps, in the myriad reasons to dance.

Le Valse

The hall is cavernous. Arches along its sides are supported by pillars in pale mustard yellow, the color of old paper, linen, and lace, the color of adobe mud and mixing bowls from the thirties, the kind with stripes at the top edge like women used to use to let the bread dough rise. The stripes are here, too, faint orange and purple and blue, running along the arches to the pillars, straight forward here then rising again for another arch, a design that echoes the invisible circles drawn by the dancers below, who hold each other, some of them smiling, some pensive as they stare into their partner's eyes as if there were worlds to be explored. Some, of course, avoid eyes altogether as they step, turn, twinkle, grapevine, separate, move side by side, and come together to glide once more across the floor. They follow the music as if it were a magic spell cast over them; the men dance forward, watching the flow of traffic and in command, skirting around obstacles; the women dance backward, sweeping, anticipating, following.

In the view from above where let us say God sits, the figures move in kaleidoscopic patterns, behaving themselves, principled, although not without an air of expectancy of something magnificent about to happen as the design reveals itself. It is the waltz, the three-minute fairy-tale, the dance of dreams, and this must be God's favorite place, where things proceed according to plan, in rhythm decisive and anticipatory similar to when things first began, before chaos was born—

something He could count on—people having a good time. Maybe He could even go so far as to say *being joyous*. Not quite free, but—well within reason anyway. Free enough to be frivolous.

And *loving*, He would say. Yes, this is an act of love, especially for those who cannot find it any other way. The loose ends, the uncherished come here. They distract themselves within the dream. *Nothing wrong with that*, He'd say. That's why they've got imagination. At least they weren't fornicating haphazardly, which of course, He never intended. Like geese, He fully expected them to mate for life, and He definitely couldn't explain what was happening now, as if anyone cared to ask Him to. He watches as the music stops and couples briefly embrace, thank each other and move on to the next partner, searching among the crowd for someone they promised to dance the fifth dance with, or looking for a prospect in someone who drifts toward the seats at the edges of the great hall or who might be looking back at them and with a nodded consent to the next dance.

Poised in each other's arms again, waiting for the music, they begin the dance and continue the echo that reverberates the wanting, that persistent, terrible longing to belong, relieving their tangled souls and pulling them in from the cold.

Nah, God would say. *You got it all wrong. They're a happy bunch. My favorite. They, above all, know how to live, how to have a good time. They're harmless. They just like to dance, that's all. Why do you have to make everything so complicated, for God's sake?*

And He's right. They wouldn't be dancing if it didn't make them happy, that elusive happiness that comes in spurts just a bit longer than a breath and not as frequent. No detached, bored, strained faces here—it's all that looking into each other's eyes, and holding each other and whirling to a beat. *It's exactly what I intended for them*, God would say.

Harmony, community, caring about each other.

And all of that is here, surely. The dancers return time and again to feel the connection, gather moments they will remember as a time when everything fit and made sense, moments so purely pleasurable they will leave and come to doubt them as they doubt their dreams in the morning. There is, after all, a certain difficulty upon entering the world again, that first treacherous step from the great hall into the April air, armed with nothing but a certain renewed and terminal hopefulness, a place where the night is always young.

The True Meaning of

The music began, the violins predominant and sweeping, inspiring everyone, even the hesitant ones, to glide magnificently on the first step. From the high old windows of the dance hall came bursts of sunlit green through the old sycamores as Jack and his partner turned again and again, dizzyingly. Nearing the windows, he was conscious of an afternoon breeze that swept in like a grand dame of the ballroom, the scent of jasmine lingering. He closed his eyes, feeling the weight of the woman in his arms, someone he didn't know. No matter. Maybe he would later, and maybe not. For the moment he knew all he wanted to know of anyone or anything, so complete did the moment seem, as though this were enough for the rest of his life.

By the time the dance ended, he was on a high with an exuberance and confidence peculiar to the aftermath of dancing. She smiled up at him—but there was something about her teeth that distracted him now, announcing that the magic was over.

"Thank you," he said. "That was marvelous." Not *you* were marvelous, but *that* was, he said to himself, wondering in a self-accusatory way at his ability to dismiss women, and whether a three-minute waltz was all he could tolerate these days. He turned from her, smiling, lest she suspect the cruelty he was capable of.

"Care to dance?" he asked an attractive middle-aged

woman standing alone. And from that moment, whether it was the magnificence of the dance before and the necessity of stepping down off that magic—and magic it was, he decided—or his own impatience to experience it again and knowing full well he wasn't likely to, he felt her weight like a stone he must compensate for as he fought for control. He couldn't wait for the dance to be over. This, plus the fact that she hinted that he looked like a gorilla, reminding him of the way Lily had made fun of him, cruelly and unexpectedly in those last violent, heated battles with her lips curling full and luscious around words he wished he'd never heard. This woman didn't name an animal exactly, but something about offering him a banana if he'd stop beating his chest long enough. Trying to make light of the situation, what he'd said to her was dancing was the only place where a man's role was clearly defined: he led, she followed. Complete submission was what he was after. He smiled; she didn't.

Lord, he was tired of bitter, angry women, that vicious vindictiveness from which he had only recently disentangled himself with Lily. Confounded, he looked away and sat out for two whole dances when a fresh-faced young woman waltzed by. He saw the trail of honey-colored curls flowing down her back and, when she turned with her partner, her green Irish eyes seemed to regard him for a moment, and he was once again entranced. She was late thirties, early forties, he figured.

He would be sixty-three on Thursday, an un-magical number. Fifty-seven was all he'd admit to. He'd celebrate the day by writing a paragraph and adding it to the forty-odd paragraphs in the leather-bound notebook his mother had given him when she'd heard he wanted to be a writer. Oh, the cruelty of that, the disappointment in looking back as he read the paragraphs that summed up where he was at a particular moment in his life and how much hope he had had. Well, never mind. He'd drum up something good for this year's paragraph. Maybe a dance partner for his high school reunion—some beautiful woman with whom he could be Fred Astaire. You never knew. *With a woman like that*—he watched her turn and disappear to his right as the dancers moved counter-clockwise before him. He waited, looking to his left for her return, and watched the smooth couples, the shuffling ones, the women with flowing skirts and the ones with short, tight ones. And then it seemed to him that the dance was much like a carousel, and he was a kid planning which animal he would ride. He couldn't hide his grin. *Yeah, right.* All this looking for a good horse was probably useless anyway; his role as a rider growing more dubious with each birthday—although with a woman like that...

A mood was coming on: the dark shades of sullenness pulled down. Better not to hope for much. Yet he needed to be in love, he thought, and here he could be, with a different partner every few minutes. And so he stood with his arms folded across his chest, beads of sweat rolling through grey, kinky hair, his black shirt darkening further at the armpits, and leaned against one of the yellowed pillars with the crumbling paint, waiting. She was just to his left now and he tried not to stare as he prepared to go forward when the music ended to ask her for the next dance. But Laura blocked him with a swish of her tie-dyed skirt and said, "Are you free for the next one?"

It was a matter of civility, an unwritten rule that one not refuse a request to dance unless it had already been promised. His mouth said, "Yes," but he kept on walking with his index finger in the air as if to say, "I'll be right back." He followed the young woman, and when he caught up with her, he touched her shoulder where a honey-colored lock lay.

"Are you free for the dance after this?" he said.

"Sorry! How about the one after?" She was breathless, a tinge of pink on her cheeks, and smiling, radiant.

"Good," he said. "Meet you here by the fourth pillar?" She nodded.

He returned to Laura. Willing Laura. The sad brown eyes that read him, the ones he sometimes unwillingly gave answers to. "So have you heard from your publisher yet?" she said, the words crisp and demanding.

He kept up the bravado as long as he could. "I'll hear something soon, I'm sure. She loved what I sent originally." He had no trouble getting the first three books published even though it was a very small press, and he did find a local publisher who might be interested in a creative nonfiction piece dealing with environment issues, but nothing solid yet. He didn't want to explain anything just now. "You're a doll, Laura—smooth as glass when you dance." She beamed. They bumped toes once—and again. Then they got straightened out, he leading the same two steps, the only ones he knew, around the dance floor, aware of her perfume which smelled expensive and her narrow waist even though she was his age he was sure because of the lines at her neck and around her eyes and down her cheeks, the peeks of white at the roots of her hair color. She'd been married for a long time to an alcoholic, borne four kids all grown now, and busied herself writing articles for the local newspaper about gardening. "I don't write a lot," she said once, "and I really don't like to talk about it because it's too much like having to have a credential. People are always sidling up to writers and saying, 'What have you published lately?'" She laughed at that, probably realizing the effect of her question to him. "Besides, when you're not young and beautiful, men seem to require credentials and I resent that."

This kind of banter made him uncomfortable. Was he supposed to say, "*Oh, but of course you're beautiful?*" Out loud he said, "There are different kinds of beauty, Laura."

"Yeah," she said. "Mine's in the credentials," and

laughed. "Or somewhere similarly obscure," and laughed again.

"No," he said. "It's in the way you dance, when the years melt away."

"Thank you, Jack," she said quietly, looking at him. "I didn't mean to ask for that, although I think I did. Sorry. Someone asked me once where I learned to dance and I said, 'Everything I've been through taught me.' I meant when you've been through enough crap is when you truly know what it is to be happy, even harmonious." Sometimes she wore bad times like a badge, Laura did. It made you ask what else there was behind the density of her pride.

"This is a happy place," was all he could think to say. "Let's concentrate on that."

"I am," she said. "Oh, baby, I am."

He turned her, then lifted his arm for her to twirl beneath it as he watched her waist which he found pleasure in, and her long back in the skin-tight leotard, as if both attributes were something *he* could be proud of. He was, he decided. She was really something to dance with.

He waited the next dance out, and when Irish eyes came toward him, smiling, lifting her arms, he thought he felt an ache in his groin. Only that. An ache. But it held possibility and hope as he said, "I'm Jack, and you are...?"

"Sherry." She had a small scar at her neck, and one on her left temple, and he realized she was plumper than he would have guessed as he put his arm around her waist. A little roll, soft under his spread fingers. He imagined her breasts, soft as a pillow, while he kept his eyes on her eyes.

"This your first time here?" he said, taking her in, the green pools of her eyes and the clear whites around them. He was conscious of the smell of jasmine again, already like a favorite, fleeting memory.

"Oh, no," she laughed. "I just come between—you know—

relationships. I've never met anyone in a romantic way who liked to dance so it's something I seem to be having to give up if I'm with someone." This by way of saying she was available, he guessed. He realized quite suddenly that she was leading, making him turn to his right, a step he was awkward about, as she said, "I get dizzy if I only turn to the left." He nodded, and followed, tripping over his right foot, stumbling on hers. "Stop a minute," she said. "Then begin it again. *Now,* two, three, *now,* two, three," dipping her head on the *nows*, the green eyes flashing and the white, even teeth directing. It might be refreshing to be with a woman like her. None of this beat-around-the-bush stuff, explosions when you least expected them. She was dressed simply, a cotton flower-print dress, looking as though she should be carrying a basket and running through wheat fields. What you saw was what you got.

"And how about you? Are you a regular?"

"I started coming a month ago. I've just moved near enough so that the dances are a possibility now. They weren't before."

"Oh. Where are you from?"

"The Eastern Shore." The truth was he was from a very expensive suburban home surrounded by gardens manicured with red-brown mulch, and from a marriage of ten years. All he had left was the dog, the white terrier, Sunny, he'd bought Lily to make her happy. Well, at least he still had the dog. And this woman in his arms, this moment—her looking up at him and smiling. He had the sense that it never got any better than this, these first moments that held adventure and mystery, seduction—and enormous possibilities thereof. You never knew, he thought, looking into her eyes to keep his balance as they turned swiftly to the music. He did not want her to say anything more or to have to say anything himself. He just wanted to hold her as if they were frozen in time. They went round and round.

Too soon the music ended. She broke away with a quick "Thank you," and began looking beyond him.

"We'll do it again?" he said.

"Sometime," she said, continuing to look over his shoulder, searching. She was dismissing him. In a second, she was in the arms of another, a youngish, tall, thin, eat-nothing-but-seeds-and-tofu type, probably an ex-runner whose knees had worn out and discovered he could get the same exercise dancing, with a beautiful woman before him to boot. What did he know of moments? Savoring? Divisions? Aching? Jack hated him and himself, knowing full well he should have kept up with his antidepressant. He was on the edge of saturnine that had been delayed for a bit but was definitely advancing. *This again*, he thought, the familiar feeling nipping at his heels.

Laura was at his side saying, "Are you free for this one?"

He grabbed her around the waist. "Why don't you come to my place next weekend?" he heard himself say. "There's a dance in Dover and a tour of historic homes. We'll just relax and have a good time," he said, almost believing it himself. She looked startled, eyebrows raised revealing a wrinkle that ran down her temple.

"That's good of you, Jack. I might take you up on it."

He never thought she would. But she did.

He lived three miles out in what could best be described as the cellar of an old farmhouse. Cellars were a rarity on the shore where the water table was usually high. People abandoned cellars after there was no longer a need to have one in which to store vegetables for the winter, but this house dated from the 1850s. Maybe this wasn't even a true cellar, but definitely the ground floor where the low dark-beamed ceiling and brick walls opened to a small greenhouse. Large windows on the adjoining wall lit up the two rooms in which he could live simply, his new lifestyle, he told himself, without a lot of fuss and the need for anything beyond the bare essentials in the way of furniture: a massive oak bed in one room, and in the other, a desk that held his computer and a brown wicker couch that creaked. Beyond that, the kitchen—a cabinet, sink, stove, a small maple table and two chairs. That was it. The large, imposing, wood-framed house rose high above him, and at night he listened to the heavy footsteps that belonged to Judith Beale, another city transplant, brusque and business-like, single, who had plans to renovate the house with a boyfriend who appeared on the weekends. In her forties, he guessed. What she needed, she said, was someone to take care of the grounds, mow, plant a vegetable and herb garden, be an all-around fix-it man in exchange for free rent. It suited him fine until he could get his bearings, he told himself. He settled in and took pleasure in walking the apple orchard and working in the garden that was just now beginning to look like something.

He had discovered an enormously thick, overgrown hedge of wild roses surrounding the orchard. There'd been similar places on the farm where he grew up, places that he called his own, where no one in his family of hard-scrabble farmer types could find him or guess the aesthetics of. They were non-dreamers who managed to tune him out. He'd always felt he was in the wrong family.

"I want to take you where the smell of roses fills the air," he told Laura when he called to give her directions. "We'll waltz there and I'll fix you a bath of herbs, as well."

"Jack, I want to make it clear that I'm coming as a friend," Laura said, "and I'll need my own place to sleep."

"Of course," he said. "I've got a couch—I'll sleep on that and you can have my bed." And then he added, "I won't seduce you, Laura," as if that was the farthest thing from his mind. He guessed it was. In fact, the idea needed more than

Laura to flourish. Time was, it didn't matter who or what she looked like; he always took the advantage. It was expected, and he expected that of himself. Trouble was, he wound up being alone for most of his life anyway. Was it in the cards or was it him? Maybe he'd get it right before he croaked.

Saturday morning with the sun low in the sky and the cool of night still in the soil, he moved among the lettuces as he cut the yellow-green leaves at their most tender and thought about how everything had an optimum moment, when he heard his name, not shouted, but sounding more like a part of a melody. "Hellooo, Jack." Laura stood at the entrance to the garden, waving, her hair in a golden glow around her head—a new hair color—her white short-sleeved sweater hugging her breasts, her long skirt slit at the sides and one smooth, brown leg peeking out at him. He came toward her, plowing through tall, wet grass. "God, you look good," he said and opened his arms in welcome. She laughed and hugged him and fussed about his directions. "You said it was the second road on the right, but it's really the third!" She was charming, pulling back now ever so slightly and he let go of her, the sun having risen enough to be beating heat down on them already.

"Whew!" she said.

He bent over and put his hands among the strawberries, and quickly picked five of them for some reason he couldn't fathom except it made him feel Adam-like. He presented them to her. "Here, taste," he said, for lack of anything else to say. And then, "I'm in charge of the garden. Place was a mess when I got here. Sandy soil. Roots and brush, pretty much. I discovered the best thing to do was to pile compost on top of it and plant everything in a hill." He began naming what was in the garden: the garlic, Vidalia onions, squash, tomatoes, broccoli, rhubarb, the lettuces of which there were seven different kinds, the herbs, lemon basil, lemon chive, dill, parsley...

She interrupted him. "Let me bring in the cooler. I've brought you pasta and bread and stuff."

He picked up the basket of lettuces. It was the only preparation he'd made for her coming. That and clean linen on the bed, the book of *Women's Poetry and Prose Anthology* on the nightstand. He stood in the garden and watched her hips swing as she walked toward her car parked on the other side of the trees and wondered what else he needed to do, feeling hapless and clueless as to what it was women saw, what they wanted of him and hated himself for saying idiotically that he was in charge of the garden when everything he'd done had finally only come down to that.

In the kitchen, he ran cold water in a pot and dropped in the lettuce leaves. Then he turned to face her as she unpacked the cooler and handed him the pasta in a plastic container and the bread, but he said, "Let's keep that in the cooler for now, and tell you what, let me show you the rest of the farm."

"Oh," she said, putting the food back. When she straightened up, she took a strawberry off the countertop and took a bite. "Yes," she said, "I want to see the apple orchard and the wild roses." She looked around the kitchen, taking in the single white-painted cabinet, the beat-up buffet with empty rectangles where drawers used to be, the silverware—two forks and two knives and two spoons lying on a paper towel, newly washed. She was smiling. Was she laughing at him or accepting things as they were, not hard to please? He didn't need to explain, but he did.

"Most of my things are in storage," he said. "I just have the bare essentials." She was nodding and looking him straight in the eye, her lips puckered like she didn't believe him, like she was filling in her own details about him. She was nothing like Lily. Lily would have believed him and later spit out a series of barbed replies when she finally got things figured out for herself. Oh, the wrath, Lilyputian style!

"Jack, let's go for that walk."

He loved the high old barn on the place and the carriage house close by with its brick exterior, and the acres of apple trees, the grounds thick with grass between the rows. He began to tell her how he was in charge here, how he had been in touch with the university and gotten them interested in courses on building sun-heated hot water systems and drying containers to preserve food for back-of-beyond places where there was no electricity, and how he was respected in each place he had been able to set up such a program. He showed her his card with the World Bank insignia, his name and telephone number staring up at them, trembling in his soil-stained hands. Another world, another time—and he wondered, once again, how he had gotten here wandering between apple trees, although it wasn't a bad place to be by any means. He would rest here, and get things figured out. He was, among other things, entirely free, something he'd always dreamed about.

He was well into his monologue when Laura stopped and said, "Are these the roses you were telling me about?" The bush rambled high into the branches of a river birch, the whole of it in a burst of small white pungent blossoms.

"Yes. I thought about pruning them back but then just left them to their own wild ways."

"Jack, you promised me a waltz!" So he grabbed her and began singing, "My Wild Irish Rose" as they waltzed, Laura holding on a little too tight as they stumbled through the thick grass and *the only flower that grows*. He flung his arms about in a performance of exaggerated motions. Laura joined him, raising her arms to the sky at the end and shrieking with an enthusiasm caused by something other than him, he was sure.

They walked through the old town, joined a tour where the old historic houses and gardens dating back to the 1850s were open to the public, the acidic smell of boxwood everywhere. The vestiges of yesterday clung to Eastern Shore soil mostly well preserved in towns along the coast. It was one of the reasons "come heres" and history buffs migrate to the shore, Laura said as they strolled to the open market, on by the old clock tower and the World War II monument of the doughboy, and into the local tavern where the sounds of a John Prine CD mellowed the stark whitewashed walls. They had a beer or two, shared a sandwich, and then he asked her to dance with him. She'd love to, she said, and it didn't matter that they were the only ones, or that the place might not have allowed it; they just went between the tables and found a space and began dancing that slow shuffle of teenage years.

"How old are you?" she asked when he mentioned that he'd just had a birthday.

"Fifty-seven."

"Oh, I thought you were my age," she said.

"Which is?"

"Sixty-three," the words spoken defiantly as if he should say, "You're not!" But instead, he said, "Actually, maybe that's what I am." She shook her head as if to say, *I knew it, you old coot.* He thought again of his high school reunion, which he both anticipated and dreaded—unless he found a young thing to accompany him. He still had dreams of erasing the clod he had been. It was important to show them—the princesses and princes he graduated with—that he'd come a long way, even if it wasn't far enough...yet. Out loud, he said, "It's nice to have someone to spend the day with, Laura." And he meant it. It *was* nice. Comfortable.

She nodded, then began humming along to "There's a

hole in Daddy's arm," her eyes somewhere in the long difficult past, he supposed. He didn't want anyone with a past, he decided just then, a flash of insight that would gnaw at his insides the rest of the day, causing a downturn and rock sliding. That was the trouble. He could never keep anything going. He felt like walking out, leaving her humming. What if he did? It wouldn't matter to a woman like her who could take care of herself. Sometimes the only thing that kept him in place for a while was if he was responsible for someone. Needed.

"Ready to go?" he said.

Saturday night's dance was a contra, traditional American folk dancing performed in two long lines to directions of patterns by the caller. At first, Jack thought he'd never get the hang of it, but people were kind and there was always an extended hand to show him the way. Nowhere else in his life could he remember such graciousness. Contra dancing was more aerobic than any other type, the two lines of dancers twirling and spinning and working patterns that brought them to the end of the lines, a kaleidoscopic pattern that someone could possibly work out with a collection of salt and pepper shakers at the kitchen table, composing new combinations of a series of five basic steps. He was not good at adjusting to so many different partners in one dance, short ones, tall ones, and having to constantly revise the center of gravity in the swing, but their eyes held him, as he listened to the calls— "gypsy" and "swing your partner," "ladies chain," "California twirl"— commands to be instantly obeyed, confusion dealt with communally as people pushed him gently to where he ought to be. It was difficult not to love everybody, he thought, so close, looking into eyes to keep balance, his nostrils filled with body smells, and with another's perspiration on his hands. It put a Band-Aid on his loneliness. Once or twice he came upon Laura in the dance pattern as they both worked their way up the line of dancers, but then he didn't see her for a long time and he was free to ask the young ones, who flirted with him and the next man equally, communally.

During intermission, he spotted Laura sitting on a folding chair at the wall, her legs crossed, arms tucked around her, her impatience poured into one madly swinging foot.

"Having a good time?" he asked.

She shrugged. "The older you get, the harder it is to find a partner—particularly here where I don't know anyone."

"So you ask them."

"I do, but if you're not used to dancing in this particular hall, you don't know who the good dancers are. I've picked a few clunkers." She said it like it was a life history.

The band began the intermission waltz, and he held out his hand to her. She rose swiftly, her arms assuming the pose, chin in the air. That's Laura, he thought. She can slip easily into illusion, assuming posture, stiff until the first step. A bit off-putting if you didn't know her, like a woman dressed too well. She took herself so seriously. But then as they faced each other and turned, bending slightly to the easy rhythm, her face softened into satisfaction, as though she were returning to something primal, her truest self. He looked away, not knowing what he was feeling. He had nothing to worry about; she carried her own weight easily, her movements reading his mind.

There was no door to his bedroom. Through the archway was the small sitting room that contained his desk and the brown wicker couch. He showed her the room and the bed, then turned away, exiting to the couch where Sunny lay at one end. Gently, he picked up the dog and put it on the floor. It eyed him with half-moon eyes and groaned.

"It's all right, girl. You can come back up once I get the sleeping bag on here," he said.

"What did you say, Jack?" Laura appeared in the archway.

"Talking to the dog," he grunted, although when he looked up at her he had to laugh. Dressed in polka-dotted pajamas, she looked Dalmatian-like. He heard her sniff as she tilted her head. As if viewing an instant replay, he imagined a lifetime spent with her, practicalities consuming them, age creeping up, daily picayune utterances over coffee, a vague coziness over everything. Boredom.

"What's so funny?"

"Nothing. I just never thought you wore pajamas."

"As opposed to—"

"Nothing. Or a black nightgown."

"Oh. Not at my age, thank you. Besides, I thought these would set the proper tone for the occasion."

"Meaning?"

"Good night, Jack," she said with a finality he was grateful for.

She read for a while, the light keeping him awake enough to wonder how or why he ever suggested her staying over—the unreasonable, adventurous flare-up he'd had—his usual response to life—impulses that later would plunge him into a kind of despair and disappointment for which he blamed himself. Was she having a good time? Should he care? What was it he had wanted when he so carelessly asked her to come? He couldn't remember, except that it would dispel the loneliness that hung on his shoulders since he and Lily parted. Not enough, really, for a night on a wicker couch.

She turned out the light and he shifted to an even more uncomfortable position, the dog lying at his feet, its weight pushing against him. He shifted again. Sunny's relaxed body flowed toward him, demanding even more space. He pulled up his knees. Then turned to face the wall. With each move, the couch creaked. Soon the dog was snoring a deep, satisfying, rumbling purr and he tried to match his breathing with the dog's, and shifted again. Was that creak his back or the couch?

From the other room, he thought he heard a stifled giggle, nothing more than a release of a puff of air, and then several in a row, and then squeals and gasps, out-and-out laughter. He was startled, wondering if she had gone mad.

"What the hell is that all about?" he called out.

"Jack, the only one sleeping is the dog. I feel bad taking your bed—I'm sure lying on that couch is only slightly better than lying on a bed of straw. Come here and talk to me."

"Talk to you?"

"Oh, for God's sake—just crawl in here and pay it no mind. I trust you."

"Well now. That's a heck of a thing. You *trust* me? That doesn't compliment you or me, Laura."

"Jesus. We're in our sixties. If we can't lie next to somebody and talk if we want to..."

"Okay. You got it." He stumbled on the door sill and banged his hip on the bedpost, but finally pulled back the covers and crawled in next to the stream of polka dots, thinking wasn't this the strangest thing he'd ever done, the epitome of his new sparse, sexless life? The harbinger of a colorless future? The final diminishment of his luxury of lascivious yesterdays?

Turning to him and laying her hand lightly on his chest, she began talking in a low murmur, first about her husband who went mad with drink, her kids, each of whom she'd put through college, her grandkids, where she lived—the house and neighborhood, careful in the details that set the stage for her life. He didn't mind, the flow of her voice calm and stoic through the dark. Once they heard heavy footsteps overhead and she stopped to listen, describing the person whose footsteps would sound like that—someone decisive, authoritative, sure of themselves, not heavy in weight necessarily but heavy in opinion. She'd never seen his landlord, and he was impressed by her perception. In fact, he began to see her in the dark plain as day, her voice her only instrument, without the distraction of her dancing. Just her. He thought about his mother reading to him in the long summer dusk, her gentle voice bringing him other worlds to fall asleep in, to distant shores to land upon as he begged for more and more. Still it was his mother's voice he remembered now, not the stories, the quiet tone, the calm demeanor, her range of expression as she spoke about events dreamed up or lived so long ago. He was quite young when he realized that very nearly everything had happened to someone at least one time before. It was comforting, as Laura's voice was now, although hers was a story he'd heard many times over, the first love, the disappointment, the parting, the grief, the brave pretenses. The ongoing search to find someone else. Yet all through the night as he stared out at the moon's passage through the rectangle of window, he listened, aware of the strangeness of her presence in his bed, the smell of her on his pillow, and her odd willingness to speak the lament of her life, which was, in the end, no more or less than anyone else's.

And he told her about Lily, how she'd stripped him of nearly everything, how he didn't care, just to be free of her. How his first wife had not wanted children, how he wouldn't have minded having one or two, how he thought of them now, the children he might have had. How it was too late for children with Lily, how they'd led a life of pleasure and passion. How his firm had regarded his inventiveness, and how he'd found himself traveling to South America and Liberia for the World Bank to help them set up businesses on a shoestring to help the poor of their countries, how after each return he realized Lily had not waited for him, how he began to have his suspicions.

Shaking his head and speaking into her hair, he suddenly said, "I don't know what love is, Laura." His voice sounded gruff and sad, confessional, and full of regret. He hated that. But he was in his own bed, for Pete's sake.

"Neither do I, Jack. But I saw it once."

"Only once?"

"Well, there are so many different ways to love, aren't there? But in the bargain one often annihilates the other—a tit-for-tat kind of game. But no, I did see true love once. I don't know what the rest of the stuff is between a man and a woman. I never could figure it out. A kind of bargain is the best I can come up with."

She moved away from him and rubbed her temples, polka-dotted elbows pointing toward the ceiling. Then her hands lay knotted across her middle. He lay on his side and held her, pulling her toward him. Her head was on his shoulder again. He sensed it was okay to talk like this. She was fine, not bitter, not weeping, just telling her story. He needed nothing more, just talk, a curiosity answered, well, not answered, it could never be answered, just opined, just something he could think about among a myriad other things. He remembered asking his mother once where the end of the world was and she said, "When you die, the world ends for you." It wasn't the answer he wanted but it satisfied him, and as time went on he could see the simplistic sense in it.

"So what did you see?" he asked.

"My friend, Bethan, when she was forty-eight, was separated from her husband, Steven. They had two teenage kids and—I don't know—I guess they just got tired of each other maybe? He was always in a bad mood and she was always picking up the pieces to placate him. I doubt either of them knew what was wrong. Anyway, they parted ways. Steven had visitation rights with the kids, of course, and one rainy evening as Bethan was driving the children to Steven's house, a drunk driver crossed the center line and hit her car. The children were okay, but Bethan got the brunt of it and her spinal cord was severed. After six months, she came home in a wheel chair, unable to move anything but two fingers on her right hand. And Steven came back to care for her. He came back, Jack. He never blinked an eye or even had to think about it. He came back, pure and simple, and did everything for her. I can't say about guilt or remorse—I don't want to analyze it—I can only say the fact is he came back and cared for her. I think only love could drive someone to do that for another—all the painful, tragic coping day after day, the giving up of one's own life for another."

Well, he had asked. He breathed slowly, sucking in air as though he were smothering. He felt the weight of her, of life, of whatever was required. He'd stick to dogs.

"Well, that is a bit of a romantic view," he said, blinking into the dark, tired now beyond all tiredness. He thought he saw the first of daylight; the room had softened to a grey-blue and the outline of the bedside lamp was silhouetted against the lightening sky. The base of the lamp was a woman's nude body, art deco style, the graceful curve of her legs, body and arms rising to hold the bulb. It was as if he'd never noticed it before, although he had, of course. He felt as though his eyelids scraped his eyeballs. Out loud he said, "Maybe he came back for some of that accident insurance money."

"Let me believe in the myth, then. Let me believe it was love."

"That's a hell of a lot to ask, Laura."

"You're right. It's rare. So is real love."

Real love. Allegiance. The great compromise.

"But there's more, Jack. He stayed for five years, while

Bethan learned how to cope. They say it takes three years or more to adjust to the confinement, to learn to accept it. As she began to take control of her life, arranging for her own caretakers and learning to communicate through a computer, she realized it was no life for Steven, still young, still virile. So she told him she was fine now, she could carry on, that he needed to go on and find someone with whom he could have a normal life. Now that was love, Jack. Love for him, to hand him back his own life."

"Maybe the trouble they'd had compounded itself, came back, and they realized they couldn't make it together anyhow."

"How could they, how could any couple make it under those circumstances? Still, she loved him enough to let him go."

"Jeez," he said. It was all he could manage. Her body next to his. There was nothing he wanted from her except comfort.

"Laura, try to sleep. A few winks before daylight."

"Jack, I know how weird this night has been. Not the usual. But at this age, nothing is as usual. Not sex, not love, not food, not sleep, not anything. I just—well, I needed this, you know?"

"Dancing not enough for ya?" He meant to sound light, bring the conversation to a different level.

"Dancing's only a substitute, a metaphor for life. And when I'm in the metaphor, I'm reminded again and again what it is I don't have. I get a glimpse of what life could be in the arms of someone who cared. Being the generic partner can be a cruelty, you know, a stirring up of old desires, things irretrievable."

She'd said too much. Better to leave some things unspoken, blurred in the back of one's mind. She was like a persistent muse or conscience. It was the dark that had made them brave, he thought, masking the longing, the strangeness

170

of everything, the polka-dotted disguise beneath which lay desire for life so strong it infuriated him. What right had they to ask for more after myriad chances at love? The two of them, swirling to one-two-three-, one-two-three. Ridiculous. They should give it up. Sixty-three and they weren't sick of it yet? Well, he was. He hoped she wasn't getting any ideas about him. He'd better set her straight.

"Laura, I hate disappointing you. I-I don't know what you have in mind. Don't go getting ideas about you and me."

"You, Jack? You haven't even got a damn refrigerator." She laughed, but she looked at him kindly. "I'd share mine with you but I know you don't want me to."

The room was definitely brightening. The dark shapes of his existence were coming into focus. Coming here to this place, living close to the bone, thinking he was free, that it was the only thing he'd ever done right, was all pretense. He knew like he'd never known anything true before, that his life was his alone. And he knew he didn't want it to be. It was Lily's. It would always be Lily's.

He turned as he rose from the bed and looked down at Laura, the golden-colored hair stiff and tousled, her eyes drowsy and half-closed after the exertion of a night considering the magnitude of love, and for a moment, for as brief a time as the whiff of jasmine on a Sunday afternoon, he loved her. But it was not the kind that lasted, he knew—and God help him—after the words, the searching and the posturing—all that was left in the morning light was the ache of the kind that lasted. *Oh, Lily.*

The Second Death

His car had a strange leak, puddling the garage floor with a thick slime he hated to mess his fingers with. Kneeling with paper towel in hand, he touched the black ooze and raised his finger to his nose. He still didn't know. It was thick but not oily, he thought. He hated the thought of the journey he had to take Monday morning to the mechanic who could tell him anything and he'd have no choice but to believe it.

This weekend, he'd invited Clairine, a frequent dance partner of his at the community dances, to be his houseguest, something he was entirely unaccustomed to doing. She was a woman who followed him well on the dance floor. They were a smooth couple if he did say so himself, and he thought he might be comfortable with her in other situations, too. Maybe. Yet it was a stranger who'd invited her, some foreign extension of himself that had calculated everything, surprising him. Maybe it meant the therapy was working, that tedious drone of his where he found himself talking to a wall while the doctor sat behind him taking notes. At times he suspected the doctor had fallen asleep, which he had, and Andrew coughed to wake him, feeling the situation was nothing more than a cliché and he was wasting money. Still, he went because he wanted to change his life. He'd gone into the seminary at the age of seventeen and remained until he was thirty, which explained a lot of things, but not everything, of course.

He had confessed to Clairine during one of the dance

breaks that his therapist had told him he must be straight with her, and let her know his frailties were not of her doing or had, in fact, nothing at all to do with her, and that he was working on them, those fears of his, which he had learned to name at least and could roll off his tongue with the same kind of reportage he noticed on the newscast—a fact he interpreted as progress. *You confess it and then it's not a big deal anymore*—and for this he'd paid good money despite the fact that he'd been aware of the wisdom of the ancients as to the benefits of confession. He'd invited Clairine to a dance and afterward, since she had to drive a long distance, to stay overnight in the guest room, while harboring thoughts that he might be able to come to terms with his fears since she was so—what he could only think of as vivacious, a woman force with such open, yet patient determination he'd not seen since—since—never. He'd never seen that before. The women he'd encountered were far more subtle and secretive, and therefore, more powerful, intimidating. He'd gotten that much figured out, and for this he'd paid good money, too.

He was disappointed about the car. Because he didn't trust it, they'd have to take hers to the dance. He'd wanted to show her he could take care of her, respond to her needs. She said there was a certain move he made on the dance floor that she "loved to pieces," that when they waltzed side by side and he held her left arm across his chest and then guided it in front of her in a kind of protective circle around her, she felt like a bird in a cage as they glided forward together, and she was so touched by that, she said, because feeling protected and being taken care of was a "rare feeling" for her. She'd insisted their eyes meet at that point which he obligingly did every time he did the step with her and she'd always smile up at him.

He'd asked her what he should get in for breakfast to which she replied, "Bacon and eggs, please, since you asked," the words spoken politely, almost shyly, as if it were too much to ask. So he'd gone shopping for the bacon and eggs which he never ate and the Coke she liked to drink in the afternoons and after that, he'd spent the rest of the morning cleaning the house, straightening the piles of work on his desk and dusting the edges of the bookshelves wondering if she'd notice his fastidiousness. Probably not a good thing in a man, he thought with a sense of panic. He wished he'd learned carelessness. It was one of the things he was never allowed, and therefore never allowed himself, he thought, as he straightened the refrigerator magnets once more, little houses with important numbers on them like the plumber and the vinyl siding salesman, the heating and A/C man, the houses placed as though they were lined up on a suburban street, a neighbor-hood with couples in each of the houses and children. The houses kept slipping whenever he closed the refrigerator door and he had half a mind to throw them out except that he would miss them, and the loss of them was more than he could deal with. It was closely associated with the fact of being in his late fifties, of time running out and his having missed some things, feelings he had to brush off daily. *Work through,* his therapist said.

He heard the car door slam. She came up the walk, her slender figure moving in the same way she danced, straight-backed, with an air about her that belied her vulnerability. He went out to meet her, cautioning her about the first step being higher than usual because the sidewalk was sinking. She took his hand, her overnight bag slapping at her knees, and looked up at him, laughing. "Some little mole living under there? Rocking your foundations?" She seemed to think it funny, the lines branching out from eyes that looked for things to laugh at. She was not beautiful, but he liked the way her face settled into something pleasant. She smiled easily.

He'd made dinner reservations at the Canton Inn for 5:30. It was nearly that when she arrived and she laid her coat on his mother's white couch which made him wish again he had a coat closet because he could see that the arm of the couch nearest the door was becoming soiled from people putting their things there as soon as they stepped in the door. He usually put a sheet over the couch which he took off whenever he was expecting anyone.

"A white couch! What are you doing with a white couch?" said Clairine.

"It was my mother's and when she died, nobody in the family wanted it. She always loved it and I couldn't stand to see it sold. Oh, we've got reservations for 5:30," he said quickly, and then he explained about his car. "Do you mind if we take yours?"

"Of course not," she said and handed him her keys as she glanced around the living room and dining room which were small and compact. The house was perfect for him though, a brick colonial sitting on a slight hill with an enormous maple outside the window that he enjoyed watching from his study—the squirrel's nest at eye level on the second floor. That was the one drape he kept open since the tree offered privacy from the street below and his neighbors, couples mostly, who seemed curious about him.

"A woman emerging from your house, Andrew!" Clairine teased as they set out. "What will the neighbors think?"

"It's about time, most likely," he said and chuckled as he held the car door open for her.

At the restaurant, he saw a colleague of his. It was a pleasure he hadn't expected. If he was not known for having a woman at his side, to be seen with one made the fruition of his goal seem possible. What he was known for was his research, being an authority on medieval history, which surprised even him at times, how he'd spent his life burrowing into books, digging into dusty library shelves with the goal of translating mysteries. So much time spent in this way but here he was,

175

trying to change his life for the better, open to suggestions, willing to grow, wanting now, ready now, for a woman by his side. His heart ached with the thought of it at times. Downright ached. Well, he was working on it.

It was Father Hager who dined alone. A scrubbed face, an impeccable life. Andrew's priest from Sacred Heart who was due to retire soon. Well loved.

"Would you mind if I asked him to join us, Clairine?" he asked. "He's a nice person and I think he'd enjoy meeting you."

"Of course not, Andrew," she said, her head dipping around to see who he was pointing to. Father lowered his head toward his soup.

On approach, and after introductions, Father declined to join them. "No, no," he said, "I wouldn't dream of intruding. You two enjoy. I'll be rushing back to the rectory soon. I'm there by myself tonight and I'm hoping they'll all be back before too long." He blushed. "I don't like being alone. I hear every noise and think it's someone breaking in."

Over salad, Clairine said, "Imagine that. A man uneasy about being alone. Seems so odd. I know women alone who'd have it no other way." Clairine lived a good distance beyond the beltway, north of the city where there were still dairy farms, which was one of the attractions for him, a woman used to listening to birdsong in the morning as she'd mentioned in one of her letters.

"Well, this is the city," he said. "People are broken into every day."

She nodded and cut her tomato in half, saying, "Even priests have to confront the world as it is, I suppose."

"Believe me, they've heard it all. Confessions, counseling—they know what's going on," he said. He felt he needed to say that because she had once said to him, "Your life seems so clean of scars, so pure, everything to good purpose. I could tell you stories that would shock the bejesus out of you." He wanted to set the record straight. He was sorry he'd mentioned to her that he'd spent a good bit of time in the seminary, something that made women back away from him. He wasn't exactly born yesterday, he'd have her know.

"How long were you in the cemetery?" she had asked then, straight-faced so that he knew it was a slip.

"The cemetery? You said cemetery." She'd laughed, a deep long, low laugh that came up from her toes. "My God," she said. "Did I really?" And laughed again, and for five minutes she shook her head trying to control herself. He was encouraged. She had family—children and grandchildren. Maybe that's what taught her to laugh like that.

Now as she sat across from him, she was subdued, her blue eyes searching his face as he told her about the car. "I think it may be one of the cylinders or gaskets or something that is leaking. I thought I'd put down clean newspaper on the floor of the garage and then measure how far in from the bumper the leak is occurring. That may help the mechanic decide on exactly where it's coming from."

"Maybe it's the radiator," she said.

"No. I don't think so. But how would I know?"

"Just fill the auxiliary tank and then check to see if the level goes down."

He didn't know if he had an auxiliary tank.

"Or maybe it's your air conditioner."

He nodded, thinking maybe the puddle was dark because it was dirty, not oily.

"Or it might even be your windshield wiper fluid."

It could have been soapy, he didn't know. "I never thought of that," he said, beginning to feel uncomfortable. "One wiper *is* dry." You could tell she'd been on her own for a while with no one to depend on about her car or anything else. Was he threatened by that, a woman who could take care

177

of herself? It *was* a bit off-putting. It was one of the things he'd have to mention to his therapist, who had encouraged him to ask Clairine for the weekend like a devil nattering behind his thoughts, saying, "Ask her. Ask her!" And before he realized it, he was asking her. He must have been mad, bursting out with an invitation without weighing the consequences.

She wiped her lips with the napkin and refused dessert. Her heavy eyelids drooped. He could see that when she wasn't laughing or smiling, her face held sadness. Her eyes sought his. "Andrew," she said, "what is it you want for yourself?" And when he told her he didn't feel that God had called him even though he'd waited and agonized for years over what to do, she said, "Somehow I thought it would have been more dramatic than that, like for a woman or something." And then she said, "What was the most dramatic thing that ever happened to you?"

He couldn't answer, although he'd thought about it many times since, puzzled that the answer about his agony didn't satisfy her. Now he repeated the words, *what do I want for myself,* looking down at the soiled plate in front of him. "I want a personal life," he said. When he looked up, she was nodding, as if seeing right through him. He'd never confessed so much before.

He drove to the dance, taking a shortcut through the city, speeding outrageously between traffic lights and timing them, the way so familiar he could do it on automatic pilot. She was impressed. "I'm lost," she said. "Haven't got a clue as to where we are!" She laughed again, as though she were on a grand adventure, and he sensed her excitement. It was the best thing about her. Then, suddenly, she said, "Does it bother you that I'm not Catholic?"

"Not a bit. Everyone has to come to God in their own way."

She looked out the window and then down at her lap,

crossed her legs and rubbed her forehead. "Andrew," she said softly, "I even have trouble with the word *God.*" He thrilled at the words. He could help her. He knew the way.

The dance hall contained his family. He'd been dancing here for years, once each week on Sundays. But this was a special Saturday evening of Viennese waltz, and much of the Sunday crowd was present. Some newcomers, he noticed, but he rarely asked a newcomer to dance, having a lineup of women whom he'd known for a long time and with whom he danced well. His regulars. He knew what jobs they held, what their middle names and birth dates were. He knew other interesting facts, too, how Sheila had recently published a paper in the *Circle Review* and that Karen was working on her doctorate. He knew Mary Ellen had been a nun and was doing a thesis on the use of puppetry in psychiatry for adults. He knew where they were from originally, their maiden name if they'd been married, and how many times they'd been married.

And he knew the signals, when to apply pressure on the woman's right hand so that she went into open position for the side-by-side, and when to guide her with pressure applied with his hand in the middle of her back to step before him in closed position. In a way, it was much like driving a car. He loved it. Through dancing, he expressed where he secretly lived deep inside. He moved possessively, aggressively, and dominantly under correctness and good manners. It was lovemaking, he guessed, the only love he'd ever made, and he was good at it. Women grabbed at him at times which he didn't especially like, but it proved he was in demand. Dancing was a duplicity made in heaven. The fairy tale satisfied him. And had done so for years. Until Clairine. For the first time, he found himself thinking there could be more.

She was a good person, a family person, a former teacher. With a generous heart. And an ease he delighted in on the dance floor.

He called hello to each one he knew, Clairine at his side, and put his things down next to hers. Then they sat side by side changing into dance shoes, exchanging breezy words to those just coming in. "Going to be hot tonight, a steamer—and no A/C—doesn't help for long anyway—more fans are what we need—the band's good tonight—heard 'em down in Georgia. Top-notch."

Then she was before him and he was safely wrapped in an odd familiarity where words and facts didn't count, his body close to hers, his hand around her waist, her face in front of him. He winked at her from his height, sweeping her along with his long strides, her skirt fanning out around them with every turn. He did the birdcage step but she didn't look at him. Maybe she just forgot. He did it again and she waited too long to glance at him although he felt her eyes on him after he'd turned away. She was just preoccupied.

He asked her for the third, fifth, and seventh dances because he knew if he didn't she'd be booked. He always looked to see who she was dancing with but he never saw her glance his way to see who his partner was. That was okay. Actually, he liked the idea of her being popular, felt it like a secret pride. She was a good dancer and men sought her out, although they themselves were not the best dancers. The best dancers had their own clique and she wasn't in it. No, the men who asked her were mostly men without credentials, artist types, men younger than her by twenty years who thought they could learn from her, or that she'd be grateful for the asking, that because of her age, she was "safe" and would ask little of them. He watched her dance away from him with one of her regulars, watched her head tilt back, the long black skirt encircle her new partner. She was laughing again. She'd said once that dancing made her feel young and beautiful, a fantasy she indulged in. "I'm in demand, Andrew!" she'd said, laughing as though it were some grand joke she was playing on them all.

Even with all the fans going, the dancers were damp and their faces shone red. The men returned to their gym bags to hurriedly change into a dry T-shirt, their bare chests white against the yellowed walls. Andrew did as well, and he glanced up to see Clairine watching him change. He was thin and self-conscious about it having been the object of much teasing by his sisters about his Ichabod Crane body when he was a kid. He'd cry and his sisters would taunt him further: *crybaby, crybaby.* He felt that same vulnerability now although Clairine was only signaling to him that she was going to the Ladies'. He watched her go, interrupted in her walk by two or three who wanted to dance with her.

He chatted with Sally, whom he'd known for years, who was unusually tall for a woman of Asian background, and a superb dancer with good balance. She painted her lips bright red, wore flowing, multi-colored skirts, and seemed mildly interested in him but he couldn't imagine it—those red lips, the generic smile. She was aggressive and that put him off, too, grabbing his arm and pulling him to the middle of the dance floor a few times. Now the red lips were giving him stock market tips about which he knew nothing. He nodded and tried to think of questions to ask but none came to him as he kept his eye on the entrance to the hall and Clairine's return.

When she entered, she looked refreshed and breathless at the same time, her hair in place, her complexion back to normal after looking as though she were on fire. She came toward him to set her bag down, laughing at nothing, the look on her face one of pure delight. He guessed it was in anticipation of a dance.

"Ready?" he said, walking to the dance floor with his

hand out for her to follow.

"This is the sixth, right? I can never keep track," she said. "I'm booked. See you for the seventh?"

"No," he insisted. "This is the seventh."

"Let me tell Paul then," she said slowly, staring at him. "I promised him the next dance. Be right back."

"It's all right," he said, but by then she was out of earshot, and he stood on the dance floor amidst the couples moving around him, not knowing whether to leave the floor or wait where she'd left him so she could find him again, the couples maneuvering around him as they seemingly had for years, his singularity so apparent to him now. He'd wait where he was.

She swooped him up. He couldn't tell what happened really, but she was already dancing when she came before him and he, in his confusion about the rhythm, began counting, ONE, two, three, trying to match her step and listen to the music all at once. He stepped on her. "Sorry!" he said. "Let's start again," and immediately she stood poised before him, ready to follow.

The way was clear. She could match his long strides and their balance was even so that he didn't feel as though he had to pull her along or support her weight. It was mutual, her hand on his shoulder exactly in the right place, the firmness in her right hand sensitive to his direction. At some point they flew, her skirt trailing, billowing around him and she grinned up at him. He blinked, crinkled up his face, hoping to send her an acknowledgment of pleasure. Their speed through the dancers caused her to slip once, but he remained steady and sure as they twirled in the open center, the eye of the movement of the main traffic, arms maneuvering until they became like vines separated to make a window between them through which he peeked and winked at her, untangled her to a left window position, then unfurled her to a left grapevine, then moved her swiftly, deftly, to the side-by-side position, and then his arm guided hers to the birdcage that she'd named, as he looked down at her and she smiled back and squeezed his hand and he brought her in front of him in a series of reverse, left-hand turns while everything spun around them in a blur—she, the only thing in his focus, steadying him and he, her as her eyes held his which he couldn't keep up, just couldn't for so long—he had to break away lest enchantment be mistaken, or entrapment, or some sort of demand come later because of it—no, he had to look away, watch the traffic, slow the speed, increase the forward direction so they could travel, spin, catch the openings—for he, after all, had to lead. At a signal dip in the music, he twirled her around on his finger, setting the rest of her loose to spin and spin and spin again as the music ended, and then with her left leg behind her, she bent low in a deep curtsy, a grand gesture, laughing. Her arm around his waist now, she said, "Perfect, Andrew. Just perfect! Don't say a word." He could hear himself laughing his high-pitched shriek that got lost in exhalations, the grand pleasure-filled pause that flowed through the pillars and out the open windows as if the entire hall expired one long sigh. The leaves, silhouetted against the street lamps outside, stirred. Was this happiness? This brief perfection? It was, he was sure of it.

He drove to his house with her yawning by his side and saying, "I'm finally relaxed, you know? The only time of the week when I truly am is after a dance." She took off her shoes and lay her head back.

"Uh-huh," he said and couldn't think of anything else to say, a growing tension in his abdomen, a cramp, maybe his diverticulitis acting up again. He sped through the streets, passed spotlighted buildings with manicured landscaping, statues black and stalwart against the grey-pink sky, through neighborhoods with storefronts and attached houses with identical stoops, passed fenced-in areas of new construction, through diamond-studded streets and cantankerous traffic lights, turning finally onto the tree-lined streets of his own neighborhood, the Victorian restorations of young couples and the wooden picket fencing of the old. To his house. He pulled in the driveway and parked, the squeak of the parking brake announcing arrival. He thought she was asleep, but when he glanced at her, her eyes were open.

"I'm going to check the leak on the car. I'll let you in the house and you can make yourself at home. I'll only be a minute."

The black puddle was larger, and he saw another one a few inches away. Were they different colors? The new one just water? He couldn't reach under that far to find out. He'd have to move the car. He unfolded a section of yesterday's newspapers and laid them in a straight line from the bumper to the leak, and from the side of the car behind the tire to the leak. Tomorrow he'd back the car out and measure.

When he returned to the house, she was in the shower, her things neatly piled on the couch, not his mother's but the one in the den where he'd already pulled out the bed that afternoon and made it up with clean sheets and his mother's pink blanket. He started a pot of tea he thought she'd like and set the table for the blueberry pie he'd picked up at the supermarket. She appeared in a smock-like something with flowers all over it and chatted about the style of the bathroom and kitchen which were straight out of the thirties, like "my mother's house," she said. Staring at the pot and waiting for the water to boil, he began humming to himself, although he didn't realize it until she said, "Do you know a different song, Andrew?"

"Why?" he said.

"Because you've been dee-deedling for some time now," and she laughed again.

"It's a habit. Here, have a seat. Tea's ready."

She was quiet. She'd washed the makeup off her face and

she looked tired, as though she'd been waiting a long time for something and it had never come. It was one of the things he sensed about her, that she would be grateful for steadiness, and thought of her as someone at odd ends, ready now like he was, her timing and his timing falling together. She'd been alone for fifteen years, she told him, the kids raised and gone, retirement upon her. He began by asking her about her mother and father, and then her sons, knowing she'd talk and talk and he need only nod and think, until she said, "So many books, Andrew! You have thousands! Have you read them all?"

"Nearly. Although I seem to collect vintage books, and I probably have too many of them."

"Any fiction? Anything to browse through before I go to sleep?"

"A few. I'll pull some out for you." She trailed behind him as he went from room to room, once placing her hand on his arm as she peered over his shoulder into the pages of a book of medieval tapestries. They traveled through the dining room, the living room, his study, the shelf-lined walls of his bedroom with his single twin bed in the center of it—how pristine it must look in her eyes—and the hallway. He ambled through, she behind him, studying the shelves, but then he walked quickly, realizing suddenly he didn't have one single book of fiction. "The basement," he said. "There's more down in the basement," thinking there must be some *Reader's Digest Condensed Books* from his mother that he'd stored down there. Or had he thrown them out, given them to Goodwill?

"It's all right, Andrew," she said. "I'll browse through this one, the tapestry book."

"No, no, no," he said. "It's no trouble," feeling his lack for there was always something he hadn't thought of that would drive him mad, make him regret later that he'd been remiss, something to make him aware that things were as they were through every fault of his own. But the truth was he disliked fiction. Didn't trust it. He was much more interested in facts, in uncovering forgotten ones in archives (somewhere, if you searched hard enough, there was always something to be dug up and brought to the light of day). He had no patience with the contrived. What did it prove? He liked it better when truth was plainly laid bare. He should have known that women liked fiction. The thought occurred to him that he wanted to provide her distraction because he wasn't ready yet—the thought of the two of them locked in embrace hardly imaginable—although her hand on his arm was okay and her hand on his back okay, too. She was asking now about his basement, "Can I come with you?" as he turned and descended the stairs, as though the basement might hold some further, deeper clue to him, the inventory of which was going through his mind as he answered as off-handedly as he could manage, not knowing how else to deal with such a question, "Sure, come on."

"What are you doing with all those cereal boxes, those Bran-wheats? Found a good sale?" she said almost immediately. He hoped she didn't notice him wince.

"Not exactly. They're empty." The boxes were stacked on a table and on two of the shelves and on top of his mother's dining room buffet. He'd been eating the same kind for years. Breakfast was one of the few things he didn't have to think about. He just did it, a ritual that brought him comfort, although now it was discomfort he could name, a reason to be ridiculed, squirreling he could give a sensible reason for but silly in the end, he supposed. Really. In her eyes. Why should he care?

"Andrew?" Laughter played at the corners of her mouth. He felt like a child who needed to explain some furtive deed in his own bedroom. He had published papers in important places, but it was the cereal boxes she wanted to know about. He already felt tricked by a world where fiction was king, happenstance contrived for purposes of entertainment, the human spirit deadened by mediocrity and privacy stolen, invaded, displayed for all the world to see. She would enjoy a caricature of his existence, the fiction she would compose about him.

"I noticed," he said patiently, trying to relax, "that the blackbirds peck at the trash bags when they are set out. If I put food scraps inside cereal boxes, the birds don't bother."

"What diligence," she said. "How about just throwing the scraps in the yard for the birds to help themselves?"

"But that would draw rats, I'm afraid." She would draw conclusions about him, and suddenly he hated the whole idea of getting to know someone, of getting too close, or opening the door to himself even a crack. His was a quiet, simple, logical life. He wished the weekend would end. What a stupid thing to do—invite her, or anyone, for the weekend.

"Here they are!" He reached for the Condensed Books series but Clairine intercepted with, "Andrew, I never read those. Thanks anyhow. It's the real stuff I'm after, unabridged. The full Monty. I don't want to miss *anything!*" and she laughed, her arm on his shoulder where she usually placed it in the dance, but he automatically looked away, an instinct of his that stayed long after it was of any use at all.

Later, as she turned toward the sleep couch, he brought out a map. "You might be interested in this," he said. "I've located the town in Germany where your roots are. It isn't very far from where my relatives came."

She looked at him as if she didn't understand at first. Maybe she didn't recall the conversation. "Remember? Klingenberg in Bavaria?"

"For crying out loud!" she said slowly and yawned, stretching her arms far out to either side and then sighing. "It's so late, Andrew."

He sat down beside her on the bed and spread the map over both their laps, her fingers smoothing the place they slowly focused on which was along the Rhine River, her hands thick-veined and plain, hands that had worked hard—not pretty hands, not pretty at all. Big for a woman, almost out of proportion with the rest of her, he thought. He'd never noticed that before. Much of the time she wore gloves when they danced. She was one of the better-dressed women at the hall, but now she appeared plain, a no-nonsense type. Her grandfather had been a blacksmith; her grandmother took in washing. His grandfather had been a tailor; his grandmother, a midwife. Salt of the earth. Handed down. Somewhere way back there was a connection, a similar culture with similar values. He liked that.

They talked about ancestry until 3 A.M. He asked question after question, although he knew it was only a tactic against any more touching, thwarting expectancies on her part. He couldn't help it. He had to think fast about deterring her because there was panic in his entrails. Perhaps she was old enough where it wouldn't matter: sex in the past, companionship enough. He didn't know but suspected he was wrong. On his part, he felt nothing beyond panic, at a loss about what to do except to keep her talking. Finally, he looked at his watch. It was 3:15. He got up with, "I better let you rest."

She nodded. There was that look again on her face, the look of waiting and wanting, the sad eyes, the lines around them deepened by the soft light. "Good night, Andrew," she said as she stood up with her hands behind her back.

In his room, he stretched out on his bed and laid his arms across his chest. The pencil-thin light from the street lamp through the gap in the drapes streaked across his bed as though marking him, canceling him out. He got up and yanked the drape an inch more so it completely closed and returning to his bed, prayed to all the saints and angels to help him and thanked God for the waltz, for Clairine's visit, for safely returning from the drive into the city and then he thought about his car, leaking quietly, steadily in the dark, while all the words about this and that but definitely not of the *you and I* variety passed between them. *Maybe it's not so bad,* he said to Hope: the leak might be trivial—only the windshield wiper fluid as she had suggested, and fell asleep worrying about the fact that they had the whole day together tomorrow.

It seemed as though he dreamed all night. Usually he didn't remember his dreams, much to the disgust of his psychiatrist, but when he awoke he remembered rollerblading through the night, all night, and now he was exhausted from fumbling with the helmet and the knee guards and the elbow guards, and leaving them places and having to go back and get them, always missing something and starting off again, rolling swiftly through the night, working to gain speed, his body at turns graceful and laboring. Hills...he remembered hills. And then a lawn mower, the motor-less kind, and he heard the sound of it again—the sound like nothing else he could think of—that soft whirr of metal brushing metal in long and short spurts, of precision and rightness as lines were drawn in the soft grass on dusky summer evenings, reminding him of his father when he was a kid, and for some reason he was being reprimanded, although for what had never been made clear. It was a general reprimand and lasted all night. His shoulders were stiff with it, his legs ached, and his hand covered himself protectively. The clock said 10:08. He made the bed as soon as he got up, then knelt beside it and thanked God for the day.

In the kitchen, he began frying bacon as he listened for sounds of Clairine's rising. The day outside was grey, the leaves heavy with rain, the sound of the bacon competing with the sound of raindrops. He was tired. There were many things he should do with this day with two publishing deadlines to meet, a paper to edit, a new research analysis to prepare, all compounded by the fact that his secretary had retired the week before, had had her retirement dinner and received her gift certificate and cried, and then returned a few days later having decided she couldn't retire, no, she just missed everyone so, and had asked, still weeping, "Can I come back, Andrew?" He'd been hoping to hire someone knowledgeable in computers this time, but he'd said, yes, of course, despite the misspelled words in her letters, the confused telephone messages and the mixing in where she had no business. That she'd infuriated him at times—well, that was something he had to bear, his cross, so to speak and he had few of those, really.

"Smells wonderful in here," said Clairine behind him, and something in his heart gave a thud, as though the sound of her voice was some kind of curtain call and he didn't know what his lines were. Nonetheless, "Good morning!" he sang out, briskly, gaily, thinking he sounded like a cartoon, buffoonish.

"I didn't mean to keep you up so late last night," she said, and slipped her arm around his waist. "I kept thinking we should not have been discussing so much history, Andrew, but you got me started."

"Yes. I wanted to change the conversation but when I looked at my watch and saw that it was after three, I thought, well, we really should get some sleep. How do you like your eggs?" She withdrew her arm.

When they sat down, he bowed his head and folded his hands. "Thank you, Lord, for the food before us, for Clairine's visit, for the night's rest, and let us go out into the day together with joy. Amen." When he raised his head and unfolded his hands, she was staring at him, unsmiling, then she quickly picked up her napkin. The corners of her mouth were tucked in as though she might say, "For crying out loud," again.

He began to think of her as haughty with a toughness that lacked humility and capable of disrespect, although she helped him clean up the dishes and the kitchen, folded up the sleeper couch again and the blankets, all the while making suggestions as to their plans for the day. She went from room to room opening drapes, saying, "Why do people in the city always keep their drapes closed? My sister-in-law does the same thing and I always feel claustrophobic in rooms where I can't see out! Even a wet day is beautiful, don't you think, with the leaves all deep green and shiny?"

"I keep them closed because I was robbed once," he said.

She stood at the dining room window with the drape in her hand, "Sorry," on her lips.

"But you can open them while we're in here," he said so she could see he was capable of compromise.

"Good," she said and the laugh returned. "Good, good, good. There's a *connection* to be made when the windows are uncovered, Andrew, with the weather, the color of the sky, the business of squirrels and robins—I'd even go so far as to say I need to sniff the air—get a good whiff, smell the currents," and she opened the window and peered out, her nose just beyond the glass. "I love it when the earth is soaking wet and you can smell it." The light revealed the lines on her skin, which were many, and some even ran down her cheeks, he could see that now, see plainly that she was older, that she had lived, that almost everything was behind her—love and sorrow and pain and disappointment and still she looked for more and eagerly sought out the day.

"God's gifts are many," he said. He thought he heard her say, "Jesus," under her breath.

"What?" he said.

"Whatever," he heard this time as she turned away from

the window with her hands on her hips, nodding as though accepting a challenge.

"What are you trying to do, save me?"

He laughed. "Catholicism doesn't work that way."

"Believe what you want to, Andrew, but don't try to reel *me* in, okay?" He was astonished at her bluntness. Strangely, he was not offended. At least he knew where she stood. No guesswork. He wondered if she'd ever had to *work through* things, or if she'd always known what to do, where she'd learned how to rattle cages or if she'd always known. He wondered if she was ever afraid.

Together they decided on the museum, there being an exhibition on Raphael's sketches and another on impressionists at the Weems Gallery, but first he had to check the leak under the car. In the garage, he listened, imagining he could hear the drips beyond the rain on the roof. Bending down, he saw the leak had continued just as he suspected. The two dark spots had converged. It would be difficult now to get an accurate measurement. He'd put fresh newspaper down except he knew he had no choice but to merely close the garage door and wait until Monday. What had he hoped for? That it would stop? Fix itself? It was going to cost him a fortune, he just knew.

They parked her car and headed toward the museum. He tried to shorten his long strides to match hers while he explained to her that Raphael had students he trained so well that much of their work was indistinguishable from his own. It was chilly, and she had the collar of her blazer turned up against the wind. He put his arm around her shoulder to warm her, and she, her arm around his waist. It was safe now, being in public, and she looked up at him as if she knew this, her eyes studying his face until he had to caution her that they had to watch out with traffic coming from both directions and the street itself uneven where part of the macadam had been removed. In the distance they heard a loud rumble, which grew louder as they neared the intersection and the first of the motorcycles appeared.

"That's right," he said, raising his voice to a shout. "It's Memorial Day. I'd almost forgotten. This is the motorcycle brigade by the Vietnam vets."

She nodded. The parade was led by a burly, grey-haired man in his early fifties dressed in black, including boots, tattoos along his arms, mirrored glasses that reflected the row of small American flags on the handlebars, and although he sat alone on his bike, behind him were couples, the women smiling and waving and holding on to men in their fifties and sixties, grey-haired, heavy-set, arms and handlebars making a circle, man and bike as one, their voices becoming the roar of the bike. *You can't deny us now, you see? There's strength in uniting and saying we were there where there was honor and sorrow and cruelty and bravery and pain and chaos mixed together, where we were changed, where America was changed, and whole villages obliterated—it was insanity, and unjust and we went because we were supposed to, and now this roaring black brigade snaking through the city says it all for we proudly fly the flag. We are part of glorious and inglorious history. We are the flow.*

For his part, he'd been out of all that. Separate, as though he'd lived on a different planet. For a few seconds he envied them, their rough manner of camaraderie, the black shirts, black bikes glinting with chrome, the women who hung on their backs like emblems. He watched as Clairine waved and turned her hand into a thumbs-up and the men and women answered back, thumbs up, nodding at her as she stood in the wind with her collar turned, her hair blown to one side and he could see it was thin and grey in this light and that her eyes held tears. He was surprised at her abandon, her mindless capability of being swept into the moment. He was shocked that she could feel so much toward strangers as she shouted, *Yeah!* into the wind and *God bless!* God bless? When she'd even had trouble with the word *God,* a concept too narrow for her liking? She was smiling now, and wiping her eyes, although he wasn't sure why except to say she'd allowed herself to be overcome, and he could see in a flash how cut off he'd been, not part of anything ever since his mother, Anna, against the sound of his father's lawn mower coming through the open window, said to him in that whisper she saved only for him, *Andrew, wet your lips. Kiss me.* He'd recoiled but obeyed, an act he got used to until he was adept. For her. For what it took to live in this world. He was no longer sure what *good* was then, it being something nebulous and contradictory. Forever after he needed clearly stated rules he could follow. All those years in seminary—all that time, all he'd wanted was to be good. He could still feel the iron band tightened around his thigh, punishment he'd sought and Jesuits condoned to erase sexual thoughts. The sting of tears he felt now was not for love or ecstasy, not for anyone or any cause but himself (an improvement he was sure his therapist would say) as he stood on the curb in the cutting wind. The tears were for time lost, for he knew as he watched the pageant of men and women that even the worst injustices could be forgiven. And at some point, he thought, as he watched their unabashed pairing on parade, he might, in the way they all took for granted, become one of them despite the panic that overtook him, fear as fierce and firmly set as the whirring of a lawn mower on a summer's evening, for he could now imagine it—her whispers silenced, her second and final death.

Mavis

Aaron Stiel, fifty-seven, sipped hot coffee in his third-floor apartment on Bakely Street. The sips were accompanied by the noisy drafts of air he took in, sounds that as a child would have been cause for reprimand but now, along with the morning sun warming his back and the newspaper comfortably in hand, reassured him that he was his own boss, could fulfill his life's desires and take his time about it, too. Recently retired, he easily stretched old routines into the empty spaces of his life, so everything took longer than it used to, and this was one of life's rewards, he told himself. One of the long-awaited pleasures. There were also a host of new pursuits he was now free to follow: dancing, for example, which he'd like to do every night of the week—international folk on Tuesdays, swing on Saturdays, English contra on Thursdays, American contra on Fridays, and waltz on Sundays. And then there was poetry. He especially liked the Main Street Coffee House where they had readings every other Wednesday—and hiking, taking the canoe out along the Choptank, and birdwatching. Especially fascinating was the community of vultures he'd discovered near an abandoned silo off river where the birds gathered at dusk, in silhouette against the orange sky. He imagined them sharing gruesome stories about their day, which tended to set him thinking about his own mortality, as if the birds themselves had decided to roost on his shoulders.

Truth was, most nights he needed to dance. It was the

only thing that settled and satisfied him. Yet he was glad he was so healthy and peaceful at this point in his life and interested in everything now that he had the freedom to be. Life was a smorgasbord after all, an inimitable feast, he told himself. Even if he'd been motivated to write a personal ad (which he wasn't), he couldn't possibly write down all the things he was interested in. Take this morning, he thought—as though he were posing in front of a TV camera emceeing his own story—our hero, the protagonist (he always had the ability to watch himself from afar) was reading the classifieds, displaying a considerable openness to life, a readiness to discover something new as he sifted through life's secondhand stuff, thoroughly committed to his new career: the entertainment of Aaron Stiel. This was happiness, he told himself. He was a self-actualized man, open to this new stage of his life, free to be creative, bring his ideas to fruition with all the tenacity of a mouse in a maze, which included polishing his moves on the dance floor.

Skimming past ads for antique washstands, a wedding band, a typewriter, a wedding dress in a size 6, a Civil War rifle, his eyes stopped at an ad for a dress form. He remembered that busty shape, stiff and prim, that stood in his mother's sewing room with bits of tissue paper pinned here and there and patches of additional gussets in strategic places to accommodate her enlarging form. A strange personification of her, it seemed to guard the house even when she wasn't there, and he felt a twinge of threat even now, across the span of years and into the security of his own apartment. He coughed, then slurped some more coffee. A dress form. Sixty bucks. Size 12. Bigger than he'd wanted. But like new, it said.

Because he knew nothing about dress forms and needed to know if this was a good deal, he turned to the computer on the kitchen table and in a minute, there they were, staring out at him, breasts pointing, hips swelling, waists permanently sucked in, $600 new, $200 used, sizes and makes listed, retail and wholesale locations, materials used, weight and height adjustments, number of wheels—more than he'd ever thought to consider, really. He was now a walking glossary on dress forms, and he shrugged off the idea that no one would be interested as soon as it occurred to him, for it was plain to him that any unusual fact could be extrapolated or embellished into a story that would fill conversation gaps and entrance his dance partners.

He shut off the computer and stared down at the brown-rimmed cup in his hand, cold coffee rings in its depths, and puzzled over the fact that he needed to talk when he danced. He was entertaining, he supposed, but what he loved was how his dance partners leaned in toward him, wanting to hear more of his facts and stories as he twirled them around and swished them into place. In the waltz, there was time for a whole story. Face to face with his partners, they were like rag dolls, so obedient to his every dancing whim that even though they often hesitated as if unsure of where he was taking them, they stayed loose, without a will of their own as they kept their eyes glued to his, straining to hear, forgetting their feet. There was a brief, harmless power in such a partnership, and the willingness he'd found among women to lend themselves to him in this captivated way was sweet. He was especially delighted when he could get them to laugh.

However, contra dancing was different. The patterns set by the caller only allowed him to entertain his partner by adding another sentence or fragment each time they came together in a closed-couple position, which resulted in a kind of serial for which his partner eagerly awaited the outcome (so it seemed to him) as they met again and again in *swing your partner, do-si-do your corner, balance and swing your partner again*. And if he wasn't finished with the story by the end of the dance, he was always assured of this partner's consent for the next dance as he continued talking, his partner fascinated, hanging in there for the story's completion. Perhaps that was it, he speculated. Assurance. He hated small talk and trying to answer silly questions about how many times he'd been married or did he have any children? *Any children? Not that I know of,* he'd reply. That always got a laugh.

Yet during intermission, he mostly sat on the side watching people as he waited for the band to start up again. Odd thing, that. He couldn't explain it except to say he came alive when he danced, a *raison d'être,* and the rest was only the gathering of facts for entertainment purposes, and for that he needed to be a good observer. If he polished his moves so that they were programmed in his brain and he didn't have to think about them, he could concentrate more on the storytelling and the observing. Truthfully, he didn't know which was more satisfying: the dancing or the story telling. The question seemed to be, did he want to live in the moment or tell about it?

But then, too, it depended on the dance. For zydeco, Cajun, and tango, only the body spoke, and he felt that somewhere in his light, short steps that often amounted to a mere shuffle with his shoulders hunched and his long arms twisting in spaghetti like configurations, he'd created a style uniquely his own. Speech detracted from the experience, and either spoiled the effect of a tango or became an impossibly breathless affair in the swing, a thought he'd never consciously realized before this moment when he found himself dialing the number in the ad, his pencil poised above the sun-splashed scrap of notepaper on the table before him, the dash of its shadow like an exclamation point.

A man answered his call. He sounded elderly, his voice raspy as he gave the address. "Like new," he said. "Do you sew?"

"I might," Aaron answered. He jotted down the address,

noting it was not in any of the neighborhoods he knew, but somewhere in the business section on the southeast side of the city. He pictured squalor, a pensioned widower getting rid of his wife's things. With luck, he could probably pick up the dress form for forty bucks.

In the car, he marveled again at his freedom, his pension check coming regularly for which he needed to do nothing. How many years had he plodded the same tedious route in the morning only to return at dusk, days gone in a blur and unaccounted for? His years in confinement. He was amazed at how many people were out and about at ten this morning, and how the street was filled with cars—people who had a good bit of freedom during normal working hours, many of them young men. What did they do, for God's sake? How did they pay the bills? He drove with the notepaper between his thumb and index finger, his hands on the steering wheel, elbow out the window. It was warm for November.

Finally he found it, jammed between the cinder block exteriors of warehouses on a treeless street. The house had an odd shape, its roundness accentuated by a curved porch. Brown-shingled with shutter-less windows, the house bore a huge, round skylight on its roof that reflected the many-storied buildings on each side and across the street, as if naming its incongruent relationship with the neighbors, like a holdout among the surrounding concrete. He walked past the uneven hedges onto the porch and knocked on the door.

A tall pole of a woman opened it, calling, "Tyler! The man about the dress form is here," and backed away to allow him to enter. In her solid presence there was nothing to give him a clue about the interior of the house, nothing that would prepare him for the palm trees that pressed against the glass of the skylight, nor the parrot that perched in one of the trees, nor the canaries and parakeets that flew from the gigantic-leaved tropical plants to palm fronds and back again, nothing to warn him about the blinding rays of the sun that streamed through the glass nor the orchids drooping from planters along the walls, their heavy fragrances already twinging his sinuses, nor the warm damp that clung to his skin like his own sweat. The space was huge, bright with blue sky and green foliage and birds and birdsong without the interruption of another room. Off to one side was a stove and sink and a few cabinets, but that was the only sign that this might be a home and not an English conservatory.

"Yeah?" he heard in the same voice he'd heard on the telephone. It was difficult to find where the voice came from, the room being so cluttered with books and newspapers and plants, but once his eyes focused, he saw a bald and grey-bearded man in the middle of the room sitting in an easy chair. "Here, sit," he said and motioned to a chair beside him. "Elise, please bring some newspapers to sit on." Aaron laughed then, feeling as though he'd entered a giant birdcage, a room claimed by bird droppings, humans allowed only by bird consent. Soon he sat down with the newspaper crackling beneath him.

"Thank you," he said, and smiled, although he could think of nothing else to say.

"There it is," the man said and pointed to a place under one of the palm trees where the dress form stood, its beige bulk plain and simple against the lush vegetation. Aaron couldn't think. He couldn't even begin to bargain. He stared at the dress form for inspiration but his words had flown with the birds, leaving him as thin and transparent as the glass above him, as if stuck inside some strange concoction of his own imagination, trapped inside a story he could never tell unless he sacrificed himself on the altar of the truly mad.

"Some coffee while you think about it?" Elise said, smiling, the road map of skin along her cheeks suiting her somehow, as if she had traveled the miles easily and thought no more of them than covering ground. "Seemed like a good idea," she said, nodding at the dress form, "but I have no need for fancy clothes anymore, and besides, my eyes aren't that good."

Aaron watched the flight of three bright yellow birds across the large, open room. "What did you want for it?" he said finally, although he knew the answer. He was interrupted by chatter from the parrot. The sound made him jump. The man laughed, and the woman, too, in deep, rich sounds filled with the timbre of years.

"I don't remember what I put in the paper!" said Elise with an astonished expression, looking at her husband. "Was it fifty dollars?"

Her husband must have once been a much larger man, he had so much extra skin. It was as if Aaron were getting a glimpse at his own coming years. In answer to his wife, the man tapped his long fingers on the arms of his easy chair. "I don't know, Elise, I don't know. You decide."

He turned to Aaron. "What do you want it for?" he said. "Sorry, that's none of my business. Just curious, you know. We thought a woman would come, but maybe you have a wife?"

Aaron smiled. "No, no. I had one a while ago. Umm," he was scratching his neck now, suddenly self-conscious at the word *divorced*, not wanting to say it, a fact in his history he hated to admit but no longer thought about unless asked. "To tell you the truth, I haven't thoroughly decided what I want the form for. But I'm curious about the house—I've never been in such an unusual home. I mean, it's—it's remarkable. A regular oasis. With a space more outdoors than the outdoors—in these parts." *In these parts.* What made him say that? He wasn't a hick. He was city-born and out of his element to the point of being embarrassed. Yet the warm, moist air and sun pouring in had a mesmerizing effect, and he was beginning to relax. In fact, he was afraid he'd drop off to sleep mid-sentence.

"Yeah. I like birds," the old man was saying. "You always know you're on land when you hear birds, even in your sleep." The woman stepped to his chair and laid her hand on his shoulder.

Aaron got up suddenly and walked to the dress form, the birds skimming his head as he went. He ducked, wiped his hand quickly along his hair, then grabbed the form with a hand on each side of the waist, pushing a little to see if it would topple. It didn't, and when he looked back at the man and the woman, realized they were watching him. The dress form was the exact height of the perfect dance partner. "My name's Aaron Stiel," he said. He just realized they hadn't introduced themselves and neither had he.

"Elise and Tyler Anderson. Stiel. What kind of name is that?"

Aaron was scratching his neck again. "Darned if I know," he said. "German, I think. Way back. It's spelled *s-t-i-e-l*."

Tyler nodded. "I learned some German in the war. Lousy war. All wars are lousy. World War, they called it. Now they say global, but it all amounts to the same thing. Soft, young, homegrown flesh torn up, blown apart, gone in an instant, although those are the lucky ones, I suppose."

"Where were you stationed?" Aaron asked, eager for a story from one who'd lived it. All original. Nothing borrowed. Firsthand. His question was all the impetus Tyler needed. With Elise sitting next to him, quietly watching, Tyler cleared his throat and began speaking in a voice fuller than his shriveled body seemed capable of. "Navy," he said. "We were all over the place. Nothing solid under our feet and danger from both the depths and the air with no place to hide."

The dress form under the palm tree seemed frivolous

now. He felt silly buying it. Maybe he wouldn't get it after all, but he'd answered the ad and was here, and probably the man and wife needed the money. Curiosity about them held him to the newspaper-covered seat and the sunny warmth, the comfort of seeing the wife's hand on her husband's arm as if it were a role long rehearsed, the richness of time reaching back on itself through a man's voice. Among the surrounding greenery, the birds, settling on their perches, preened themselves. He no longer needed to think of anything to say. Like his waltz partners, he was being guided toward something grander than either person could manage alone, and it lay in the unspoken bargain between teller and listener.

The voice went on and on. "It was in the night, January, with the decks slippery and the lines frozen, you see, when the ship was in the North Sea, which had just begun to calm itself after a terrible ice storm. We were taking a breather—that's when the torpedoes hit and the air raid began, almost simultaneously, and the sounds of the ship's sirens went on in their own hysteria. The ship, essentially, broke in two. We didn't know it right away. We only rushed to shut the hatches and doorways to cut off the rush of water, but later, in the dead of night, when some of it actually broke away—broke, mind you, like a child's toy—when it was rumored that we'd try to make it back to the coast for repairs—that we began to hear the shouts of the men across the water, men on the sinking half of the ship—men desperately calling and calling over the water, their voices fading..." His voice broke. "In my dreams, and awake—the ship is always moving forward with its terrible orders to leave them."

Aaron was not ready for this. Nor did he want another man's grief. What trust it took to be a listener, he thought, suddenly feeling angry. Tyler kept on, but Aaron, eyes glued to Tyler's eyes, began to think of how soon he could leave with the dress form without seeming rude. He continued looking in the old man's eyes—thinking what strange bonds we find ourselves in. Yet he couldn't look away even though he was ashamed at the wellspring of tears in his own eyes.

He nodded and finally looked away, broke away like the torn ship and began idiotically to think about the dress form, about one of those Styrofoam noodle things that kids played with in swimming pools. They were five or six feet long, weren't they? And he could probably take one of those and thread it through the shoulders for arms, maybe cut off the Styrofoam with a knife to get the length right. He hoped the wheels would be easy rolling. If not, he might be able to replace them with ball bearings. He couldn't see what type of wheels was on her—funny he was already thinking of it as her, like a kind of adoption.

Tyler, with Elise still with her hand on his shoulder, was saying, "We made our way back to the States, but it took several weeks since we could only go at a very slow speed. Day and night, with the ship rolling beneath us, I never stopped hearing their calls, and even now, sometimes, if I don't hear the birds, I hear the voices of the men and feel the pitch of the ship, the iron-clad cold."

Aaron didn't consider himself to be cold-hearted. Maybe it was just that he'd rather laugh than cry. Maybe this story asked too much of its receiver, left the receiver helpless in the wake of its grueling monstrousness, its unrelieved suffering. It definitely was not a story he could ever repeat. Was it worth repeating? What could anyone do except feel pain, and why would one choose to do that? Tyler obviously had some issues to deal with. Things that didn't pertain to Aaron. He was perspiring now. He'd smother in the heat of high noon.

Tyler went on. "But when we pulled into port—that was the most difficult of all. The families that waited. The wives that sought their own among the faces that had returned..."

If he weighted the dress form at the bottom, say with an

extra set of wheels, she'd never tip over. He'd have to see. Test her with a rope around her middle. Pull her toward him, fling her out with a push of his hand, stop her sharply, just far enough for a good retrieve. Tyler was clearing his throat again. "Well," he said, as if suddenly self-conscious. "It's always interesting to get visitors, and putting an ad in the paper to get rid of stuff is a good way to meet people."

Suddenly the tension eased, like the release of a bird. Elise laughed and left Tyler's side. "Well, you can't leave yet," she said to Aaron. "The coffee is ready."

When she'd left, Tyler tipped his head toward the dress form and said, "It was a present for her. But she never owned up to disliking it, or at the very least, not wanting it. She never used it. You can think of the dress form as virgin, if you like." His laugh now was a bit thin, a little forced. "How about forty dollars—is that a deal? Forty and you take it," he said.

Aaron nodded, as though he was considering everything thoughtfully, but he began to think in terms of how he'd been made to sit and listen, almost as if he'd been invited under false pretenses. Actually, they should pay him for his time. He would never think to bother anyone with his personal stories. The ones he told were made up, his declaration of facts entertaining, carefully sifted through so as not to ask too much of his listener. He had his own stories, his originals, but he kept them in the past where they belonged. Trained to stay there.

It occurred to him that somehow his anger was connected to the reason he needed the dress form. It was boring for a partner to go over and over the same moves with him while he practiced. It was too great an imposition. No woman he'd ever known tolerated practice well, especially while he practiced for hours on end the most complicated moves of his style, the pretzel, for example, in the swing. He was arranging his life so he could practice whenever he needed to without bothering anyone. Not that Tyler was practicing his story, or was he? Practicing the telling of something that had happened fifty years ago until it was tamed into being just a story, maybe.

The warm coffee mug in his hand, he knew he was much angrier than the situation called for. He looked at Elise as if to ask what she thought of forty dollars, wondering how many times she'd had to hear the story of the ship, how many times she'd had to put her hand on Tyler's shoulder, wondering how much of her sainthood was mere tolerance, how living with him in the cocoon her husband had made for himself stripped her of all desire for anything of her own. Aaron found himself growing impatient with her, and with her husband, and the consuming heat of their manufactured paradise, dulling their senses to everything else. An exceedingly narrow point of view.

For it was desire that gave color to life, wasn't it? The reach toward—even in a brief future—a wanting that reached beyond the bond imposed on another, something not committed to, only asked of? Surely the truest part of life was often kept on the outside rim of haunting facts and histories, just as the most significant thing in that room was that Elise had elected to stay with him, even love him, despite the fact he'd given years of attention to a story he repeated over and over and over...How easily she carried love's burden. What Aaron felt now was envy.

For him, there had been a different set of facts. There was the fact of his split with Mavis, his wife, and the fact that one night after she'd left, she came back, but only for a few hours. "Let's do it," she'd said, her words delivered in a saucily spoken demand with a tinge of sappy rose-hued nostalgia. "For one last time. But it doesn't mean anything, okay?" Something a man would say. Something he himself might have said once or twice in a situation where it really *didn't* mean anything.

He looked again at Mrs. Anderson, the one with whom he felt the bargain should be made.

"Forty dollars?" he said.

She nodded. He was stifling now and needed air—needed his own life back. He set the cup down, and when he arose, the parrot screeched as if it had forgotten he was there, annoyed at the second intrusion of its idyll in one morning. He picked up the dress form. He'd call her Mavis. For old time's sake. He could see himself with a dance partner in his arms, telling her the story about Mavis's conversion and purpose, making it light and brief enough for one whole waltz.

Inside Out

"So what have you learned from your relationships since your divorce?" George asked. He was serious, standing there with his hands in his pockets, his shirt pressed, shorts belted, clear, blue eyes peering down at me, and me, sixteen years older, looking off to the trees, trying to come up with an answer, annoyed at his impertinence.

What did I learn? *What did I learn?* I learned about pain, I thought. Nah. The point was not to sound bitter. Immediately, I began composing. "Well, I guess I learned mostly about myself. Starting over each time, always something new to learn, how I react to people, how they bring out different aspects of me I didn't know were there."

"I don't know," he said. "I think I'm always the same. Nothing goes too deep. I wish I could feel more."

"No, you don't, man. I wouldn't recommend it."

The first band was warming up and getting loud. They were on a portable stage, speakers stacked two high. Bales of hay marked off the dance floor and beyond lay a congregation of picnic tables surrounded by buildings that would house cows and goats at the county fair in September. The Rotary Club members were cooking hot dogs and selling beer. People walked in with lawn chairs, blankets, and coolers. A few kids, two- and three-year-olds, ran among them stumbling on tree roots. My hand reached out to save one kid's fall. Reminded me of my Carrie, always falling and skinning her knees. She's thirty-one now and still has the scars, but she's not afraid of anything. Rides around in that ancient Nova with the bottom falling out of it. "Mom," she says, "Have you got a piece of rope? The hood flies up sometimes." Good Godfrey.

"How do you do that? Not feel too deep?" Maybe I shouldn't have asked this out loud. Actually, I had to shout it because the band was revving up.

"What?" he said, holding his hand up to his ear.

"How do you *do* that? Not feel too deep?"

"I don't know. I figure my first marriage didn't work out. Not that she was a bad person, but she had some problems. And this time, things are pretty good but you never know." He shrugged. "I might be alone again at some point, and I've got to prepare for it. Better not to have things go down too far." He patted his chest with his hand.

Why was I talking about this with him? He was Ben and Lolly's guest, on the loose for the weekend because his wife was away on business. I didn't even know him really. The kids just invited me along because I like live music. But there was too much bait on the hook. I couldn't let it go by. So I said, as if it were *pass the salt*, "In my last relationship he calls up out of the blue and says, 'It's over,' just like that. I said to myself, 'I've been through this before. I can handle it.' But the truth is, I went crazy. Things I thought I had worked through welled up again. Maybe when you have a history, you don't exactly start over fresh with each relationship, come to think of it," I said, switching tracks. "You'd be amazed at what you can dig up—things you thought you were done with." I wanted to go off somewhere now, get a hot dog or something. I hadn't meant to say so much.

George looked at me a long time, it seemed. I didn't like it. I felt wrinkled and old, a crone, minus the wisdom.

"I wish I could feel that much," was all he said.

I'd give it up if I could. Here, take it. Take this load off my back.

A couple of dancers were on the roped-off area before us. Mottled sunlight splashed over them like a strobe light, the man in an over-sized T-shirt and jeans and the woman, older than he, in shorts and a tight shirt, bosoms bobbing as she jumped up and down. She looked defiant, knocking her arms about, fighting the air with clenched fists, but grinning all the while, and ducking her head, feet slamming down on the ground sending up puffs of dust. When the dance ended, she applauded, hands high in the air, while the crowd kept streaming in, finding places to settle under the trees.

We were on blankets, passing the fried chicken that John and Susan, friends of Carrie's, had brought. My daughter-in-law, Lolly, thought to bring cups, a jug of lemonade, and apples for everybody. I wondered why I hadn't thought to bring anything. I used to pack a carload of stuff for the kids, picnics at the beach my specialty. Now I never think about it, even when the family's all together. Always had to bring that little stuffed dog of Carrie's, too. She'd hold its ear to her top lip and stroke herself to sleep with it. Had to have that.

The Tom Turkey started dancing then. John poked Susan and Lolly and Ben stopped talking to watch. The kids kept weaving in and out of the grownups and May, John's sister, faced the opposite direction, her eyes tracking her Amy through the maze of blankets and around sheds, but everybody else saw the Tom Turkey, cowboy hat pushed back, full beard, plaid shirt, suspenders over paunch, high-jacked jeans, boots, drumstick arms, all moving together and rippling from head to toe, dancing alone in the center of the ring. He held out his arms, palms up, beckoning with his fingers for a partner. Anyone? He had a taker as one woman rose from her lawn chair and danced toward him. His hips cocked, ready for a fan tail, his left foot pawing the ground, raising sand, then the other foot, elbows in and out, head jiving like a turkey's. He stopped for a second, swung his hat down to his boot in a sweeping bow as far down as he could bend, and came up again for the turkey walk. He nodded at his partner and winked, keeping up the dance.

With the next song, he looked around and beckoned, but the women seemed not to notice, turning in their chairs. I avoided his eyes but got up before I knew it, my feet itching to dance. "Just like you," Edward, my ex, would have said. "Always plunging in with both feet." Ah, what did Edward know anyway? Twenty-seven years and who was he anyhow? Don't think I ever knew for sure and he certainly didn't know me. The one inside. The one who went nuts. The one who kept swimming against the tide in the ocean between us, and then drowning in it. Once in a while I still get to dance, Edward, even if it's with everybody's Tom Turkey. One good man can keep a lot of women satisfied these days, especially if he likes to dance.

There was nothing special about dancing with him, and yet everything I know had to come buzzing around my ears at that moment. The two-ness of it and how comfortable it felt, a couple on this worn-out, dusty mound of earth moving at the same time for a change and liking it, and the brevity of it, three minutes, and the knowledge that everything was really good for three minutes but with the rest being eons of not-so-good. God, what a mood I'm in, I thought, and everybody watching, too. The kids are probably looking the other way, busy distracting their friends, talking about—what do they talk about? Oh yeah, fad diets, organically grown food, and doing everything better than their forebears. You believe that at thirty.

The lead guitar groaned up the scale, laboring under a lot of static. The leaves trembled. There wasn't a breath of air. The music stopped, yet for some reason, the turkey grabbed me and pulled me to him for a kiss on the cheek in front of all those people. It was the suddenness of it, I guess. I bolted a little, but caught his eyes, which were smiling with nothing more than gladness in them. It *was* nice.

I didn't want to go back to the blanket just then. The band was unplugging, and a DJ began playing tapes. Maybe I'll just go and sit in the car for a while, I thought, and figure out what I did learn from my relationships since Edward. Maybe it's not a question of learning at all. Maybe it's only snatching at illusions of happiness. Maybe it's only enjoyment, and then you quit before things get rough. Maybe there isn't supposed to be anything more. Maybe that's all there ever was, just three minutes. And all there ever will be, three minutes. Three-minute relationships. Like Carl. The three-minute expert. "It's over," he says. A sniper, a thief, and a liar. "You're the neatest person I ever met," he says. "You're the perfect woman. You're beautiful, baby. I want to hold you and hold you. I love you," he says. And just when I was believing it— finis. He was a lot like Tom Turkey, come to think of it. Palms up, welcome, dance is over, good-bye. Next? Oh, the single life.

"Bird Dog and the Road Kings coming up next, folks, so get yourself a hot dog and a beer while the gettin's good. Bird Dog is next," the announcer hollered. The line at the bathroom wound around the shed as I headed for the car. When you're feeling vulnerable, there's nothing like a big '84 Oldsmobile to pull around you. Been driving it a long time. With the windows up and the doors locked, I could only hear the faint muffled sounds of the Rolling Stones' song, "I can't get no..." Pulling down the lighted mirror on the back of the sun visor, I began combing my hair, slowly, as if I could pull away the snarls and tangles of my life. I had never sat in my car like this before, dead still—no plans to go anywhere, no revving up for the smooth takeoff, no positioning the mirror and the electronic seats, no turning up the a/c, then the radio, humming off someplace, free, floating over bumpy byways, passing, stopping, exploring, the dotted line and the solid line parting in an unending welcome, my own unfolding cinema, me, in the driver's seat, hermetically sealed, arriving fresh, ready for more.

Don't think I'd ever sat in the passenger seat before, come to think of it. Not since Edward. He actually came back to help me pick out this car. "It'll last you a long time if you take care of it. Don't forget the oil changes every three thousand miles." He seemed to be more worried about the car in my hands than me. I guess it's easier to worry about a car. Well, it has been a great car. I hope it lasts the rest of my life. Ben said, "Well, if you kick off Monday morning, Mom, you'll get your wish." I couldn't help laughing although that only encourages him.

I caught the drumbeat, so I got out of the car, clicked the electric lock button and slammed the door. Glancing back, I caught sight of the keys, fanned out and glinting on the brown velvet upholstery. My heart beat in rhythm to the bass drum, kaboom, doot-doot, kaboom. I leaned back against the door, feeling its heat and my own. How do I do it? I amaze myself. No, it can happen to anybody. It's an hour and a half back to the farm for the extra keys. I'll borrow Carrie's car. Or I'll get Ben. He'll know what to do. No, don't get Ben. Take your time. You can solve this yourself. Helpless now, without the car. Stupid. Combed my stupid hair! I wandered around under the trees, hands in pockets, wondering who saw me in my foolishness. The ticket takers at the gate, arms crossed talked among themselves; a pair of kids, arms around each other were engrossed in other matters. I headed toward the restrooms where an ambulance was parked. The stretcher, white and expectant, awaited true catastrophe.

"Help you, lady?"

"I locked my keys in the car. Have you got a slim-jim?"

"No, we don't have nothin' like that. Officer Travers is in

the bathroom. I'll ask him when he gets out."

Standing there with my hands jutted into my very empty pockets, who should come by but George.

"You okay?"

"Yeah, thanks."

"Can I do anything?" He wouldn't quit or go away without an explanation. "Somebody grope ya?"

I laughed. "George, I locked my stupid keys in the car!"

"Oh, we can handle that." At least he hadn't said, "Stupid keys?"

Officer Travers stopped. "Somebody need help?"

"Yeah, do you have a slim-jim?"

"No, sure don't, but the state police do. I'll call 'em."

George disappeared. I waited.

Officer Travers said, "What kind of car do you have? Oldsmobile? Electric locks? I don't know." He shrugged his shoulders. "They're hard to open."

I could see George leaving the refreshment stand with a hanger, striding toward my car.

The rest of us arrived at the car a few minutes later, three town policemen, one state trooper, the aproned ticket takers and me, to find George with one end of the hanger groping its way between the car window and the door frame. The state trooper took the slim-jim and ran it down the other door under the window again and again, back and forth, up and down. Then he and George switched doors.

"I've opened only one or two of these electric locks in my day, lady," said the trooper. "It's rare. Looks like this one isn't gonna give." Bird Dog's fiddle was doing a slow waltz. I thought I could see Tom Turkey through the trees, hovering over his partner.

George's hands worked steadily, bending the wire hanger at different angles to see what worked best. Once the wire touched the lock handle but skidded by as he applied a little pressure.

"I could get Carrie's keys and use her car to drive home, George," I said quietly.

He peered at me again with those very clear blue eyes, his self-assurance born of the knowledge of how things worked.

"Well, that will be the last resort. That'll take you almost three hours. I'm sure I'd have the car unlocked in that time."

The other men offered suggestions occasionally, eyed me and George, asked how it happened, told about times the same thing happened to them. George kept on working.

Once the hanger got caught in the seatbelt and he twisted and turned the wire till it finally broke loose and snapped on the window. Another time he got the wire looped around the lock knob and one of the Rotary Club men banged at the door to joggle the lock loose. No luck. The state trooper got another call and left with his slim-jim.

"Sorry, ma'am."

"Thanks for trying."

George pulled the hanger out, bending it a different way.

"What about breaking the little side window?" I said. "It probably won't cost that much to replace."

"No," said George. "Seems like just when you're ready to smash something and announce a few expletives, if you stick with it just a little bit longer, things go right. Give me a bit more time. If I really feel dead-ended, you can get Carrie's keys. But if we can get this, nobody needs to know what happened."

"I'll bet one of those Bronx kids could open this in three seconds," said one of the town policemen. They began to drift away.

By this time, George had a loop fashioned at one end of the wire at the exact angle to lift up the knob and a bend in the metal at the right distance from the knob to the edge of the window. His hands, working steadily at shaping the metal,

215

sensed its tension. The patient probing of the wire brought about a communion of sorts and transformed the hand and the wire into a determined whole, a working of matter to a resolution, an ability that linked George to my father, my sons, and even Edward. The guys who dreamed up the Oldsmobile must have had it, too. I read somewhere that the only true acts of creation occur in music and architecture, that all the rest is imitation of nature. What about machines? What about the Olds? What about the human hand and a wire?

George said calmly, "One more try."

To tell the truth, the action on the lock was always very stiff and I doubted so much that he could do it that when the knob gave a thunk and George sprung open the door, I shrieked in disbelief.

"My God, you did it!" I grabbed him, whirled him around, laughing. "May nothing bad ever happen to you in this life! May everyone always smile on you! You did it, George! Thank you! Thank you!"

He grinned, a bit shy at my outburst. A few minutes later, we stood drinking beer at the edge of the dance floor. "Let's just stand here and calm down," he said. "Let me know when you're ready to go back to the others."

"George, I hope your wife knows what a good guy you are!"

For the first time, he threw back his head and laughed.

Tom Turkey was still dancing, mopping his sweat with his sleeve and occasionally tipping a silver stein to his lips. His smile to his partner was magnanimous. She was almost his size and dressed in a black halter and black skirt. She could make her body ripple just like he could; in fact, she might have been a belly dancer. The fiddle screamed at them, skimming the notes down their backs to their feet and across their arms to their fingertips. They were helpless till the fiddle gave out. The crowd applauded and yelled for the fiddler and the Tom

Turkey and the belly dancer who had the spirit. A healthy swig from the stein was the grand finale.

The sun was sinking. We waited for a band called Tranzfusion. I'd danced to them before and they were extra good. Lolly wanted to borrow the keys to get everybody's sweatshirts from the car and George winked at me when he said, "Don't lock them in the car." Little kids were dropping next to mothers, rolling themselves in balls of towels and favorite blankets. It was sweet. As the children slept, people paired off to dance.

Then there was George and me.

"Maybe this is a time in my life when, along with all the reflecting I've been doing, I need to learn to dance," he said. "I'm taking ballroom dancing lessons on Tuesday nights."

"George, you don't need to know anything for this kind of dancing. You just listen to the music and let your feet go."

"Well, I'll be out there all night if you can put up with me."

"Trouble is, you're not forty yet. When you get to be forty, you stop worrying how you look. I finally figured out that it doesn't matter what people think anyway. And after fifty— after fifty the dance is all that matters. You know that line in a song by Crosby, Stills and Nash, *Did you envy all the dancers who had all the nerve? So much water underneath the bridge.* I wasted too much time *not* dancing." I stopped mid-tracks. Why did I keep blurting out?

Truth is, they were playing "Pink Cadillac" and the nerves in my feet were sending out sparks to all the other little nerves in every particle of my skin and the tension was unbearable. If the energy wasn't released I would go into a spasm, maybe wrinkle up like a piece of bacon on the fire or burst into flames. The keyboard player was swinging his shoulders from side to side. The lead guitarist and his long, silky hair shivered together, tense as a cat watching a bird. Nearly everyone was dancing: Tom Turkey with a new partner, Ben and Lolly, Carrie and what's-his-name, and May with Amy in her arms, and John and Sue, and everyone from the motorcycles and picnic tables and lawn chairs.

I pulled George out to the center of the crowd. George watched his feet. He seemed to be sending messages to them as separate beings, reacting in astonishment when they began to move. He watched my feet for a while, then his again. It was as if his long, thin frame hung from the nearest tree by two invisible threads, head down and his arms dangling at his sides. His feet crossed over each other, stepped to the side, stiff and unyielding, unwilling as a tree trunk.

It occurred to me then that there must be two types of men in the world: those who move with grace in the physical world with two feet on the ground, who understand the mechanics of life but who seldom dance, and those who understand little of the practicalities of the world and find some way to either escape it or celebrate its mysteries. And then I figured out that maybe I was in a stage of my life that was sitting smack-dab in the latter category, the elusive one of illusion, and that if Carl had only been dancing with me, then I had danced right along with him and that I could *celebrate the dance itself*, however brief. And Edward, too. And our family, and our days together.

George and I faced each other but every once in a while, I danced around him so that he began to turn a little, and then we began dancing in a moving circle around each other. Everyone has what they need in this life to survive, but to really live well, that's much more of a secret.

Tranzfusion was charging up the dancers now. Bodies sweating, fingers snapping, feet tapping and stomping, dust clouds billowing all around, dust in noses and ears and embedded in toenails, down inside T-shirts and under belts, dust between teeth and under eyelids. We danced between

Carrie and Tom, stealing them for a moment, and then danced on. We found Ben and Lolly and John with Amy on his shoulders with Amy holding on to his ears, then Sue and May, and danced between them and around them all. George still watched his feet and looked up occasionally to see what the rest of us were doing, trying to figure out where we were headed. Some people cleared out to rest and we formed a circle that included a girl we didn't know. She studied our faces as she danced and smiled. We welcomed her and smiled back. Carrie floated across the circle like a silk scarf, and then Ben picked up his feet high and fast like a tarantula had gotten him and his life depended on how fast his feet could move, and John flung his arms wide and threw his body side to side and kicked his feet in the air and May, looking as if she just came out of the rain with her hair plastered to her shoulders, sailed by, and I, trying to save my breath, stepped slowly and listened for the guitar to tell me what to do and George—by God—George kicked his feet up high and forgot to watch them, setting them loose, off by themselves with a new-found freedom. His shoulders became undone and sent his arms flapping and with his face flushed and dusty and his shirttails out of his belt, he was dancing—I mean really dancing, the kind you do when your heart is pounding and you love everyone and that love is beaming energy to everything that is, to the lawn chairs, the motorcycles, the trees, and the black sky, right up to other worlds.

He was laughing, throwing his head back and laughing with the rest of us, as if turned inside out, at how ridiculous it was, and upside down, at how important and simple at the same time, to have our insides out and our outsides in and our downsides up, twisting right sides left and left sides right and agreeing with our eyes and smiles and kept dancing until our fears left us completely and roosted in the trees, leaving dreams and angels room to enter. We danced harder and harder till the band gave up its encores, and the dust stuck to the backs of our throats and gravity once again anchored us to our earthly home.

Upside right again, there was George looking sheepish with his hands back in his pockets, staring at the ground, and Ben clapping him on the back, saying, "You're all right, man," and me, gathering up the chicken bones and paper plates and folding blankets. We walked back to the car, too high to let the dust settle, dragging our feet and calling back and forth to one another.

Of course, the Olds had a few nicks in the paint on the door and as I opened it I could see how the rubber around the frame had torn, leaving it to flap in my hand. We piled in, Ben and Lolly and John and Sue, George and May with Amy on her lap, filling the velvety seats, the windows open to the night air, joyful noises floating up to the stars. I finally expected nothing more and realized how peaceful that was.

ABOUT THE AUTHOR

A native of New York City, Barbara Lockhart lives on a nature preserve on the Eastern Shore of Maryland. She is the recipient of two Individual Artist Awards in Fiction from the Maryland State Arts Council for her short stories and her first novel, *Requiem for a Summer Cottage*, as well as a silver medal from the Independent Book Publishers Awards for her historical novel, *Elizabeth's Field*. She has authored and co-authored four children's books and a nationwide program for the teaching of children's literature, *Read to me, Talk with me*. Her short stories have appeared in such venues as *Indiana Review*, *The Greensboro Review* and *Pleiades*.

CPSIA information can be obtained
at www.ICGtesting.com
Printed in the USA
LVOW11s0856050317
526179LV00001B/123/P